COMPELLED BY PASSION

"Matthew, I'm not sure how long I'll be here. You see, I planned to return to Asheville, to my home. I've a great deal of work to do on the house before Sula and I can move back in."

"You had not intended to tell me this," he said. Matthew's hands were on his hips and he looked down at the ground as he spoke.

"No," she whispered.

"Why?" He looked at her in disbelief and a hint of his old anger.

"I . . . I didn't think it would matter to you, and I want to see my home," she said.

"Didn't think it would matter?" He shook his head and gave a disgusted sigh. "This is your home now, Kathryn! You belong here with us at Foxfire. Don't you think it's what Robert intended? And Mother?"

"But what about you, Matthew? What do *you* want?" She had become brave now that the time had come to say goodbye.

Matthew gripped her arms and pulled her to him. With a soft moan he covered her lips with his warm mouth. Her heart leapt as she felt an instant response to his touch. He kissed her hungrily as if he never wanted to let her go. And when he did they were both left shaken and breathless.

With his arms still around her he whispered, "I'm sorry you even had to ask what I want."

THE EMERALD TEARS OF FOXFIRE MANOR

CLARA WIMBERLY

ZEBRA BOOKS
KENSINGTON PUBLISHING CORP.

ZEBRA BOOKS

are published by

Kensington Publishing Corp.
475 Park Avenue South
New York, NY 10016

First printing: April, 1990

Printed in the United States of America

For Wayne, my husband and best friend,
and for my children Wayne Jr., Mark
and Suzanne, with all my love.

Prologue

The tall, broad-shouldered man swung one long leg over the saddle and stepped down from his massive black horse. He walked toward the campfire and threw his hat on the ground, rubbing his forehead as he sat down cross-legged before the fire.

One of the soldiers walked around the wagon behind him and immediately came to attention. "Major Kincaid!" he said.

"At ease, soldier," the man before the fire said. His voice sounded flat and weary and he hardly looked up at the boy.

God, but he was sick of this war! He could hardly bear to look at the faces of the young men of his command without wondering just how much longer they would be alive.

As the last, long grueling months of 1864 drew to an end the Confederate troops were tattered and starving. Lee's Army of Northern Virginia existed on scarcely a mouthful of food per man per day. Earlier in the war, provisions had been sent from homes or provided by ladies' groups in Southern cities; now even those civilians were suffering from the food shortage and could no longer help.

Major Matthew Kincaid had seen all too often how

his fellow Southerners were suffering and how desperately they tried to hide it. While he was in Richmond he had even been invited to a civilian 'starvation party,' at which the only refreshment was James River water. His neighbors were proud, fiercely trying to hang on to the last vestiges of a dying way of life.

But Matthew was weary of it, weary of the pretense and the high price that had been paid for their pride. He could see for himself that the Confederate army was now operating strictly on determination, discipline, courage and the *élan* of its tired soldiers. For after four long years of fighting, exhaustion was as much the enemy as the Union troops.

Matthew worried about his mother at Foxfire Manor, his home high in the mountains above Asheville, North Carolina. He wondered how she was faring, well aware that some Southerners were paying as much as twenty-five dollars per pound for butter and an unbelievable twelve hundred fifty dollars for a barrel of flour. Of course, it was easier in the mountains, isolated as they were, but the war at this point had left no one untouched.

He pulled the letter from his pocket and turned it toward the firelight to read again the troubling words his mother had written.

"My darling son," he read. "Try not to worry unduly about your brother Robert. I am thankful that he is alive and that his spirits are good. When I received word that he had been wounded I feared I would never see him alive again. If we are lucky this paralysis will be only temporary and he will come home a healthy young man again. I hope if you are going to be nearby you will stop at the hospital in Asheville and visit him."

Matthew stared unseeing at the fire, feeling the pain of his young brother's injury. If this war had taught him anything of value it was that home and family were irreplaceable. He vowed that if he lived through it his main priority would be to return to Foxfire and care for the ones he loved. That thought was all that kept him going some days.

His troops were escorting a supply wagon through the mountains, and within a few days he would be there visiting his brother if nothing delayed them.

They had received word that Sherman's troops were on their way to the coast of Georgia, heading toward Savannah after his infamous devastation of Atlanta. Matthew expected from there the federal troops would head to the Carolinas. But it was not only the army that worried him now. Renegades on both sides preceeded the armies, discarding their uniforms in favor of outlandish outfits stolen from their victims. They were hardened men, unmoved by the plight of the civilians they terrorized and murdered. The regular soldiers called them "bummers."

So now the citizens of the Carolinas could only wait and pray as Sherman turned his wrath toward them, not knowing which path he would take or what would be their fate.

But as Matthew sat before the fire he could hope for nothing more than this one chance, possibly his last, to visit his brother and family, to make sure they were safe before returning to the uncertainty of the battlefield.

We are not only fighting hostile armies,
but a hostile people, and must make old
and young, rich and poor, feel the hand
of war, as well as their organized armies.
General Wm. Sherman

Chapter One

December 1, 1864
Asheville, North Carolina

The muffled sound of rifleshot echoed eerily through the mist-covered mountains of the Blue Ridge and seemed to hang in the cold winter air. In the valley below, the muddy streets of Asheville were deserted as residents sought the uncertain safety of their homes.

In the parlor of the house on Montford Avenue, two women sat silently before the small flickering blaze of a fireplace. The room was sparsely furnished and there were bare spaces on the wall where paintings once had hung.

The large black woman rose suddenly, causing the cane-bottomed chair to creak and groan loudly in the still house. She walked abruptly to the windows facing the street and pushed aside the heavy velvet curtains to peer outside.

"Lord! I wonder how long they gonna keep up that racket! Do you think it's that General Sherman coming?"

The girl glanced up briefly from her sewing. "Mr. Simmons says it's nothing to worry about, Sula—

only a few stragglers fleeing from Georgia. He said the main body of soldiers passed through the mountains this morning. Mr. Simmons said it's believed that Sherman will move up the coast and not through the mountains."

Kathryn McClary looked young, with the too-small, simply made cotton dress drawn snugly across her breasts. Her light auburn hair was thick, its mass of curls framing a small, perfectly shaped face.

"Well, I hope he's right," the black woman said. "I sure do hope so!"

The girl sitting quietly before the fire, her slippered feet crossed before her, did not look her twenty years. Perhaps if circumstances had been different—if the War between the States had never come—she would be at a fancy dress cotillion tonight, celebrating the coming Christmas holidays and doing nothing more strenuous than plying her lace-covered fan and flirting with the young men of Asheville.

Her mind wandered to the days before the war when this house was always filled with young people. Her papa had held court every Saturday evening, speaking with eloquent passion about politics and the law, his life's blood and greatest love beside his daughter. Here at McClary house, political opinions and ideas could be bandied about freely.

Kathryn smiled to herself in the dimly lit room. Her skin tingled with excitement at remembering some of the discussions. The arguments over secession and states' rights had raged for months and her father had listened attentively to them all.

Her father was a tolerant man, denying her nothing—absolutely nothing. And when, at sixteen, she had been too outspoken and opinionated for a female, he had only smiled and indulged her all the more, often saying that he could refuse her nothing since the death of her mother years earlier.

But Kathryn was not spoiled, not in the sense that her character had ever been in danger. Sula had seen to that, lending a down-to-earth philosophy to the girl's upbringing and supplying the discipline Kathryn's father could not bring himself to deliver.

She glanced around the gloom-filled parlor. There was not much left in the way of material things to remind her of those glory days. Much of it had been sold in order to buy food. After her father rode away to join the South's fight, life had slowly but surely become a daily struggle for Kathryn and Sula. But unlike Sula, she didn't blame Judge McClary—after all, how could he have known that Confederate money would become virtually worthless or that the war would last so long?

Kathryn knew he worried about them, and she had not even told him in her letters about the departure of the house servants more than two years ago. His knowing that the passing armies confiscated all the food and livestock would not have made anything better. And although she had not admitted it to Sula, Kathryn was just as worried about Sherman's army as she.

Kathryn sighed.

Sula turned from the window. "What's wrong?" she asked.

"Oh, nothing, Sula. Just wishing, I guess. Wishing that the war would end and Papa would come home . . . things would be the way they were."

"Things ain't never gonna be the way they were, child," Sula said gently.

"I know," Kathryn replied with a note of wistfulness. "I know, but sometimes on nights like this, it helps to think they might."

Sula returned to her seat across from the girl and reached out to pat her hand in comfort. It angered her more than she could say to see Kathryn's young life shattered by the war and the years that should be her happiest made into a struggle that many women much older and wiser found hard to bear.

"Judge McClary should not have left you here like this!" she declared.

"Oh, now, Sula, don't start on that again," Kathryn said. She smiled indulgently at the woman who had cared for her so devotedly most of her life.

"Well, it's the truth! Menfolk got no more sense than a blind goose when it comes to women and fightin'. They'll just up and leave their responsibilities and women behind, thinkin' they fightin' for glory and honor. But I tell you the truth, I thought your daddy had more sense than that!" Sula fairly huffed with anger.

"We've managed as well as we could, Sula. No one has escaped the effects of the war," Kathryn replied.

"Well, sometimes I wish you'd jes get mad! You're too young to be acceptin' all this the way you do. Just when you should be dancin' and havin' fun. It jes don't seem fair."

Kathryn sat silently, picking at the cloth she held in her lap. She had heard Sula's speech so many times she practically knew it by heart.

"Oh, now, I didn't mean to go and get you all blue-eyed—" Sula said.

"No, you didn't. I'm just tired that's all." Kathryn smiled at the woman across from her.

"Well, let me fix us some tea. We still got rose hips and sassafras in the kitchen."

"No," she answered. "I think I'll go to bed. Besides, I need to be at the hospital early tomorrow. Pastor Morgan says they need all the help they can get, and with this shooting in the mountains today, there may be even more casualties."

"Kathryn McClary! I thought you was goin' to quit that. You know how I feel about you workin' at that place!" Sula snapped, her large black eyes shining with agitation.

"I never said I'd quit," Kathryn replied firmly. "And I certainly know how you feel . . . you've told me often enough. But as I explained to you before, I need to do something besides sit in this house day after day. Besides, all the young ladies are doing it now."

"Well, I don't like it! Down there seein' all kinds of things. It ain't no fit place for a lady, I tell you!" Sula insisted.

"I'm not going to stop working there." Kathryn raised her chin the way she did when her mind was made up. "And you know, Momma Sula, that all your preaching is not going to make any difference."

"I know that for certain. You're as stubborn—"

Kathryn smiled and a flash of firelight reflected momentarily in her emerald green eyes. For all of Sula's practical and protective ways Kathryn knew she was as soft as cotton where she was concerned. Besides, Sula knew working at the hospital would take Kathryn's mind off the fact that she had heard nothing from her father in months. And Sula was as worried about the Judge as Kathryn was.

As Kathryn climbed the cold, dark staircase the

small stub of a candle she carried flickered crazily, reflecting off the damp, mildewing walls. She had stopped even noticing the decay of the house that once had been a showplace in Asheville. Besides, there was nothing she could do. Yet somewhere within her remained a small spark, a tiny ray of hope that when the war ended and her father returned everything would be the same again. For all her new-found independence, she still sometimes cherished the dream of being cared for and protected. After all, it was still a man's world and one that did not look kindly upon a young woman who, except for her black nanny, was alone in the world.

She shivered as she entered her cold bedroom—the only room left with some semblance of the elegance her home once had.

She quickly undressed and climbed into bed, drawing her legs up for warmth under the heavy layering of quilts. Lord, but she was so tired of being cold! Always cold and always hungry.

The next morning Kathryn bundled up and set out on the short three-block walk to the hospital in the old depot at the edge of town. The building was a long gray rock structure that sat on a slight rise above street level, accessed by wide stone steps.

A lot of the patients were here as a result of illness; others had been sent from other battlefields to recuperate. And there were always casualties from the few skirmishes, such as the one they'd heard yesterday, in the mountains surrounding Asheville.

Kathryn walked through the doorway and found her senses immediately assaulted by the smells and sounds that greeted her. It was something she had never grown accustomed to—that or the suffering she'd seen within these walls.

"Ah, Kathryn, you're here." It was Pastor Morgan. "I need you to help with a few letters before you begin with the patients."

Kathryn did not mind. It was one of the more pleasant duties she had at the hospital. Pastor Morgan was a kind, hard working man, and she was willing to do anything she could to help him.

The remainder of the day passed, as it usually did, in a confusing blur. Nothing ever fully prepared her for the anguish and suffering she saw. And yet, as always, by the end of the afternoon she was glad she had come and more sure than ever that she could not stop working here. There was not much she and the other women who volunteered could do except make the soldiers comfortable, sit with them, or sometimes write letters for them. But the look in their eyes—the gratitude she saw reflected there—made her certain she was doing the right thing.

The week passed quickly with Kathryn often returning home, exhausted, to tell Sula all about the events at the hospital.

"Ain't no fit place for a lady," Sula would declare. But there was pride beneath the quiet criticism, and Kathryn knew that Sula no longer truly objected.

One Friday as Kathryn left the hospital and stepped out into the frigid night air she saw a young boy rushing up the steps toward her. She recognized the towheaded youth as Sam Bennett, the son of one of her neighbors.

"Why Sam," she said. "Whatever are you doing here at this time of evening? It will be dark soon and your mother will be looking for you."

The twelve-year-old boy paused and bent over to catch his breath before looking back up at her.

"You got to come quick, Miss McClary," he gasped, pulling at her coat.

"What is it, Sam? Is it your mother—is she sick again?" Kathryn knew his mother had not been well the past few months, and with her husband in the army there was only Sam to help her.

"No, ma'am. It's the house! You've got to come quick!"

"The house? What about the house?" Her voice was puzzled as she began to follow quickly behind him.

"It's burned! Your house—it's burned!"

"Burned?" Her voice sounded flat, reflecting the confusion she felt. How could the house be burned?

"Yes'm. Them marauders came today." The boy was breathing hard as he spoke, and now they both began to run.

"My God!" she whispered. "But Sula . . . is Sula all right, Sam?"

"Yes'm, she's fine, but she told me to fetch you real quick!"

As they rounded the last corner Kathryn could see the house—its aged rose-colored brick walls still standing. The fire seemed to be out, but the open doors and broken windows were a testament to the fire's destructive force. The once white Doric columns on the front portico were black with smoke stains. On the lawn sat several pieces of furniture and other items from the house.

Several neighbors who stood looking up at the house turned as Kathryn ran into the yard. They stepped aside to let her through. Sula saw her and came forward to put her arms around the girl.

"Sula . . . oh, I'm so glad to see that you're all right. What happened?"

"It was them renegades that's been plaguing the countryside. They was crazy drunk, demandin' food and whiskey. I told 'em we had nothin' left but they didn't believe me. They tore through the house and took what little was left. They shot out the windows . . . and one of them knocked a lamp over onto the floor." She began to wring her hands as she saw Kathryn's incredulous expression. "They went tearin' out of here shootin' and hollerin' and somebody said they ransacked another house up the street."

"Sula, you could have been killed!"

"Humph. Well I ain't killed!" she answered.

Kathryn stood trembling, as much from rage and frustration as from the cold night air. After offers of help, the neighbors drifted away, back to their own homes. Finally only Kathryn and Sula stood looking at the smouldering hull of the McClary house.

"Mistress Simmons says we're to come stay with them. They were the first of the neighbors to come a'runnin' when they heard the racket."

Kathryn hardly heard Sula's words as she watched the dying thin gray smoke drift away into the twilight. She had been oblivious to pain and suffering when the country was plunged into the cruel conflict that some called the "Great War." And now she could hardly remember those days or the young girl who was only interested in beautiful dresses and gala parties. Since then her world had collapsed around her with the sure, steady beats of each drummer's call to battle. Yet still she clung to a stubborn resolve to go on.

Kathryn did not remember her mother, who had died of a fever only a year after her only daughter was born. But if fate had decreed that the child should grow up without a mother, Kathryn was still blessed to have Sula. Oh, her papa had always been there, so alive and full of zest, and she never doubted that he loved her intensely. But in her childhood it was Sula she turned to.

She stood now, a bedraggled woman, helplessly gazing at the blackened, gutted house. There seemed to be nothing left of the feisty carefree girl that Sula had so fondly called a devilish little Manx cat.

Kathryn had faced the day-to-day struggles to survive, the loneliness and the fear, somehow managing to weather it. But the loss of her home seemed to be the final grievance. How would she survive this?

"Damn this war!" she said, her emerald eyes burning with anger and frustration. For the first time in months she allowed bitter tears to come, streaking her soot-blackened face. She pushed back her tangled mass of auburn hair impatiently and her shoulders slumped in defeat.

"What does it matter, anyway?" she sighed. "What does any of it matter?"

"It do matter, missy!" Sula turned to Kathryn, her black eyes snapping in her round shiny face. "It most certainly do *so* matter! Now when this war is over and the judge come back we can fix this place back again, jes like new. But first we got to run them Yankees back up north where they belong to be!"

For a stunned moment Kathryn looked at her before beginning to laugh. "Oh Sula, how can you always be so optimistic?" she asked, wiping away the last of her tears.

"Well, I don't know about that big word, missy, but if it means I got hope then you're right—Sula's always got hope!"

Sula put her arms around Kathryn and shook her shoulders gently. "Now listen here—we got to see good in things, honey. Why the good Lord—now he don't intend all these bad things to happen. And He's bound to fix it soon! Look—we still got most the house left. It ain't so bad, ain't beyond repair, now, is it?"

"No, I suppose not," Kathryn answered.

"All right then, we're goin' over to the Simmons and have some supper. You'll have some company your own age and everything is gonna be jes fine." Sula's eyes sparkled with determination.

"I know you're right, Sula," Kathryn said tiredly. Then, with her arm around Sula's round shoulder, she turned to walk across the street to the Simmons house.

"That's right—I am!" Sula said. "I promised your dear little mama before she died that I'd take care of her sweet baby girl and that's jes what I'm gonna do. Ain't nothin' gonna keep me from it, neither!"

Mrs. Simmons had obviously been waiting for them and met them at the door. She was a small, plump woman with graying hair and plain country features. She had always been kind to Kathryn, and it was the Simmons family whom her father had asked to keep an eye on the place while he was gone. Mr. Simmons was her father's law partner and oldest friend, and their daughter Tilda was the same age as Kathryn. They had even attended a small private school together when they were children.

"Kathryn, you poor child. Come in this house. You should never have tried to stay by yourself in that big old place. It frightens me to think of what could have happened if you'd been home today!"

Kathryn smiled. She knew it would do no good to protest, so she allowed the woman to fuss over her as they walked into the parlor and took a seat before the fire. Mr. Simmons and Tilda waited for them there.

"Please, Sula, you sit down," Kathryn insisted. "You're the one who was almost killed today."

"Of course, Sula," Mrs. Simmons agreed. "Do sit down."

Mr. Simmons, a tall thin balding man with kind brown eyes had risen from his chair as they entered. Tilda brought shawls to place over Kathryn's and Sula's laps. But it was Kathryn they all watched, waited for her to fall to pieces so that they might properly console her. If she disappointed them with her calmness they managed to hide it, bringing hot soup for the two homeless women.

Tilda sat beside Kathryn. She was tall and thin like her father, with dull brown hair pulled back behind her ears. She was not a pretty girl, but the light that shone in her dark eyes and her effervescent personality more than made up for her lack of beauty. As a result, Tilda was always the life of any gathering. She was smart and sometimes irreverent, which Kathryn supposed was one of the reasons she enjoyed being around her. Even in the midst of bad times like these Tilda could always make you laugh.

The Simmons family was kind and sincere in their desire for Kathryn to stay here indefinitely. She had no doubt about that. Still, it rankled Kathryn to be obligated to anyone. She did not like the way they treated Sula, as if she were a servant, not that the black woman would ever complain. But Kathryn could not make this her home any longer than she had to.

"You'll never guess who they brought into our ward at the hospital after you left, Kat," Tilda said animatedly, barely able to sit still as she spoke.

"Who?" Kathryn asked. She was distracted and the day's events had left her spent. She longed only for the comfort of a bed, but she did not want to be rude to Tilda so she listened halfheartedly to her excited words.

"Robert Kincaid! Why you know he and his brother Matthew are the two most eligible men in these parts!" Tilda's voice rang with enthusiasm.

"Robert Kincaid?" Kathryn asked.

"Surely you remember Robert, don't you? From school?" she persisted.

She did recall a Robert Kincard from school, but his family lived west of Asheville in the mountains, at least three hours away. He had attended school for only one year. Of course she had heard of the Kincaid family since then, if only because of their wealth. But she had not seen Robert in years or even thought of him. And she couldn't recall ever meeting the one Tilda called Matthew.

"Yes, I do remember him, Tilda. Has he been wounded?" Kathryn asked.

"I'm not exactly sure what is wrong with him. I didn't actually see him when they brought him in. It will certainly give the other girls something to gossip about though, won't it?"

Kathryn almost laughed aloud, for she knew Tilda was the most likely gossip at the hospital.

"Yes, I imagine so," she said, trying to suppress the yawns that rippled up from her chest.

Mrs. Simmons interrupted before Tilda could do any further speculating.

"Dear, I know Kathryn is tired and both of you must be up early. Why don't you show her to her room now? Sula, you may sleep in the room off the kitchen with Betty and Roxanne."

"Yes'm," Sula said obediently, flashing a look of warning at Kathryn that told her not to complain.

As they climbed the stairs to the bedrooms, Tilda was still chattering to Kathryn.

"Robert Kincaid was one of the handsomest and nicest boys in school, remember?" she whispered. "But Matthew, oh my, he used to frighten me to death. He was always so intense and serious."

"I don't remember Matthew, I'm afraid," Kathryn said.

"Oh, but he's just about the handsomest thing you ever saw! So tall and dark. I'll bet he could just sweep a girl right off her feet with those smoky gray eyes and his charming good looks."

Kathryn looked indulgently at Tilda. The girl fairly twittered and was beginning to sound more and more like her mother every day. Kathryn smiled and accepted Tilda's quick kiss on the cheek as they said goodnight.

That night Kathryn lay in bed for hours, conscious of every unfamiliar lump in the bed and each tick of the clock on the mantle. Each time she closed her eyes she had a frightening vision of Sula, alone at McClary house, surrounded by ugly, dangerous men who might just as easily have left her dead. It hurt her to think of Sula, always so uncomplaining, forced to be apart from her for the first time in her life—put in the servants' quarters like a common slave. And for the second time that day, hot tears spilled from her eyes, running silently down her cheeks to dampen the pillow beneath her head. Her heart ached with concern for Sula and the loneliness they would have to endure. She drifted off to sleep praying that something would happen soon to make things right for them again.

Life belongs to the living
and he who lives must be
prepared for changes.
Johann W. Von Goethe

Chapter Two

Kathryn had forgotten her conversation with Tilda until the next day at the hospital when she came to the bedside of the new patient. She hardly recognized Robert Kincaid.

"Kathryn?—Kathryn McClary—is that you?" the man asked.

The man who had spoken her name had a thin, ravaged face, and his once shining blond hair was now darkened with dirt. He smiled at her, but she could see in his eyes the dullness caused by pain.

"Robert?" she managed to say as she took his thin hand in her own. "What has happened to you? Is it bad?" she whispered sympathetically.

"Bad enough," he replied, with a glimmer of a smile. "I got in the way of some shrapnel as we were falling back from Petersburg up in Virginia. Can't move my legs yet. . . . Doctors say part of the metal is lodged near my spine." His voice grew tired and weak.

Kathryn gasped and touched his frail chest, patting him softly in mute sorrow. The world had turned upside down during this war, had gone crazy. No matter how many times she saw this devastation of the country's best young men she never grew used to it. She could remember Robert as a little boy, running and darting about in a game of tag. He had been a quiet, gentle boy, more considerate of the girls than some of the others.

"Don't fret for me, Kath. The best part of it is I don't feel any pain from the waist down. It's this damned broken collarbone that hurts so much!" he laughed feebly.

She smiled at his unselfish attempt to put her at ease.

"What can I do for you, Robert Kincaid?" she asked, ready to do anything she could to comfort him.

He smiled at her, a glow in his gentle blue eyes as he looked at her fresh, dewy skin and thick lustrous hair. She had grown into a beauty such as he'd never seen. And there was a goodness about her, an honesty that one rarely saw in a girl so young and beautiful. For the first time since his injury he felt a terrible ache within for all he had lost, knowing even if he did not admit it to her, that this injury would probably be permanent.

In the following days Kathryn was impressed with Robert and he became her special patient. She found herself wanting to be with him any time she had a free moment. She made sure he was clean and fed and kept as warm as possible in the drafty rooms of the old depot. When she could she would bring newspapers and read to him about the war's progress.

Before long he began to look more like the Robert she remembered from childhood. And she could not believe how, in such a short period of time, things had changed and how happy she had become.

One morning Kathryn arrived just as the doctors were leaving Robert's room. He was sitting up in bed, propped against his pillows.

Dr. Logan turned from the doorway and looked toward Robert. "I'm sorry, Robert," he said. "Good morning to you, Kathryn," he added as she came in.

Robert wore a clean, neatly starched night shirt that helped give his skin a healthy looking glow of color. It was hard to believe, just by looking at him, that he could be so terribly injured.

"Robert?" she asked.

He looked up at her and in his eyes was an emptiness and sadness that made her want to comfort him.

Quickly she sat beside him and reached to take his hand. "What is it?" she asked.

"Doctor Logan says there's nothing more to be done for me here," he said quietly.

"Oh Robert . . . , I'm sorry."

"I had hoped that one day I could move my legs. They tell me I'm lucky to have a family and a home so near, so I can go home in a few days. They say I'm lucky to be out of the war." His voice shook as he spoke.

"Lucky!" he growled, hitting a fist against his unfeeling legs. "They call this lucky!"

She sat watching him sadly, waiting for his anger and bitterness to subside.

"Robert, I'm so sorry," she murmured. Then with a pause she said, "But there are boys here—"

"Please, Kathryn, not you too!" he snapped, turning slightly away from her.

"Robert . . . look over there at the Johnson boy," she whispered. "His legs are fine and he can walk about, but he has the mind of a child now, and his wife will never again know the comfort of her husband's strong and loving protection. She can never even have a conversation with him! I couldn't bear it if that had happened to you."

Robert turned back toward her and took a deep breath of air, breathing it out disgustedly through his mouth.

"And what about Johnny Everett? Would you trade

your legs for his poor blinded eyes? At least you're still here with the people who love you. . . ." Kathryn stopped, saddened by the words she spoke and afraid she had said too much.

"The people who love me?" he asked. His eyes were filled with longing as he looked at her questioningly.

"Yes . . . your family and friends," she replied. "We care about you."

"And do you . . . care about me, Kathryn?" he asked.

"You know that I do," she smiled.

He grinned sheepishly at her and seemed satisfied and pleased with her answer.

"You're right Kath . . . I know you are. I should learn to count my blessings, I suppose."

"I didn't mean to minimize your injury, Robert, truly I didn't. It's just—"

"No, you don't have to apologize. I need someone like you to tell me the truth when I'm feeling sorry for myself. You know . . . I can't wait for you to meet Matthew. I'd like to be the one showing off a beautiful woman for a change," he grinned.

She watched his eyes darken and his face grow serious as he took her hands in his.

"You realize, of course, that you're the one bright spot in all this misery?" He made an effort to keep his words light. "Kathryn, you mean so much to me."

Kathryn looked down at her red, work-worn hands in his, and a feeling of apprehension began to gather within her. She hoped he had not misinterpreted her words about caring for him. But she could not deny that it was becoming more evident each day that Robert cared for her in a much different way than she did for him. She could see it now in his eyes as he spoke.

"I almost wish we had more time here . . . that I

could take it slower, but I'll be leaving soon and I need to say these words to you."

"Robert—" she began.

"No, let me finish. The days here with you have meant so much to me. What I'm trying to say is . . . is that I've fallen in love with you, Kathryn. I often think of how you'd look, dressed in fine gowns once more . . . your auburn hair shining, done in the latest style. I long to see those green eyes spark with fun and mischief again."

"Robert . . ." she began. "I don't think those days can ever come again—"

"Yes, they can! And they will. The war can't last much longer. Grant's leadership and our lack of supplies is already taking its toll. When the war is finally over we can begin again . . . together." His words were questioning.

Kathryn said nothing for she didn't know what to say without hurting him.

"The Kincaid family is not ruined, you know, no thanks to me," he laughed. "Matthew made sure of that. I can remember how angry I was at him . . . oh, how long ago that seems. I was furious with him for being what I thought was disloyal to the South because he refused to give all our fortune to the 'great cause.' "

Robert gazed up at the ceiling, reflecting on his memories.

"How green and naive I was when I accused him of being cynical and ungallant, and how correct he was in his judgment. God, I was so wrong. What I'm trying to say is that, thanks to Matthew, I can give you everything you want . . . materially. It's just . . . Lord, I don't know exactly how to put this . . ."

Kathryn looked at him with affection, for she did care for him. Placing her hand on his arm, she stilled his words. Before the events of the last few years she knew that a young man and woman would never be allowed to speak privately of marriage, much less the subject Robert was trying so hard to broach. Indeed, they would not be allowed to visit alone in the hospital as they did every day. But she wanted to spare him any further embarrassment in trying to explain what she already knew.

"I know, I think, what you are trying to say, and I thank you for being so gallant. But we both know it would not be fair to you, Robert. I have nothing. . . ."

"You have nothing?!" he interrupted. "Oh, my sweet, adorable girl," he laughed. "You have everything! With your intelligence and compassion . . . your beauty . . . what more could a man—"

"No, Robert, what I mean is . . . I don't think . . . I mean, I'm not sure about love. Oh, I'm saying this all wrong." Kathryn took a deep breath and made an effort to continue more calmly. "I love you as a very dear friend, but as for marriage . . ."

"I know that, Kathryn, and I can accept it. Maybe in time . . . but you're what I want, who I want to spend the rest of my life with, such as it is." He looked directly into her eyes, his blue gaze never wavering. "I admit it would be an unconventional marriage, but I want to take care of you, provide a home for you. We will base it on friendship, Kathryn, if you wish . . . companionship. It would not be much different than a marriage arranged by our families."

She sat quietly, thinking of his words. At that moment they sounded so comforting and reassuring. She was weary of the day-to-day struggle just to exist. But marriage to someone she did not love? A lifetime of living with a man who could never be more than a friend? No, she had always presumed there would be more than that, much more, when she married.

"It's not fair for me to ask this of you, is it?" he said,

doubt beginning to slow his words. "To marry a cripple?"

Quickly she looked up, frowning, startled by the anguish in his voice. "No, don't ever say that, Robert," she said firmly. "That has nothing to do with my hesitancy. Please, don't convince yourself it does."

"All right. I've rushed you. We shan't speak of it again until I leave for home. But I warn you, Kathryn McClary, I'm not going to give up on you," Robert said, his voice firm and steady.

She smiled. How could she not smile at his sweet persistence? He was a kind, gentle man, and the last thing she wanted was to be impatient with him. She bade him goodnight and left the hospital for the short walk to the Simmons house.

As soon as she walked into the entryway of the house she sensed something was wrong. The house was deathly quiet, save for the low murmur of voices coming from the parlor. Like a wake. The thought flashed briefly through her mind before the icy grip of fear struck her. She wanted to turn and run as fast as she could out of the door of the house and never come back, rather than face whatever it was that brought the certain chill of death into the Simmons warm and comfortable home.

Kathryn stood frozen where she was, still and breathless as the parlor door opened, almost as if someone had sensed her presence. Sula came forward and clasped her young charge to her before wordlessly leading her into the room. She was crying. "We got somethin to tell you, honey," she said.

Kathryn's feet felt leaden and her teeth had begun to chatter. She saw the look of stark pain in Sula's eyes, pain and something else—in her face was a distinct and very personal look of pity. It was then that Kathryn realized what they had to tell her.

"Daddy?" she cried softly, her voice sounding very young, a keening sound filled with such anguish that it brought forth a soft groan of sympathy from Sula.

Mr. Simmons stepped forward solemnly. In his arms were a few articles of clothing and in his outstretched hand he held her father's gold watch, its long chain dangling crazily down between his fingers.

"No, no, no . . ." Kathryn backed away from the man and his small, sad bundle of belongings. This then, she thought, is the end of it . . . of the man who had loved and taught her all her life. Even if the thought had entered her mind the past few months that he might be dead or wounded, she knew now that she never really believed it could happen, not to her own father.

Kathryn's knees buckled beneath her and she sank to the carpeted floor, overcome by a great wave of weakness. She was never unconscious, but her legs simply refused to hold her any longer. Even in her grief she was aware of the disgust she felt with herself for showing such a loss of control in front of the others. But there seemed to be nothing she could do as she watched all of them through a cool, white haze.

Mr. Simmons quickly laid her father's belongings down with the watch sparkling beneath the glow of lamplight and rushed to help her. Kathryn could not take her eyes off the glistening object. It was the last thing she remembered before the numbing rush of darkness came and carried her away from the terrible pain tearing at her heart.

The doctor came later in the evening and administered a small dose of laudanum to the distraught girl.

"Nothing I can do except provide her with a little rest through the dreamless, thoughtless passage of time," he said.

As the minutes passed into hours and the hours into days, Kathryn became numb with grief, refusing to eat or drink or even to speak to those around her.

"Happens that way with some," Dr. Logan told Sula and Mrs. Simmons two nights later as they watched Kathryn sleeping. "Grief can destroy the mind in those not able to face the truth."

"Kathryn's not like that—she's a strong girl," Sula declared. "She's gonna be all right. I know she is."

"Well, nothing to do now but wait, Miss Sula," he said looking at her with sympathy. "It's up to Kathryn now—but you're right, she is a strong girl. She may pull herself out of it yet."

It was the third morning after the news of her father's death and Kathryn sat staring blankly out the bedroom window. Sula placed a cup of herbal tea on the small walnut table before her. The girl did not move or acknowledge her presence in any way. Sula tiptoed quietly to the door, where Mrs. Simmons stood watching anxiously. Kathryn was vaguely aware of the voices that spoke softly behind her.

"How is she this morning, Sula?" Mrs. Simmons asked.

"Jes like she been the last two days, ma'am. She won't talk, won't eat. Lord, it breaks my old heart to see her like this. It's like the light done gone out of her. Her daddy never should have gone and left her in the first place. He always did treat her too grown up for her own good. And her . . . why, she spent all her time tryin' to live up to his belief that she was a grown woman. She never even had the chance to be a little girl!" Sula shook her head worriedly.

"I agree with you completely, Sula," Mrs. Simmons

whispered. "Men! Why do you know they've made a big thing of the judge's death in town? Even got his picture on the front page of the weekly, as if his dying was some kind of glorious sacrifice. I for one can't find anything glorious in what our poor Kathryn is suffering right now."

"Amen," Sula agreed.

Kathryn focused on the steady downpour of sleet falling outside her window. The tiny pieces of ice made the smallest rattle of noise on the trees and rooftop, causing the winter birds to dart about from limb to limb. The sleet fell heavily, straight down, becoming interspersed with large feathery flakes of snow. She could feel the cold through the glass panes and the rush of wind around the window sash. She picked up the cup and drank the dark, bitter tasting tea.

"Sula, would you bring me the newspaper, please?" she asked, her unused voice hoarse and low.

At the sound of Kathryn's voice Sula clasped her chest in surprise and turned from Mrs. Simmons. She hurried forward to the girl and brushed the thick cloud of hair back from her shoulders.

"Kathryn, love, let me get you something to eat," she said gently, as if tentatively coaxing a wild kitten. "You had nothin' to eat for goin' on three days, child."

Kathryn looked up at Sula, at the anxiety on her face. She never intended to hurt this woman, and yet she knew she had. She smiled at her.

"All right," she said. "I'll eat if you will sit and eat with me. And when you bring our supper, please also bring the paper."

"Kathryn, honey . . ." Sula began, her voice pleading.

"Now, Sula, it will be all right. I need to see it . . . I need to." Kathryn's voice broke slightly.

Sula looked toward Mrs. Simmons, who nodded

from the doorway.

"All right then. I'll go get us some supper," Sula said, great tears welling in her black eyes.

Later, under the watchful eyes of Sula, Kathryn managed to eat the hot soup and bread placed before her, trying to quell her anxiety to be done and reach for the paper. When she did she appeared outwardly calm as she hungrily scanned the dark picture of her father on the front page and read the glowing report of his brave and heroic death during the siege of Atlanta. It had taken three months for the soldier to bring his few belongings and the news of his death. But as he explained, it was something he wanted to do personally for the judge.

The paper began to shake in her hands and the print became blurred as hot tears dimmed her vision. Sula, ever watchful, agilely rose and took the paper from Kathryn's trembling fingers and laid it carefully on the table.

Kathryn bent forward, placing her face in her hands, unable to stop the torrent of grief that overwhelmed her and shook every inch of her slender body.

"I hate crying . . . I hate feeling this way, this terrible way . . . and I hate this war!" she cried.

"Oh, my baby," Sula murmured, holding her close and crying with her. "It's all right, it's all right."

"What are we going to do now, Momma Sula? Whatever are we going to do now?"

Sula held her and soothed her for long moments, and a tiny smile lit her face. For even though it hurt to see Kathryn suffering so, she knew instinctively that this was a turning point for the girl. She knew now that despite the grief that would haunt her for a long time to come, her little Kat would get through this just as she had everything else. She was a survivor.

Who does the best his circumstances allow,
Does well, acts nobly—angels could no more.
Edward Young

Chapter Three

Sleet continued to fall through the night, pattering softly against the windowsill. Firelight lit Kathryn's bedroom with a warm glow of topaz-colored shadows.

She had finally convinced Sula to leave her and go to her own bed. Sula reluctantly did so, leaving one candle lit beside the bed, a candle that Kathryn now extinguished. She had cried until her eyes ached and her head throbbed, now she wanted only the peace and darkness of her room. It was the kind of night she once would have enjoyed, with the wintry elements at bay outside the cozy confines of her darkened hideaway.

But this night was one for saying goodbye and for making plans. It was late in the night when she had finally made all her decisions and at last let her weary mind rest.

She was up early, even before Sula came to check on her. She had dressed in one of the few worn, faded day gowns she possessed, one which she had long since outgrown.

"What on earth are you doin'?" Sula asked, setting the breakfast tray down with a clatter.

"Getting dressed to go to the hospital," Kathryn answered.

"Oh, no—huh, uh, you get right back in that bed!

Its freezing cold outside . . . and you ain't well. No ma'am, you are not goin'!" Sula fumed.

"I'm going Mom Sula," Kathryn said quietly, with the familiar tone of stubbornness in her voice that Sula knew so well.

"Girl, you're as stubborn a lass as ever drew breath!" Sula snapped, obviously frustrated.

"Learned it from you," Kathryn said with a hint of her old mischievousness. "Now! Sit and eat with me before I go off into the cold, dreary world."

Mr. Simmons drove the girls to the hospital because of the bad weather. Kathryn sat silently as the exuberant Tilda rattled on and on about the news of the war and the tragedies of their various patients. She seemed to know the life story of each of them. Kathryn suspected she was in conspiracy with Sula and Mrs. Simmons to keep her occupied with silly, meaningless chatter.

It was an exceptionally busy day at the hospital, with new soldiers arriving from South Carolina by special train. During the busiest part of the afternoon Pastor Morgan called Kathryn aside.

"We're going to need more bandages, Kathryn. Mrs. Mulligan over at the saloon has some for us, but until one of the orderlies can get free, you'll just have to do the best you can."

"I suppose I could go over and get them," she said.

"Oh, I don't think you can do that. The saloon will be crowded with soldiers that brought the supply wagons into town. A young lady like yourself . . ."

"Of course I can go," Kathryn said. She was eager to be away from the hospital for awhile. "I'll wear the nurse's band on my arm and I'm sure there will be no problem. Besides, I work with soldiers every day."

"Well . . . if you're sure. We do need those bandages badly with all the new patients. I suppose it will be all right, after all it's only across the street."

As she walked outside she saw that Pastor Morgan was right—the streets were filled with soldiers. But she got the bandages from Mrs. Mulligan, the saloon keeper, and hurried back out toward the street. She smiled as she thought of what Sula would say if she knew Kathryn had actually stepped foot inside a saloon.

She walked into the crowded street and was trying to make her way back to the hospital when one of the soldiers jostled her, causing Kathryn to drop some of the bandages.

"Well now, ain't you a pretty little nurse," one of them said, coming up close beside her.

"Excuse me," she said.

"Wait a minute now. I just want to talk to you. Its been a mighty long time since I've seen such a pretty woman . . ." He clamped his dirty hand onto her arm.

"Soldier! Let the lady pass."

The man released her arm as he and the others turned to see who had spoken. The man shouldering his way through the crowd was tall and dark; his eyes were shaded by the gray officer's hat he wore. He looked at Kathryn only briefly, his glance quickly appraising her as she stood staring up at him.

"What's your outfit, soldier?" the uniformed man asked sternly.

"Fifty-third North Carolina, sir!" the soldier replied, saluting the man before him.

"Then I suggest you get back to it."

"Yessir, Major, yessir." The man quickly hurried away, obviously relieved to have received no other reprimand.

The major turned to Kathryn and she saw his face more clearly. He was one of the most devastatingly handsome men she'd ever seen and she could only stand speechlessly looking at him.

"You work in the saloon, miss?" he asked.

"Me? . . . Why no . . . I . . . I work at the hospital." She lifted the bandages for him to see. "I just went there to pick up these bandages."

"I see. Then I suggest you return to the hospital before some other poor soldier succumbs to your charms." His voice held the same sarcastic, cold quality as when he had spoken to the soldier moments before.

Angrily she gathered the bandages up in her arms and whirled away from him. On impulse she turned and shouted over her shoulder. "I'm not one of your soldiers, Major!"

His eyebrows lifted in surprise and he gave a soft chuckle as he pushed his hat back on his head. She knew he watched her as she stalked angrily up the steps and into the hospital.

But once in the hospital Kathryn scarcely had time to think again of the brash Confederate officer who had angered her. Her whole mind was concentrated on the wounded who had been brought in.

She found herself thinking of Robert constantly, more anxious than ever to see him and assure herself that he, at least, was all right. Now that she had come to care so much for him, his handicap seemed less and less important, but still she worried.

When she had finished work in the evening she went

to Robert's ward. She had worked three hours past her five o'clock schedule and many of the soldiers in the low row of beds were already asleep. The room seemed especially dark and depressing by lamplight. Most of the rooms in the old building were badly in need of repair, the stuccoed walls cracked and damp. It was no wonder recuperation took so long in such a place.

She found Robert sitting up in one of the new, wheeled chairs. Beside him stood a well-dressed young black man whom she did not know.

Robert's eyes came alive when he saw her. She particularly noticed how handsome he had become since regaining some of his weight. As he reached out to take her hand there was sympathy in his clear blue eyes. It was evident that he had heard about her father's death.

She pulled a chair close to his and sat down, still holding his hand.

"Kathryn, this is Joseph," Robert said. "He has taken care of everything at Foxfire since Matt and I left and he's also an excellent coachman. Joseph, this is Kathryn McClary, the young lady I've been telling you about."

Joseph was tall and handsome, with the same clear, dark features as Sula. But his eyes were a pale gray instead of snapping black like hers. He bowed solemnly to Kathryn, his attitude friendly but restrained, more that of a servitor than a family member.

Joseph soon excused himself and Robert immediately brought Kathryn toward him. His sympathy for her was evident in every motion of his body and every look he gave her.

"I'm so sorry about your father, darling," he said,

holding her in his arms.

Kathryn had never felt as close to anyone as she did to Robert at that moment, and she was surprised to find just how much she needed him now. His tenderness quickly brought a lump to her throat and she found it difficult to speak. But she was tired. It had been a long night and an even longer day and she wanted nothing more than to go home, take a bath, and change into something warm. Her worn gown was soiled, her hair had fallen from its prim chignon, and her work-worn hands felt chaffed and red.

"Darling," Robert began slowly. "Now that this has happened, what will you do? You can't go back to your home in its present state. The South is falling as surely as I speak, and soon the Union will squash the homeless and unprotected in every Southern community. You must get away from the city!" He paused, watching her face.

"Surely you can see that?" he asked.

When she sighed and did not answer, he continued. "I'm sure the Simmonses would love for you to stay with them indefinitely, but I have a feeling it's not what you really want, for you or Sula. Is it?"

She took a deep breath and looked at him. Her eyes were large and luminous, filled with a sadness and desperation she had not allowed him to see before. He reached out and touched her cheek softly.

"You're too perceptive, Robert," she said quietly, "and you know me entirely too well."

"No, never. I'll never be able to know enough about you," he said almost shyly.

"Actually, I thought most of the night about what we're to do and I have still found no solution." She lifted her chin slightly as she spoke.

"To be perfectly honest . . . I had hoped your solution would be much more clear-cut . . . for both of us."

"Oh, Robert, I wish . . ."

"No, don't wish—or wonder if its the proper thing. Just do it, Kathryn! For once in your life, do something for yourself, something *you* want to do," he pleaded. "Marry me and let me take care of you. It can be such a wonderful life, I know it can," he pleaded.

Kathryn took another deep breath. She had already considered it, mulling it over in her mind a thousand times during the long cold night and still she could not say with a certainty if it was what she truly wanted. It seemed lately she could not make even the most basic decisions regarding her life, much less one of this magnitude. Perhaps he was right. Perhaps she did need someone to care for her. Tonight, here with Robert, it seemed right.

All she knew for certain was that she was exhausted, both physically and emotionally, and in this worn state of mind she longed only for peace and security—the warmth of a real home again. Was that so wrong?

Sula had always told her she would meet a man someday whom she would love so deeply and desperately that she would know it was right. But perhaps Sula was wrong. Perhaps what she was feeling for Robert was love, perhaps not everyone found a deep, all-consuming love in their life. Besides, she could not imagine anyone wanting a tired, worn, penniless girl like herself with nothing to offer. And yet miraculously Robert did.

Could she afford to toss away this opportunity, expecting to find something, someday, that might never come?

Robert waited patiently, watching her face all the while as she stood lost in her own thoughts. Yet he would say nothing to persuade her—knowing it must be her own decision.

Saying a small, silent prayer, Kathryn looked up into Robert's eagerly waiting face. She smiled at him and pushed aside all her doubts.

"Are you sure, Robert?" She wanted to give him one last chance to be certain.

"Does that mean yes?"

"Yes," she said.

He took her face tenderly in his hands and kissed her cheeks and her closed eyelids, then almost reverently he kissed her warm, upturned lips.

"You have made me the happiest man in the state of North Carolina . . . in all of the Confederate States . . . and in the Union too," he said, lowering his voice conspiratorially.

They both laughed, and Kathryn felt her fear of making a tragic mistake lessen somewhat in his happiness.

One of the orderlies stepped inside the room and looked toward Robert. "You got a visitor, Cap'n Kincaid."

Kathryn and Robert both looked down toward the hallway, where a man walked toward them. The light was behind him, outlining only the tall, erect figure of a man in uniform, striding purposefully toward them. He wore a great coat that flared out about him as he walked, and he filled the doorway with his imposing presence.

Robert frowned and squinted into the light. The man moved forward and Kathryn found herself captivated by the mystery and sense of adventure that he brought into the room. The very air seemed to vibrate with his presence and she found herself curiously trying to see his face.

"Robert," he said, his voice as deeply masculine as Kathryn would have expected, and it sounded strangely familiar.

Robert's face broke into a wide grin of surprise and pleasure as he recognized the man.

"Matthew! God, I can't believe its you! How did you get here? When . . ."

Matthew stepped into the light of the small lantern and Kathryn gasped as she saw his eyes upon her. His face held the same surprise as they stared at each other. It was the Confederate officer she had met in the street earlier that day. So this was Matthew Kincaid!

The man bent and embraced his younger brother, clasping his shoulders tightly in his gloved hands. Robert was obviously pleased and moved by his brother's sudden appearance.

"Never mind answering my questions, Matthew. We'll get to that. First let me tell you my good news. This is Kathryn McClary and she has just moments ago consented to be my bride." Robert beamed at Kathryn, proudly displaying her to his brother. "Kathryn darling, meet your new brother-in-law."

Matthew pulled himself up to his full height and turned to Kathryn, towering over her as he looked solemnly down into her face. He made no mention of their previous meeting as he tucked his gloves into his belt and removed his greatcoat. Then he stepped forward rather formally and took her hand in his. In a coolly courteous gesture he barely brushed his mouth against the back of her fingers, causing a shiver to ripple up her spine.

Kathryn became painfully aware of her rough, calloused hands in his and she knew he did not miss that detail, either. Why it should matter to her she did not know.

Matthew's eyes scanned her face curiously and she had to admit he did a splendid job of concealing his surprise that Robert was taking a bride. Not once did he allow his cool gray eyes to flicker toward Robert's lifeless legs beneath the woolen coverlet.

He pulled a chair forward and sat down, listening attentively as Robert told him of his proposal and his eagerness to go home. All the while they talked Kathryn's attention was focused on Matthew.

Beside Matthew, Robert appeared slight and boyishly handsome, almost pretty. Matthew was so different, with his dark skin and black hair that grew a bit long about his neck and fell thickly over his forehead. He had high, wide cheekbones with a straight nose, giving him an exotic, almost foreign look. His features were hard, bringing to mind the image of a privateer. Yet his lips were well-formed and sensual, even sensitive. If anything Kathryn found him even more handsome than before. She continued to study his ruggedly handsome face. It had the look of one hardened by life, one not given to standing aside patiently to await the actions of others. Kathryn would guess him to be a man of fast decisions and quick observations. Everything about him exuded energy and vitality. He had a tense, waiting quality about him, almost as if he might spring up at any moment to pace restlessly about the room.

Matthew's dark glance flicked suddenly toward Kathryn, catching her off guard as she watched him. His eyes met hers briefly before traveling to her disheveled hair and thin, worn dress that fit too snugly in all the wrong places, then to her worn shoes and blunt, ragged nails. Things that had not bothered her before when she was with Robert now suddenly seemed obvious and glaring, and made her want to run and hide from his quick, knowing eyes. Just as suddenly his attention turned again to Robert, leaving Kathryn with the feeling that she had just been summarily dismissed.

"What are you doing back here in North Carolina, Matthew?" Robert asked. "Last time I heard you were in Kentucky."

"We're escorting a supply train through the mountains to Greensboro. I took a slight detour to visit you," he stated simply.

"You detoured a whole supply train just to visit me?" Kathryn could see his pleasure as he spoke to Matthew and she knew it meant a great deal to him that his brother had come.

In answer to Robert's question, Matthew only smiled. It was obvious that the two of them cared a great deal about each other. As they talked, she thought it odd that they did not speak of Robert's injury, but then the Kincaids were, as gossip had it, a rather enigmatic family.

"Have you been home to see Mother?" Robert asked.

"I'm going there as soon as I leave you, little brother,

which should be soon if I'm to get back to my company by morning."

"Well, I'm glad you came—you can't imagine how good it is to see you and know that you, at least, are well." Robert's face was unusually serious as he spoke.

Matthew frowned as if the words pained him, but he quickly hid it as he again embraced his brother. He picked up his coat as they said their rather formal goodbyes.

"Oh, Matthew," Robert said, glancing over at Kathryn. "Could you escort Kathryn over to the Simmons house? She's living there temporarily, and I believe Tilda Simmons has already left. I promised her I'd find Kathryn a way home."

Kathryn looked startled, surprised at his unexpected request. "Oh, no, Robert. I'm sure Major Kincaid is in a hurry . . ."

Matthew turned his cool gaze toward her and with a slight tilt of his head said, "On the contrary, Miss McClary, I'm never too busy to escort a beautiful lady home. And with all the troops on the streets, you might not be safe." His full lips curled upward in a deliberately flirtatious smile.

"No, really . . ."

"Kathryn," Robert scolded. "Let him do this for you. I know you're tired, and if you wait for Pastor Morgan, you won't get any rest at all tonight. All right?"

She glanced at Matthew, who was watching her closely.

"All right," she agreed reluctantly, unwilling to make a scene in front of Matthew.

"She has an independent mind," Robert said fondly, gazing with adoration at Kathryn. "But it's one of her most endearing qualities."

"I'm sure," Matthew drawled.

If the sarcasm of his reply failed to register on Robert, it did not pass Kathryn unnoticed. She had a feeling from the first that Matthew Kincaid did not approve of her, but she had no earthly idea why. The look on his face now, thoughtful and challenging, made her wonder just what it was about her that seemed to irritate him so and cause his instant disapproval. She drew in her breath and lifted her eyebrows proudly, meeting his eyes with a challenge of her own.

Matthew read the look, his only reaction a slight smile before motioning with his gloved hand that she should go first.

She bent and kissed Robert briefly on the cheek, instinctively aware of Matthew's look from the doorway.

"See you tomorrow, darling," Robert said. "Goodbye Matthew, take care of yourself and tell Mother when you see her that Joseph and I made the arrangements today for my trip home."

Matthew did not speak as he escorted Kathryn down the hall and out of the hospital. She felt awkward and unsure of herself as she walked beside him, his confidence evident in the way he held himself, the way he walked. After arranging for a buggy, he helped her into the passenger side, then walked around to climb into the driver's seat.

The pale winter sun had long since set behind the surrounding mountains, and the night had grown cold and windy. Above them thousands of stars sparkled across the black sky, as a few scattered, wind-whipped clouds pushed past the silvered moon. The streets were almost empty and few lights shone from the houses. Kathryn felt an isolation from the world here in the rugged mountains. It was not usually an unpleasant feeling, but tonight it caused a tremble to race up her spine.

"How long have you known Robert?" Matthew asked from the darkness, his deep voice much closer than she thought.

"We knew each other as children," she said quietly.

"And how did it happen that you became reacquainted?" he asked.

"I met him at the hospital. Tilda Simmons mentioned that Robert was there," she replied.

"So you looked for him?"

"Why, no . . . I . . . I saw him one day while I was working." She looked over at his profile in the darkness, wondering what he meant. But he was looking straight ahead, as if he had not heard her reply.

If this was his idea of polite conversation, she found it very unusual.

Matthew said nothing more and soon they arrived at the steps of the Simmons place, where he came around to help her down from the buggy.

Rather than take her hand he reached up to place his hands at her waist. She hesitated only slightly, surprised at the intimacy of his gesture, before placing her own hands on his broad shoulders, allowing him to lift her easily to the ground. But he did not step away from her immediately. She looked up at him, startled and a bit puzzled by his actions. She could see the glint of light from the house as it reflected in his eyes.

"I don't want my brother hurt, Miss McClary." His voice carried a hint of warning.

She stepped back as if she'd been burned. Now she understood a little better where his questions were leading.

"Major Kincaid," she said coldly, "I wonder why you find it necessary even to mention such a warning to me."

"I wouldn't call it a warning," he said.

"Then what do you call it?" she insisted, her cheeks growing warm with anger.

"You're a young, beautiful woman Miss McClary, as I'm sure you're well aware." His mouth was curved in a sarcastic smile as he spoke. "My brother is vulnerable right now, perhaps willing to let his heart overrule his head. If I may be so blunt, I couldn't expect you to be a faithful wife to him under the circumstances, but I would suggest an understanding . . . between the two of us."

"An understanding?" she asked, frowning. She turned her head to one side, curious to know what he could possibly be suggesting.

"For your part, I expect you to treat Robert with respect and an outward display of affection when in the presence of my mother or his friends. Never give him any cause for embarrassment. I don't think that's too much to ask." His words were measured and impersonal, but she could see the tension in the set of his jaw and the repressed anger in every gesture he made.

"Be discreet," she answered sarcastically. She could not believe her ears. How could he be speaking to her in this manner when he barely knew her? And in her usual way she could not reveal exactly how deeply he had wounded and insulted her.

"Exactly," he answered.

"And in this 'understanding' between us, Major . . . just what is your part to be?" She kept her voice steady, careful not to let him see her rage.

"I shall see that you have everything you could ever wish for . . . that money can buy, at least. And that is your whole purpose for marrying Robert, isn't it?" His look was cold and disdainful, as if the very sight of her disgusted him. "And of course, if there are any other brotherly 'services' you might require . . ."

She slapped him then, her hand stinging where it met his hard, unyielding jaw. Her breasts rose and fell rapidly in anger and her green eyes glistened with fury.

"How dare you!" she said. "How dare you speak to me this way! You know nothing about me or how I shall behave. Whether you believe it or not I happen to care very deeply for Robert. You're as arrogant and overbearing as—"

"Spare me, Miss McClary," he cut in, never betraying a sign of the anger she knew he must be feeling. It was as if the slap had not happened. "Use your energy to convince Robert just how deeply you care." His words reeked with sarcasm.

He stepped toward her, his face very near to hers, but he carefully avoided touching her. His words were slow and carefully chosen and this time there was no mistaking the warning they carried.

"For if he should spend one moment of pain because of you, then you, my dear, shall answer to me."

He turned abruptly on his heel, the cape of his great coat swinging out from him as he climbed up into the buggy. He drove swiftly away, never turning to look at her again.

Kathryn stood shivering, her arms and legs trembling and her heart pounding at her throat. She sat on the steps and took long shuddering gulps of the cold evening air. The doubts she'd had about her marriage to Robert came crashing in upon her, threatening to overpower her, but she knew it was too late. She was responsible now both for her own life and Sula's welfare, and marrying Robert was simply the best she could do. She would try to show him her appreciation every day of their lives for what he was doing for her. That was the least she could do. But no one, not even the infuriatingly arrogant Matthew Kincaid, had the right to condemn her before she even had a chance to prove herself.

A man is too apt to forget that in this world he cannot have everything. A choice is all that is left him.

H. Mathews

Chapter Four

Telling Sula of her decision was onc of the hardest things Kathryn had ever done. At first Sula just looked at her in disbelief.

"Married? Why child, you can't get married . . . I mean you can, but . . . who is this man and what do you know about him? Do you love him?" she asked, obviously too stunned to know what to say.

"His name is Robert Kincaid—don't you remember Tilda talking about him? And I've known him most of my life," Kathryn said, not meeting Sula's questioning look.

"But do you love him?" Sula insisted.

"Oh, Kathryn!" Tilda said, bursting into the room. "Is it true? This is just the most exciting, the most romantic thing I've ever heard!"

Kathryn looked up from her packing, relieved by Tilda's interruption.

"Yes, Tilda, it is," she said.

Tilda threw her long thin arms around the smaller girl and squeezed her tightly, bouncing on the toes of her feet as she did so.

"But this is wonderful! Sula . . . isn't this wonderful? Married into the wealthy Kincaid family. And Robert is *so* handsome . . . and even if he is crippled right now, why I'm sure . . ."

"Crippled?" Sula asked, looking at Kathryn oddly.

"Oh, Sula," Kathryn said breezily. "You'd better see to the items we're taking from home. I think they're waiting downstairs to help you load some things into the wagon."

Sula's eyes flashed angrily but she left without another word. Kathryn knew, however, that it was not the end of the discussion.

Nothing Kathryn said in the next couple of days could make Sula happy about her decision to marry Robert. But after seeing Kathryn's determination she yielded quietly, as usual, hoping that perhaps she had been wrong. She left for the Kincaid home a day before Kathryn and Robert, taking the few remaining heirlooms that had belonged to Kathryn's mother.

It was December twenty-second when Robert and Kathryn left Asheville. The weather had grown progressively worse and the numbing wind rattled limbs in the huge bare trees along the road, making them crack loudly through the forest. Still, the view of the mountains was breathtaking and the blue haze that covered the surrounding peaks gave a mystical glow to everything.

The carriage wound its way through the lowlands and rattled up the road into the foothills as Kathryn held Robert's hand and watched him anxiously. His eyes were bright with anticipation, although he still appeared weak and tired. She worried about the prolonged exposure to the cold and hoped they would soon reach the top of the mountain and his home.

Almost three hours later they rounded a long curve and Kathryn saw the house ahead of them. Foxfire Manor had been built on the side of the mountain rather than at the peak. It probably had been placed there because this view gave a good vantage point, overlooking the vast holdings of Kincaid land below. They owned the valley as far as could be seen from the house—the valley of the tranquil French Broad river. As they reached the first plateau, the mountain leveled off onto a long, sloping grass-covered knoll. At the top of the knoll stood the house, the most magnificent house Kathryn had ever seen.

She was reminded at once of Matthew Kincaid as she viewed the dark, mysterious structure. It seemed quite fitting that he should be master of such a place—much more fitting for him, really, than for the gentle Robert.

The house was not built in the typical antebellum style now so popular in the South, but instead had been fashioned from native stones of gray and brown. There were many long, shuttered windows along the front of the house, with tall, cream-colored columns on the porch that reached up to the second level.

Kathryn turned to Robert and saw his look of longing at his home. He clutched Kathryn's hand in his. "Well, what do you think of your new home?" he asked proudly.

"It's . . . it's magnificent, Robert, just beautiful," she replied.

But she shivered as she gazed up at the house. As beautiful as it was, there was a brooding, mystical quality to the place. It seemed so alone and closed in, leaving her with a vague, unexplainable feeling.

The sloping front lawn ran right to the edge of the mountain. There, jutting out from the mountain, was a large granite ledge. Kathryn smiled with pleasure as she imagined standing there with the strong updrafts from the valley blowing across the rocky cliffs. From this place could be seen the rich bottomland below and the bright shining strip that was the river as it cut through the middle of the fertile plains.

Kathryn looked away from the view and back to the house. She was shaking as they grew nearer, but it had nothing to do with the cold wind. For a fraction of a moment as she looked at the house, the gray afternoon light fell blankly on the windows, giving back no reflections. In that moment the manor looked like the giant face of some dark being, waiting and watching.

She shrugged her shoulders, trying to shake the unpleasant feeling, telling herself she was merely tired from the last few tumultuous days and weeks. Her emotions and fears had overstimulated her imagination, that was all.

She wondered if the wind always blew across the clearing as it was doing now, fiercely whipping the horse's mane and tail. In the distance the tallest peaks of the mountain stood covered with the winter's first snowfall, while dark clouds hung low as if ready to dump even more.

They drove slowly up the circular drive to the large stone front porch. She could feel the tension in Robert beside her and his anticipation at being home after all the months he'd been away. Though it was bitterly cold, the servants stood awaiting them, with the huge double oak doors flung wide. Lamps had been lit within, sending a welcome glow out into the cold and darkening winter afternoon.

Kathryn sighed in relief, for by now the vision of the frightening face she'd seen on the house earlier had disappeared. It was, after all, only an ordinary house.

The large manor was unique in the way it seemed to blend into the surrounding forest and the perpetual mists that swirled around the Blue Ridge mountains. The house's twinkling lights looked suspended in air there in the mist. She could see why Joshua Kincaid, Robert's father, had named his home Foxfire Manor. From a distance, it did indeed look like the luminous and mysterious foxfire, the flickering lights that were said to move through these mountainsides in summer.

Kathryn had heard of mountain people who sought the foxfire lights for years, but no one had ever found an explanation for them. Kathryn could remember being told that as soon as one grew near to the lights they would disappear or flicker deeper into the forest. Sula used to tell stories about the foxfire, or how some people never returned from their pursuit of these elusive glimmerings. Kathryn shivered again and tried to shake the feeling of unease that kept returning to her.

Joseph pulled the horse to a halt and stepped down and to the rear of the carriage. He lifted Robert into his arms and carried him onto the porch, placing him in a chair with large spoked wheels. The black man's powerful arms barely seemed to ripple at the effort.

From the shadow of the doorway appeared a tiny, gentle-faced woman. Her green Zouave jacket and skirt reflected the simple elegance of one accustomed to the finest comforts that wealth could afford. Her dark blonde hair was drawn back into a chenille net. But Kathryn could see that she was no different than any other mother, for her face reflected the love and the agony of seeing a child hurt. Kathryn knew she was Thursa Kincaid.

Kathryn could almost feel the woman's sadness as she reached down to embrace Robert.

"Welcome home, my darling, darling Robert," the woman said.

Robert was visibly moved at his mother's loving welcome. His blue eyes were misty as he kissed her cheek.

Kathryn had been standing back, feeling very much a stranger among the watchful eyes of the Kincaid people.

Thursa noticed her slight reluctance and moved toward her. With a kind look she said, "And you, of course, are Kathryn. Welcome to Foxfire Manor, my dear. Please come into the house—its grown so cold here on the mountain."

"Eugene is here, Robert," Thursa said.

The man she spoke of stepped forward to shake hands warmly with Robert. They seemed genuinely happy to see one another.

"Eugene, this is the woman I've brought home to marry . . . Kathryn McClary. Kathryn, this is Eugene Davenport, my boyhood chum and closest friend."

The tall, slender man bowed slightly, taking Kathryn's hand in his thin pale one. His hazel eyes blinked nervously as he looked at her.

"Welcome, Miss McClary," he said. "My friend is indeed a lucky man." His eyes surveyed her with admiration.

Robert reached out to touch Kathryn's arm lightly. "I'll leave you with Mother now so that she may introduce you to the staff and your new home." She could see the tiredness in his eyes.

She nodded to him, knowing he probably could see how nervous she was.

"Thank you for coming, Eugene. It means a lot to me. I'll expect you Christmas Day for the wedding," Robert told his friend.

As Joseph pushed Robert's chair deeper into the hallway, the household staff that had been waiting moved forward to greet him before he went to his room.

Mrs. Kincaid introduced Kathryn to the servants who stood in a row shyly waiting to meet Master Robert's bride-to-be. It was then that Kathryn spotted Sula, standing behind the others in the spacious foyer. She lifted her hand in a little greeting. Sula smiled at Kathryn, her bright eyes shining with pride for her. Kathryn could see on her face the happiness Sula felt that Kathryn was being welcomed so graciously to the big elegant house on the mountain. Nothing in her manner today betrayed the disapproval Kathryn knew she must still be feeling.

Moving down the line Kathryn made mental notes, trying to remember each name. Then Mrs. Kincaid stopped before an older woman with dark, almost black hair that was braided and twisted around the crown of her head in a harsh style. Her pale, amber eyes that boldly assessed Kathryn were cold and distant.

"And this is our housekeeper, Lila Spencer . . . and her daughter, Cynthia," Mrs. Kincaid said.

The girl standing beside Mrs. Spencer was also dark. She reminded Kathryn of the Cherokee people who lived in the mountain further west of Asheville. She looked to be seventeen or eighteen. Cynthia Spencer was a pretty girl, but she appeared extremely shy and uncomfortable when being introduced, leading Kathryn to assume she was not used to meeting many strangers here in the mountains.

Robert had mentioned earlier that Mrs. Spencer's husband once fought with Joshua Kincaid in the Indian uprising, and when Mr. Spencer was killed, the family took Mrs. Spencer and her daughter into the home.

Kathryn's glance came back to the girl and she noticed that her eyes held a strange, lackluster look, almost as if she had no conscious thoughts and didn't really see the person she was looking at.

Kathryn found the interior of the house to be quite lovely, warm and inviting. While it was elegant, there was still much of the country feel to it, with the shining wood floors partially covered by small rugs. In the entryway where they stood, the floor was oak parquet, gleaming in the light from the large brass and crystal candelebra overhead. A large mirrored hall tree and oak sideboard were the only other pieces of furniture, although several potted plants brightened the area with their greenery. A graceful stairway to the left of the entryway curved up and around toward the second floor.

"Come into the parlor, Kathryn, Eugene. We'll have tea while Kathryn rests," said Thursa, handing Kathryn's coat to a waiting servant.

"Thank you, Mrs. Kincaid, but no, I must be going," Eugene replied.

"Eugene," Thursa said, her voice growing more serious. "Thank you for being here today to welcome Robert . . . and his bride-to-be," she added, looking toward Kathryn.

"You're entirely welcome, Mrs. Kincaid," he said, bending to kiss the woman's outstretched hand. "I'll be back in a couple of days to check on my old friend. In the meantime, if there's anything you need, you've only to send Joseph down to fetch me."

Then to Kathryn he said, "Miss McClary, once again, congratulations and welcome to our part of North Carolina." He looked at her steadily, his eyes frankly admiring.

"Mr. Davenport," she murmured, feeling a bit uncomfortable at his candid look.

She followed Robert's mother into the parlor, which lay to the right of the entryway. A bright fire burned cheerfully in the grate and many beeswax candles lit the room. Oil for lamps was very scarce, regardless of a family's wealth or status, but Kathryn preferred the atmosphere given by candles and thought the room looked inviting and warm.

Mrs. Spencer carried in a tea tray and did not look up or speak as she left the room and went down the hallway toward the kitchen.

Thursa handed Kathryn a delicate china cup steaming with the fragrant aroma of real tea.

"I'm sorry we've no sugar, but since we have our own beehives there is honey if you like. I've grown so fond of it I may never use sugar again." She laughed gently, her voice reflecting the accent of her English birth.

"Oh, just having tea again is wonderful," Kathryn said gratefully. "I confess I never grew used to the taste of raspberry leaf tea."

Her feet and hands were still numb from the long, cold ride up the mountain, and the warmth of the room and vaporous tea made her feel deliciously pampered. Soon the comfort of her surroundings whisked away the strange feeling she'd felt about the house earlier. She almost laughed now at her silly, foolish imaginings.

"Raspberry leaf teas, persimmons for dates—my, but we Southern ladies have managed to make do, haven't we?" Thursa laughed. "But I'll disclose a little secret to you my dear. Knowing how his spoiled mama loves her tea, Matthew makes sure that I always have a generous supply. He has a friend, you see, who is a blockade runner, scandalous I know . . . so he usually brings a few little luxuries like tea with him when he can manage to visit."

"How very nice of him," Kathryn murmured politely. She managed to hide her doubt that the enigmatic Major Kincaid had a soft spot for anyone, even his own mother. She had found him to be a hard and unyielding man, somber and too demanding of those around him. It was hard to imagine anything would change her mind about him. Indeed, she could not picture him showing tenderness or concern for anyone. Living in the same house with him after the war would certainly be a challenge, to say the least, and a challenge she did not look forward to.

"Kathryn, my dear, I just wanted this little moment alone with you to formally welcome you into our family and let you know how happy I am that you're here." Her look was warm and sincere. "I know you will be very good for Robert and for me as well. I've always longed for a daughter, and I wanted to tell you how sorry I was to hear about your father. I never got the chance to do that. He was a fine man and I hope you will let us be your family now." Her voice softened as she mentioned Kathryn's father.

Kathryn felt the sting of tears at her eyelids. She was more touched by the woman's words of kindness than she would have thought possible. It had been a long time since she had felt such comfort and sincere concern. Since learning of her father's death only two weeks ago she had managed to push her feelings so far inside herself that it was surprising to feel them surface again so readily. She was reminded of the fact that she had not cried since that night with Matthew when he had made her feel so angry and hurt.

"Thank you, Mrs. Kincaid. Your welcome means a great deal to me . . . more than you know," Kathryn said.

"Please call me Thursa. We are all alone here on our mountain and we do not always observe the social amenities. I confess I like it just that way." There was a hint of defiance in her voice as she spoke.

Kathryn was beginning to see for herself that the Kincaids were indeed a unique family. She was surprised and pleased to call her new mother-in-law Thursa, and she was also relieved to be accepted so kindly.

"Well!" Thursa said in her bright, enthusiastic manner. "I know you must be exhausted. Why don't I have Mrs. Spencer take you up and show you to your room?"

Kathryn was escorted up the stairway by the stony-faced Mrs. Spencer. She left Kathryn in the middle of her room with no conversation, no polite mentionings of any further family routines.

A large canopied bed, made of gleaming cherry wood dominated the room. The canopy was covered in an airy, fringed lace that matched the counterpane. In the center of the room was an oval carpet of emerald and rust colors. Other pieces of furniture, a dresser and armoire were of the same cherry wood. The flickering firelight bathed the room in an amber glow. Over all, the atmosphere was one of simplicity and beauty.

Kathryn heard a sound from outside the house. It sounded like the high-pitched laughter of a child. She walked to the large windows and looked out, but while she could see the fir trees and branches of thickly clumped mountain laurel whipping about in the fierce wind, there was no child there. There was no one. Perhaps it was just the wind around the eaves of the house, she told herself.

She was walking about the room, touching various items, reveling in the luxury surrounding her, when she felt a prickle of fear along her neck. It was a strange sensation, as if someone were watching her. She turned swiftly, expecting to find someone behind her. She turned completely around, scanning the shadowy corners of the large room. But no one was there.

"This is ridiculous!" She laughed nervously. First the imagined face upon the facade of the house and now this. Feeling childish and a bit foolish she lifted the bedskirts, peering underneath, then walked across to open the large cherry armoire in the corner. Nothing. Still the feeling persisted. She wanted to run from the room and from the disturbing feeling. But she had never been one to run from her problems, so instead she willed herself to stand perfectly still, hoping the feeling would vanish.

As she stood there quietly she heard a small noise at the door. Turning toward the sound she could see the doorknob turn ever so slightly. She held her breath as the door swung slowly open.

The woman who stood there looked much like Thursa Kincaid . . . except for something . . . Kathryn could not quite name what that something was. For one thing she was dressed oddly, almost raggedly, in faded clothes that once would have been almost garish colors. The small feet beneath her skirt were encased in leather elfinlike shoes. She had Thursa's features, the same golden blonde hair, but instead of the simple, dignified coif, her hair stuck out about her head in short, frizzy curls.

On her face was a sly, conspiratorial grin. She reminded Kathryn of a small child who'd been caught dipping its hand into the pudding.

"You're Robert's bride," she stated. "I've been watching you—yes I have." She spoke in a singsong manner.

"Yes, I'm to marry Robert on Christmas Day," Kathryn replied, trying to hide the burning curiosity she felt. "And how have you been watching me?" she asked.

"Oh, that's for me to know and you to find out!" she cried, breaking into a gleeful, raucous laughter. Just as suddenly the laughter stopped and her face became solemn.

"You should not have come, you know. Foxfire does not welcome strangers," she said.

Kathryn shivered at the woman's words. "Who are you?" she asked.

Once again she broke into near-hysterical laughter. "I wasn't invited to your welcome tea party—no. Nobody wants Teresa around. They don't want her to meet Robert's pretty bride." Again she laughed.

"Teresa! What are you doing in here bothering Kathryn?" Thursa asked from the doorway.

Seeing them there together, Kathryn thought the resemblance was not quite so strong, although she was sure they must somehow be related.

Joseph and Mrs. Spencer appeared and led the tiny childlike woman away. As they walked down the hall she turned to watch Kathryn intently—her eyes bright and glittering.

Thursa saw the slight tremble that ran through Kathryn's tense body. She appeared ill at ease and embarrassed. "I'm sorry, my dear. I should already have warned you about Teresa," she said.

She walked to the loveseat and stared into the fire for a moment before she spoke again.

"Teresa is my sister, you see. Actually, she's my twin sister. We never looked exactly alike, but when we were young—before . . ."

It was evident that whatever had happened to Teresa was painful and difficult for Thursa to talk about. But even as Kathryn sympathized with her anxiety, she wondered if they had deliberately planned to keep the woman hidden.

"When we were young, Teresa was a beautiful and vivacious young woman. She was the more popular of the two of us, always having young men fall in love with her. I married first and came to America with Joshua. Later, Teresa married too. Their first child was stillborn, and afterward, when Teresa came down with a terrible fever, they thought she would also die, but she did not. Instead the fever did this to her. The doctors said she would never be the same. That was almost thirty years ago.

"Her husband, poor man, was never able to accept what had happened to his lovely young wife. He finally left—simply disappeared. The sadness was she barely knew he was gone. By that time our parents were growing old and unable to care for her, so we brought her here to live with us. Oh! but it almost broke my heart when she arrived—to see her that way. She had been such a joyful person, intelligent and full of life . . ." Tears welled in Thursa's eyes as she recalled that day so many years ago. Helplessly Kathryn touched her arm, but she could think of nothing comforting to say to this woman whom she had just met.

"I'm sorry. You'd think after all this time I'd have grown used to seeing her this way," Thursa murmured. "I want to assure you Kathryn, that Teresa is totally harmless. In fact we rarely see her unless she wants us to. She likes to wander in the woods, gathering herbs and flowers. She seems happiest doing much the same thing a child would do."

"There's nothing to apologize for. I do understand. Please don't worry about it on my account. I'm sure Teresa and I shall get on well together," Kathryn said.

"She has a strange, imaginative mind, often filled with ideas that . . . well, just don't pay any attention to any of the odd things she might say to you," Thursa said.

Kathryn could not miss the way Thursa turned from her as she spoke, almost as if she had not told her everything.

Long after Thursa had left Kathryn sat thinking about the unusual events of her day, wondering what it all meant. She did not know what to make of this place or its unique occupants. A most curious and mysterious family to be sure. She sat before the fire until it was almost gone, hoping she would not regret her decision to marry Robert and come to live here at Foxfire Manor—a house that, if her intuition was correct, did not look upon strangers kindly.

There were only three days left before Christmas and the wedding. The house came alive with preparations. For Kathryn it would be her first real celebration of the holiday since the war began.

Despite her uneasiness about the coming marriage, she soon found herself caught up in the holiday atmosphere. She had brought the few small gifts she could afford with her from Asheville and spent an entire afternoon wrapping them in gaily colored tissue paper and writing the accompanying cards.

Sula seemed happy those first few days at Foxfire, and Kathryn was delighted that both Thursa and Robert made sure she was treated as a member of the family. Kathryn was sure Robert must have told his mother how close she and Sula were. Sula seemed so contented that Kathryn had not the heart to confess to her the doubts and worries she herself had about being here, just as she had never mentioned Matthew's rude warning to her. She often caught herself wondering about Matthew—where he was and when he would be home. It was an event she dreaded. From the talk around the fireplace in the evenings he seemed to be the very heart of the Kincaid family, the hub around which everything turned. Somehow that did not surprise Kathryn, for she had sensed immediately that he was a man of action.

They had decided to exchange gifts Christmas Eve so as not to interfere with the wedding and its preparations the next day.

Kathryn told Robert she would bring a basket to collect his gifts and place them under the tree downstairs. She dressed and walked through their sitting room that separated the two bedrooms.

The sitting room was a long narrow chamber, filled with light from the row of windows all along its outside length. It was brightly decorated in lemons and greens, unusual in that most decor was somber dark velvets and heavy fringed brocades. But it certainly seemed in tune with Thursa's spirited personality and Kathryn liked it very much. In the corner behind a settee stood a unique tiled stove, like those often used by the Moravians. It, too, was a pale yellow, dotted with tiny blue and green flowers. No room could have been more perfect for the afternoon teas that Kathryn shared with Robert. It had also become their habit to take meals here when he did not wish to join the family downstairs.

Passing through the room, she knocked at the heavy oak door leading to Robert's bedroom.

"Come in," came his muffled reply.

He was seated in a large wing-backed leather chair. His room was more somber than hers and of course more masculine. It smelled of the pleasant spicy shaving balm he favored. He smiled and held out his hand to Kathryn. Taking it, she knelt beside his chair.

"How's my beautiful bride holding up?" he asked, looking deeply into her eyes for any signs of doubt.

"I'm fine," she assured him. "I can't quite believe that I'm really here. It seems so far from the war I could almost believe it was all just a horrible dream."

"It makes me happy to hear you say that. We have been lucky here, I suppose, although from what Mother tells me, we've had our share of renegades, but no close battles, thank God."

He paused for a moment, looking at her tenderly. "So tell me, you haven't changed your mind, have you? You still plan to marry me?"

Kathryn smiled at his easy way of bantering with her. "Don't worry, you can't get rid of me that easily."

But behind his joking manner she knew he was totally serious. He seemed desperately afraid of losing her. She cared for him and wanted only to see the tired, anxious look finally vanish from his eyes. How could she not be grateful to him for rescuing her from the drudgery she faced in Asheville? Matthew's threats came to mind once again as they often had lately, and she vowed once more to spend the rest of her life showing Robert her gratitude.

"I'm sorry Tilda won't be able to come to the wedding tomorrow," Robert said.

"So am I, but there was not enough time," she answered. "I did ask her to come for a visit as soon as possible . . . that is, if you don't mind."

"Of course I don't mind!" he smiled. "Whatever makes you happy is what I want. And I want you to be a part of this family—a real part," he declared. "I'm just sorry you won't have any of your friends here."

"I have Sula, and that's enough," Kathryn said.

"Yes, and if Matthew could be here, it would be perfect," he said. "Just you wait, Kath. When he comes home we'll have this old place back on its feet once more. We'll have parties and dinners—it's going to be grand!" He sighed in contentment as he spoke of the imagined return to the grandeur they once knew.

"Speaking of Matthew, I never had a chance to ask what you thought of my big brother," Robert said.

"Oh, I thought he was . . . very nice. He seems to care a great deal about you." That at least was not a lie; his protectiveness toward Robert, where she was concerned at least, bordered on the excessive.

"Yes, I suppose I'll always be the little brother he has to look after," Robert grinned. He did not seem to resent Matthew's protectiveness at all.

"Robert, I'm going to take your gifts and put them under the tree for tonight, then Sula and I have some work to do on my dress."

"Ah, yes, the wedding dress. I don't suppose I could

see it . . ." he teased.

"No, you may not . . . until the wedding," she smiled.

When Kathryn returned to her room, she walked across to the bed where her mother's lovely velvet wedding gown lay. Earlier, Sula had gathered it from the trunk where it had lain all these years, wrapped in tissue paper and sprinkled with rose potpourri.

The veil, aged and yellowed, was in tatters and simply could not be worn, so Sula and Thursa had quickly gone downstairs to see what could be found as a replacement.

Kathryn ran her fingers lightly across the soft material as the door opened and Sula and Thursa entered. They behaved like old friends, both of them doting on Kathryn and Robert. As they came toward her they were both laughing with excitement.

"That is a beautiful bridal crown, Miz Thursa," Sula said.

"Why thank you, Sula, but it would not be complete without the lace veil you fashioned for it," Thursa answered.

Kathryn smiled with bemusement at the two and wondered how long this great wealth of compliments could continue. Yet she could not help being pleased by the way Robert and Thursa had so readily accepted her Sula.

Sula placed the dark green wreath of magnolia leaves atop Kathryn's head. Nestled here and there on the crown were delicate sprays of dried gypsophilia. A shoulder-length piece of fine lace had been gathered and attached to the ornament.

"It's perfect," Kathryn said, turning about as she looked into the mirror.

"Oh!" Thursa exclaimed, clasping her hands together at her bosom as if she were a young girl. "Sula, isn't she going to be the most stunning bride?"

"Yes'm," Sula agreed. "Jes stunnin'!"

They all laughed and Kathryn could feel their excitement catch fire within her. It was the only time she had felt anything other than apprehension about the wedding.

All day the darkness and the cold
Upon my heart have lain,
Like shadows on the winter sky
Like frost upon the pane.
John Greenleaf Whittier

Chapter Five

After a Christmas Eve supper the family gathered in the parlor for the opening of the gifts. The entire household was there and a spirit of friendliness and gaiety filled the room as they admired the huge decorated fir tree that stood in the corner.

"Everyone's here," Thursa declared. "Let us begin. Joseph, will you do the honors?"

"Wait Thursa," Kathryn interrupted. "Cynthia's not here yet." She looked about the room for the girl.

"She won't be here," Mrs. Spencer said sharply.

"But its Christmas Eve . . ." Kathryn began. "Is she ill?" She looked toward Robert and was surprised to find him looking the other way as if he had not even heard the comments. Thursa appeared disconcerted and embarrrassed. Had Kathryn said something wrong by mentioning Cynthia?

"Yes, that's right, dear, I believe Cynthia is not feeling well tonight," Thursa said, handing identical packages to the housemaids.

Kathryn frowned, wondering why she should have such a strange feeling about something so trivial. Surely there was nothing wrong with anything they had said or done, nothing sinister or devious about the girl's absence. And yet the joy and gaiety she'd felt earlier began to dissipate, leaving her with a curious, isolated feeling.

Everyone seemed pleased with the gifts Kathryn distributed, although there was nothing spectacular about the lace hankerchiefs and tobacco tins given to the servants. She had bought books for Robert and one for Teresa with beautifully illustrated pictures of various mountain wildflowers. Her gift to Mrs. Spencer, lace caps, was more practical and was received with a curt "Thank you." For Sula she had picked something deliberately unpractical and extravagant, a new black turban hat that sported a feathery ostrich plume on one side. She smiled as she watched Sula place it carefully on her head.

"Kathryn dear, this is the loveliest little brooch." Thursa beamed, placing the cameo pin at the neck of her white silk blouse.

Kathryn placed to one side the small gift she had picked for Cynthia. She had been more extravagant than she should, buying her a cut-glass perfume flacon, but something about the girl touched her and made her want to give her an especially nice gift for Christmas. Her life here seemed so bleak and uneventful.

"Happy, darling?" Robert's voice intruded on her thoughts.

"Yes, it's been lovely. I can't remember a nicer Christmas," she said. "How can I ever thank you for the lovely gowns and jewelry? Really, you'll spoil me."

"You deserve all of it and more!" he declared. "I just want you to be happy here."

"I will be," she said, smiling into his bright blue eyes. "I want to learn all about your home and the mountains where you grew up. I can't wait to be outside, exploring every part of it."

"You should like Matthew," Thursa interjected. "He

was always the outdoorsman, the explorer. Our Robert was the one who stayed indoors and read or played games."

Once again Matthew had intruded upon her moment of happiness. Kathryn wondered sourly if he would always do so.

Christmas Day found the household still filled with the exuberance of the holidays. But they all agreed it was the wedding which would add the final, perfect touch.

For Kathryn, the ceremony passed in a blur as her emotions threatened to overwhelm her. Now that it was actually happening she could not remember ever being so confused. There was no one to talk to, least of all Sula, who would not understand. She would want to whisk her straight back to Asheville and the Simmons house if she had even the slightest hint that Kathryn felt doubts about what she was doing.

They were married in the parlor before the windows that looked out upon the brown lawn and wind-lashed forest surrounding the house. Kathryn, dressed in her mother's velvet gown, was quiet and subdued, her green eyes appearing large in her pale face. Robert was splendidly handsome in his blue jacket and cashmere waistcoat. He did not notice Kathryn's solemn mood, nor did anyone else—not Eugene, the best man, or Pastor Morgan, and certainly not the ebullient Thursa.

It was only later as they were enjoying refreshments that Sula stepped closer to frown questioningly at Kathryn.

"What's wrong?" she asked quietly.

Kathryn could not hide the worry in her eyes, certainly not from someone who knew her as well as Sula.

"Nothing," she lied. "I'm just a little nervous."

"Huh!" Sula said pointedly, doubt wrinkling her brow.

"Sula, please . . . I don't want to spoil the day for everyone."

"Well, you done spoiled it for me all right, and worse than that it looks like you done spoiled *your* whole life!" Her whispered words were nevertheless fiercely spoken. "Is that right?"

"We'll talk about this later," Kathryn said between clenched teeth.

"Well, you can be sure of that, missy!" Sula said, turning to leave the parlor.

Kathryn thought the day would never end and that any moment Robert would turn to her and read the doubt on her face the same as Sula had, but that didn't happen. Robert was too occupied with his happiness at the marriage and he seemed intent on letting everyone know it.

When at last they were alone in the privacy of the little sitting room he told her time and again how happy he was, how lucky he felt that she had consented to marry him. Then he kissed her goodnight and retired to his bedroom as if it were the most normal wedding night in the world. Kathryn walked to her own room.

Well, what had she expected? She knew from the beginning how it would be. They had certainly discussed it many times. But she knew that her disappointment had nothing to do with the lack of a normal physical relationship between them as husband and wife. It was more than that. It was this place and her feeling of isolation and fear. And it was her lack of an emotional commitment to Robert, for try as she might, she could feel nothing for him except friendship and gratitude. That was not the way she had always dreamed it would be when she married. In her daydreams she had imagined she would marry someone who would challenge her, make her feel alive and vibrant. Someone strong, someone like her father.

Unbidden, the image of Matthew Kincaid, strong and vital, came to her mind. She frowned, disgusted with herself for letting him intrude upon her private thoughts now. Quickly she began to undress so that she might put on more comfortable clothes and sit for a while in front of the fireplace before Sula came. For she knew without a doubt that Sula would come.

Kathryn wasn't surprised to find Sula much calmer when she appeared, for that was her nature. She might become very upset at the first sign of a problem, but after time to think about it she always became calm and reasoning.

Sula sat on the loveseat beside Kathryn and propped her feet upon a nearby footstool.

"So, you want to talk about it? she asked.

"Not really, but then I don't suppose you planned on giving me a choice," Kathryn smiled grimly.

"That's right," Sula answered.

Kathryn rose and walked to the fireplace, stirring the fire to life. "Robert was very convincing. I was hurt and confused. We had no home, nó money. Somehow I reasoned it would be the best thing to do. It's as if I were another person then. I don't know . . . it just seemed the only choice I had," she sighed.

"You shouldn't have made such an important decision while you was grievin' for your daddy. Why didn't you tell me this? Why didn't you come talk to me?" Then Sula slapped the palm of her hand against her leg. "I should have seen it! I should have! But I was as bad as you, thinkin' only of havin' a new home and a little peace and comfort, too. I guess I told myself it was what you wanted."

"Now, Momma Sula, don't blame yourself. Besides we do have a lovely new home and we have been welcomed like royalty. That's not so bad, is it? No worries about where our next meal will come from. Robert loves me. . . ."

"Humph!" Sula snorted. "And you're a young, beautiful girl with your whole life ahead of you. Trapped in a marriage to a man who . . . well, even that would be all right if you loved him too . . . but now!"

"Robert knows I don't love him. I realize that's no excuse, but at least I don't have to feel guilty about that!" Her voice held a slight ring of defensiveness.

"And what, pray tell, is goin' to happen when some tall, handsome man comes along and you fall head over heels in love?" she asked, her eyes large and shining.

"That won't happen. That will never happen," Kathryn insisted.

"Child, you are just foolin' yourself if you think that!"

Kathryn sat back down beside Sula. Both of them were silent for a long moment. Finally Sula pushed her large body up tiredly, placing her hands at her back.

"We'll just have to make the best of it then," she declared. "Is that what you say?"

"Yes," Kathryn said. "It's all we can do."

"Then there'll be no more fussin' about it. Goodnight, baby," Sula said, bending to kiss Kathryn's cheek.

But as Sula left Kathryn's room her face was troubled. She had been afraid of this very thing, of her Kathryn, seeking shelter, taking the first warm den she stumbled into. The Kincaids were a good family, she had no doubt about that, but what troubled her most was that Kathryn had married a man like Robert. It wasn't his handicap that was the problem. He was just not the right kind of man for her. And Mister Robert wouldn't have been her kind even if he were perfectly well. Kathryn needed a man to oppose her sometimes, make her think . . . a man who lived and loved fiercely, not someone to cater to her every whim, someone who was content to let the world pass him by.

But Kathryn's strong will to make the most of her situation and her stubbornness to fulfill her obligations surprised even Sula. In the next few weeks she saw the young, inexperienced girl take over the responsibilities of running the large household, a job Thursa had long wished to relinquish. Kathryn did it with love and generosity, never showing resentment. It was as if she truly enjoyed it. Maybe it would be all right, Sula hoped, watching Kathryn blossom amidst the luxurious comforts of Foxfire.

It was true Kathryn was thriving at Foxfire. But whenever she could get away from the house and her newfound responsibilities she would steal away for a few minutes alone. The granite overlook she had spotted that first day had become her favorite place. Here she could lift her face to the heavens and let the wind or rain wash away all the pressure she felt when she was inside with the family.

This view from Foxfire where the end of the lawn met the mountain's edge was a spectacular one in any weather and at any time of day. It became Kathryn's retreat, her one haven from the sometimes stilted life of Foxfire and the demands of a marriage that she had realized immediately to be a mistake.

Sometimes she would stand looking into the valley, longing to throw open her arms and shout with pure joy at the beauty before her. It gave her a wonderful sense of freedom.

Sometimes in the early morning as she stood at the overlook, a blanket of fluffy clouds covered the valley and the river below her, a strange phenomenon in the mountains. At other times snow fell softly, quieting the sounds of the mountain, covering the large hemlocks in a thick, frosty white blanket. She loved the exhilaration of watching an approaching storm roll across the distant summits, coming ever nearer until with a roar of the wind it raced through the trees below and up the mountains to envelop her in its mists. She found the storm both frightening and beautiful in its thundering magnificence. The waves of rain or sleet would send her running back, wet and dripping, to the house, excited and tingling with life.

Sula and Thursa, even Robert, would scold her for her foolishness, telling her she would make herself ill. But it was the one release she had and one she would never relinquish.

One snowy day in late January, she took a different route back to the house after a visit to the overlook, walking into the still, waiting forest. She loved the quite of the forest after a snowfall. She looked for animal tracks in the snow the way she had as a child. Suddenly she stopped and frowned. She turned her head to one side, listening. She heard something that sounded very much like a child's shouted laughter.

She stood quietly, trying to find the direction from which the sound came. She turned quickly to look about her when suddenly she was thrown to the ground by a small squealing bundle that came bounding out of the forest directly at her. Kathryn sat in the snow, stunned. She looked up into a pair of very blue eyes in a small, dark face. The boy appeared to be about four years old and his face reflected as much surprise as hers.

His fringe of dark thick lashes could be the envy of any fashionable lady. Thick black curls tumbled from beneath his brown cap. He stared gravely at her, his chin trembling slightly as if he'd done something terribly wrong. In that fraction of a second as Kathryn looked into his frightened little face, her heart was lost.

"I'm sorry," he stammered.

Kathryn looked at the hand holding the child's and up into the startled face of Cynthia. Both of them were speechless as the little boy began to chatter, making apologies.

"It's all right, really," Kathryn said as she picked herself up. She brushed the wet snow from her coat. "I'm not hurt."

"What's the boy's name?" she asked Cynthia.

"Woody," the girl answered, almost defiantly. "He's my boy—but most folks hereabout don't know it."

"Oh," Kathryn replied. "Neither did I. Well, he certainly is a beautiful child." And indeed, she thought she'd never seen a more handsome or appealing little boy. Her calm voice did not betray the shock she felt on hearing Cynthia's words.

"He didn't aim to hurt you—just got a lot of spunk, I reckon," his mother said.

"Please," Kathryn said, "don't give it another thought. There's no harm done and I should have paid more attention to where I was going." She was still stunned by the existence of the child and wondered where he'd been kept and why no one had told her about him.

"Woody," Kathryn said. "Do you think we could be friends?"

"Yep," he replied seriously. "I reckon." He looked up at his mother for approval.

Cynthia nodded curtly to the boy.

"Yep, I can," he confirmed with a big grin.

"Good!" she laughed. "My name is Kathryn."

"You're bonny Kath . . . Kath . . . what did you say?" he asked.

She smiled at his use of the word bonny. It sounded so old a term for such a young boy. But here among the mountain people many Irish, Scottish, and British words were scattered generously in their speech. She could not keep from making a comparison between his happy face and his mother's unsmiling one.

"Kathryn," she answered. "But my daddy used to call me Kat when I was a little girl about your age, because I had a hard time saying my own name. If you like you may call me Kat."

He laughed, a lyrical, carefree sound. "Like a kitty cat?" he asked.

"Yes," she answered. "Like a kitty cat." She felt a happiness inside her each time she heard his childish laughter and she smiled.

Kathryn wondered about the circumstances of the boy's birth and who his father might be. Cynthia could not have been more than fifteen at the time of his birth.

Woody's presence explained many things—Cynthia's strange absence Christmas Eve and the times Kathryn thought she heard a child's voice. And she couldn't help wonder if his presence was kept from her deliberately during the weeks she'd been here.

Surely they could feel no need to keep this from her. She realized that the existence of an illegitimate child was not discussed publicly, but after all, she reasoned, this girl was little more than a servant here. Her actions were in no way a reflection on the family she worked for.

The little boy's sweet face continued to pull at her conscience after she had returned to the house to meet Robert for tea. She was not entirely fair to Robert that day, she knew, blurting out the news of her discovery with no warning.

"I met Cynthia's son today," she said, looking at him

steadily.

Robert looked startled only for a moment, before quickly managing to hide his surprise by taking a sip of the hot tea.

"Did you?" he asked coolly.

"I can't keep from wondering why you felt it necessary to keep his presence a secret from me." she said.

He laughed—a stiff, unemotional laugh, a rather patronizing sound, she thought.

"My darling Kathryn, why would we do such a thing? It's a trivial matter I assure you . . . one I'm sure we simply overlooked," he said.

"Robert . . . how could anyone overlook a boy—a real flesh and blood boy? Don't you know me well enough to know I would not be scandalized? Nor would I pass judgment on the poor girl . . . and certainly not on you or your family."

He watched her carefully with something like relief in his eyes. Then he smiled sweetly, looking at her apologetically.

"I am sorry, sweetheart, if you felt left out, but with all the pain you've suffered the past month I only wanted you to get settled in before we drag out all the family skeletons."

"And just what is the family skeleton in regard to Woody?" she asked.

"I only used the term loosely. Of course Cynthia's indiscretion has nothing to do with our family." With a wave of his hand he dismissed the subject and went on to something else.

It was a side of Robert she had not seen before, and it made her feel as if she'd never fit in at his home. During the next few days his attitude toward the boy never changed. Whenever Kathryn spoke of Woody, Robert's eyes became blank and uninterested, his eyes cool and unreadable.

Kathryn was finding it more and more difficult to face the fact that her own husband could be so cold and unfeeling toward such a delightful child. But she refused to let Robert's obvious disapproval interfere with her joy in Woody. In a life filled with regrets, he became her godsend.

In him she found an eager partner with which to wander the countryside. Even at his young age he seemed quite knowledgeable, in his own childlike way, of the abounding nature of the Blue Ridge. She felt like he had been left pretty much on his own before she came.

In late February the weather turned unseasonably warm and one day Eugene rode up the mountain to visit with them. He and Robert sat outside on the wide front porch watching Kathryn and Woody walk back toward the house from one of their daily explorations.

She saw them watching her as they talked quietly and she sensed they were discussing her. She knew it was true as she stepped onto the porch and found that Eugene could not meet her eyes. That was one of the things she had noticed about him as they became better acquainted.

"Run along Woody and find your mama," she said. "Let her know we're back."

"Well," Eugene said a bit too heartily. "As I just told Robert, I really must be going. Good to see you again, Kathryn."

"You too, Eugene. Good day," she said.

Robert watched the tall sandy haired man ride away and disappear down the winding mountain road.

"Eugene certainly seemed uncomfortable just now," Kathryn mused. "What were you two talking about?"

"Darling, don't you know why he's uncomfortable?" he asked.

"Why . . . no, I'm afraid I don't," she said.

"Kathryn!" he said laughing aloud at her puzzled look. "You are such an innocent. You don't mean to say you haven't noticed the way my friend Eugene looks at you whenever you're near, how nervous he is in your presence?"

"No," she insisted, frowning at the odd excitement in his voice. "I haven't noticed."

"Why, my dear, I believe you're blushing! And its quite becoming. Could it be you are attracted to Eugene as well?"

She looked at him, startled into silence by his insinuation and shocked even more by the fact that he seemed oddly excited by the idea of her and Eugene together.

"Robert . . ."

"Oh, don't be upset, love. Can't you see I'm only teasing you?" he said, quickly smoothing it over.

She said nothing, but there was something in his manner that troubled her. It was almost as if he *wanted* her to be interested in Eugene. For the first time since their marriage she felt angry at him, even a little repulsed by his presence.

"Excuse me, Robert, I think I'll retire for the evening," she said, walking past him.

He reached out and caught hold of her wrist and pulled her down to him. His blue eyes glittered oddly as he kissed her cold lips.

"I hope you aren't feeling ill," he said, smiling as if nothing out of the ordinary had happened.

"As a matter of fact, I am," she said pulling her arm from his grasp and walking into the house.

She was shivering by the time she reached her room and her stomach quivered uneasily. She must be coming down with a fever. That, at least, would explain the odd, sick feeling in the pit of her stomach. Perhaps she needed to rest, she told herself. After all, she had been very busy since coming here. Yet as the evening turned to darkness and the night passed slowly she found herself tossing restlessly, unable to sleep or to chase the uneasy feeling away. She could hear small noises in the house, and once she thought she heard the sound of hoofbeats outside.

Jumping quickly from the bed she drew the curtain aside and looked out, but she saw no one. She picked up her robe and thrust her arms into the sleeves. It was no use, she could not sleep in the hot, stuffy room.

Peeking out the window once more she saw the outline of the moon behind midnight clouds. She felt a rise of excitement within her at the thought of being outside at the overlook with the wind blowing through her hair and the moon illuminating the valley below.

Quietly she tiptoed down the stairs and out the front door. Her slippers made no noise on the graveled drive as she ran toward the ledge.

She did not hear the clatter of hooves until they sounded directly behind her, causing her to spin around quickly in alarm. With horror she saw that the horseman was already upon her, his silhouette tall and menacing against the night sky as he sat on the prancing black horse.

She screamed and began to run toward the overlook, not thinking where she would go when she finally found herself trapped there. Abruptly she was caught from behind as the man leapt from the horse and captured her in two swift strides. He clasped his hand over her mouth, his other arm tightly encircling her waist, holding her close against his tense body. She struggled frantically, kicking and turning within his grasp.

"Kathryn!" he warned.

Instantly she went still in his arms and was quiet. He turned her about to face him.

"You!" she hissed. "What are you doing here?" she demanded.

"I live here . . . or have you forgotten?" Matthew drawled.

"Let go of me. You almost frightened me to death!" she said jerking away from his disturbing embrace.

"Imagine my own fright. I was convinced we had acquired a beautiful ghost at Foxfire," he said wryly.

She glanced toward Foxfire, shivering at his use of the word *ghost*.

"You're cold," he said. "Whatever are you doing out here at this time of night, dressed only in . . . this," he taunted, his fingers reaching out to flick the satin ribbons on her robe.

She caught the ribbons from his hand and pulled them to her.

"I . . . I couldn't sleep. I often come here when I can't sleep." She avoided his eyes that glinted down at her in the moonlight.

"Oh, I see. Restless? Married . . . how long now . . . two months and already you're growing restless? Ah, my little green eyed nightingale, that is not good." His voice had grown low and husky. Reaching out he pulled her toward him before she could protest. He held her arm behind her back, trapping the other between their two bodies so that she could not escape.

"Such a shame," he murmured, his lips dangerously close to her own. "That lovely mouth going to waste."

He ran his thumb lightly along her lower lip and along her cheek, causing a tremble to pass through her body. From deep within his chest came a low rumble of laughter as he felt her reaction. He pulled her even closer. "This soft, warm body . . ."

"Stop it, Matthew!" she said, finally finding her voice. He couldn't know that it took every ounce of willpower she possessed to resist him. "This is wrong

. . . you know it is. Why are you doing this?"

"Why indeed?" he whispered. "I've wondered myself why I should be thinking so often of my brother's wife." His breathing was as ragged and heavy as her own as they surveyed each other warily.

His eyes studied her in the moonlight, traveling over her defiant face and parted lips and on to her hair, which fell loose and full about her shoulders.

There was no time for further protest as his mouth descended to her, parting her soft lips, surprising her with the sweetness of its touch. She would not have expected it from such a man as he.

When finally he pulled away she found herself gasping for breath and staring helplessly into his eyes. She was disturbed by the strange excitement he elicited from her. Never would she have expected to react this way to the kiss of a man she despised.

She pulled away from him, and this time he did not protest but stood watching her cautiously. She imagined she saw a flicker of surprise cross his face, as if the kiss had disturbed him also.

"Such a sweet kiss to warm me on my cold ride down the mountain, dear sister-in-law . . . an almost innocent one, if I did not know better."

Kathryn pushed past him, ignoring his words. She was torn with confusion about what she was feeling. Part of her wanted to scream at him with all her might and denounce his insulting manner; the other part longed to cry because he was leaving, perhaps never to return. What was wrong with her? She turned quickly toward the house, afraid he would see the tears gathering in her eyes and taunt her even more.

"Kathryn," he said.

She stopped, wiping her eyes before turning to look at him.

"What?" she asked.

He pulled himself into the saddle. "I'm leaving tonight for Virginia. I spoke with Mother but I did not want to wake Robert. Would you tell him I love him?" His words were soft with a tinge of sadness, leaving her to wonder if he had some sort of premonition that he might never come home again. That thought frightened her more than anything and she had not the heart to do battle with him any longer.

"Yes, I will," she said. "I wish . . ."

He pulled the big black horse closer and sat looking down at her.

"You wish what?" he asked softly.

"I wish . . . I wish you a safe journey."

Silently he tipped his hat, acknowledging her comment, and turned the horse toward the road.

Kathryn watched until he was out of sight then walked back to the overlook, sobs choking her, her heart aching at the unfair resentment she knew he felt toward her. Finally she cried for the guilt she felt within her own heart, for God help her, she had wanted him to hold her, whisper those forbidden words to her, to kiss her and never stop.

Spring with that nameless pathos in the air which dwells with all things fair.

Henry Timrod
Poet Laureate of the Confederacy

Chapter Six

The next morning, at Thursa's request, Kathryn met with her and Robert in the parlor. There had been little other discussion at breakfast except about Matthew's unexpected midnight visit and consequent move onward to Virginia. Still, Kathryn was surprised when Thursa produced a letter from him which she wanted to read.

At the mention of his name Kathryn felt herself blushing slightly as an unexpected vision of his face appeared before her.

Part of it she knew was guilt because she had not given Robert the message Matthew asked her to. But how could she? How could she explain their presence together in the middle of the night while she was dressed only in her nightclothes? Or was it something she didn't want to admit, even to herself . . . that Robert might see something else in her eyes when she mentioned Matthew's name?

"Dear Mother," Thursa began to read. "I'm thankful I was able to visit home before we go to join Lee's army in Virginia. The Union forces have kept us on the move all over the southeast for the past year, but there is a feeling now that what we are about to face will be the final confrontation. There is no way of knowing how it will end, or whether the triumph shall be to the North or the South, but whatever happens, I want you all to know how much I love you and miss being with you at Foxfire. Tell Robert and Kathryn I wish I could have been home for the wedding."

Thursa's voice grew shaky and hoarse with unshed tears as she struggled to continue the letter.

"I hope you will think of me in the coming weeks, as I shall of you, and that spring will find us reunited once again. All my love, your son, Matthew."

Kathryn was touched and more than a little surprised at the poignancy of the letter. It shook her image of Matthew as a hard, unfeeling man, and she wanted nothing to interfere with that opinion, for after last night, she dared not let herself.

But in the weeks to come, Matthew's words continued to haunt her, as did the last meaningful look he gave her that night near the overlook. She began to have sharp, frightening images of something terrible happening to him. She even woke in the night trembling from the realism of the dreams. She became more and more convinced that he had felt some premonition. It frightened her so terribly that she filled her days with even more activities, until she was so exhausted at night that she fell instantly asleep as soon as her head touched the pillow.

It didn't help that Robert had become moody and distant. She knew he was concerned about Matthew too, and the news of the war was not good. But she could not keep from wondering if Cynthia had anything to do with his moodiness.

Twice she had walked into his room after hearing the sound of angry voices from within, only to find Cynthia, red-eyed and upset. As usual, Robert brushed it aside, saying that Cynthia was an emotionally troubled girl.

"But what were you arguing about?" Kathryn asked.

"We weren't arguing at all," he said offhandedly. "It's certainly nothing for you to trouble yourself about."

Along with Robert's moodiness and her own sense of isolation, Kathryn felt more and more resentment from Lila Spencer and her daughter. She could attribute it to the fact that she had usurped a bit of Mrs. Spencer's authority, which obviously didn't sit well with the woman. As for Cynthia, it puzzled Kathryn why the girl still did not take to her. She could not imagine she was actually jealous of the time Kathryn spent with Woody.

However, all the petty mysteries of the house were forgotten one quiet morning in early April when Eugene rode into the yard, jumped from his horse, and hurried toward the house.

Kathryn had seen him coming and opened the door as he bounded onto the front porch.

"Eugene, what is it ?" she asked.

"The Yanks have taken Richmond!" he said breathlessly.,

"Is it over then?" she asked, her voice quiet and sad.

"Not yet, thank God, but it doesn't look good!"

Hearing Eugene's agitated voice, Thursa came into the entryway.

"Eugene," she said, as if she were afraid to ask what news he brought.

"I just came to tell all of you that Richmond was evacuated and her warehouses set fire by the Rebels before they fled. The ironclads and ordinances at the James river defenses were blown up and the bridges burned by our retreating cavalrymen."

"But nothing of Matthew?" Thursa asked.

"No, ma'am, I've heard nothing," he said.

"What will happen now?" Kathryn asked.

"There is speculation that Lee has gathered his troops and plans to join Johnston here in North Carolina. If that happens we may still have a chance," Eugene said.

Kathryn turned from him to pace the hallway. His enthusiasm for the continuation of the war disturbed her. "Eugene, don't you think there has been enough killing? Isn't it time we admitted defeat and ended this . . . this slaughter?"

"Why, Kathryn, I'm surprised to hear such defeatist words from you—the daughter of a Confederate hero and the wife of one who almost lost his life for the glory and . . ."

"Eugene, please!" Thursa interjected. "I agree with Kathryn. And as the mother of the one you seek to martyr, I too am willing to see an end to it. All that is important to me now is that Matthew come home safely."

Eugene looked surprised, but his boyish spirits were brought down to earth somewhat by her plain language.

"Of course," he said, bowing slightly. "I should not have expected genteel ladies such as yourselves to accept or understand the last gasps of a valiant army's battle. I apologize. If you will excuse me now, I'd like to go up and give Robert the news."

"Certainly," Thursa said.

Thursa turned to Kathryn with a spark of anger, but a hint of a wry smile on her face.

"Sometimes I wonder how we poor feeble-brained ladies get by."

Kathryn sighed, but could not resist a smile in return. "Eugene can be such a pompous jackass sometimes," she whispered.

They both laughed despite the fear in their hearts, for what they knew would surely happen now.

By mid-April the news had reached Foxfire that Lee's attempted flight southward had been blocked at Appomattox and that he had surrendered his army of Northern Virginia there to General Ulysses S. Grant. The war has finally over.

For Kathryn it was both a relief and an agony, for she knew what the soldiers were suffering. But there was nothing to do but go on and wait for news of Matthew.

Woody had been pleading with her to go with him to a place he called the old cabin, but the weather had been too cool.

The news of the war was depressing and worries about Matthew became overwhelming now as Thursa waited for news. A picnic seemed like just the thing. Perhaps a trip to the old cabin would help Kathryn forget for awhile.

Sula packed a lunch basket and waved gaily to them as they left through the kitchen door and started across the back lawn toward the forest beyond.

Kathryn could see the road that led to the barn that stood in a clearing in the woods. In their few wanderings she had not been any further from Foxfire than the barn.

After they passed the barn Woody led her to a well-worn path at the edge of the forest as he chattered and giggled with sheer happiness at being outside with his Kat.

"There it is, Kat, there it is!" Woody shouted, running ahead of her along the rocky path to a small log cabin sheltered by huge overhanging oak and hickory trees. The greening leaves built a canopy above them, bathing the cabin in its cool, dark shade. The forest floor was thick with fallen leaves and large clumps of deep green moss.

It was upon the beds of moss that they spread their lunch. They ate with the healthy appetites of adventurers. After they had eaten, Woody lay on the moss pretending to be an Indian.

Kathryn looked about at the place where Joshua Kincaid had built his first home for his English bride. It was hard to imagine the genteel, ladylike Thursa living in the small cabin deep in the forest, particularly as in those days there had been Indians here.

She liked the place immediately. It had a quiet sense of peace and tranquility, with its graying logs and huge stone fireplace. It had been kept in good repair over the years. Kathryn could imagine being here in the summer beneath the great old trees, and in the winter when gray smoke trailed from the chimney, they would be snug and cozy indoors.

Woody soon tired of his game of Indians and tugged at Kathryn's hand, breaking into her reverie. He pulled her further along past the cabin to a small cemetery encircled by a fence of gray stone.

"Here's where Grandpa Spencer is buried, and Mr. Kincaid," he said.

Kathryn walked for a while among the graves where bright sprouts of flowers and grass, some ready to bloom, had pushed through the winter soil. There were several graves other than those Woody pointed out, most likely the graves of servants of the family. There was also a tiny grave beside Joshua Kincaid. Upon examination, she found it to be the resting place of a girl child, unnamed, who died at birth. The daughter Thursa never had the chance to raise. Perhaps that accounted for the easy way she had accepted Kathryn into the family.

They spent more time than expected there, and before Kathryn realized it she knew she would have to hurry to get back in time for her afternoon tea with Robert. She knew how much he looked forward to that time with her each day and didn't like to disappoint him by being late.

Woody had grown tired; she forgot sometimes that he was only a little boy. She carried him from the barn to the house, handing him gently to Sula as she entered the kitchen door.

Kathryn pushed his dark hair from his forehead as he rested in Sula's arms.

"I think he's ready for his nap," she said.

She ran quickly upstairs to change her dress before joining Robert. Afterward she stood looking at her reflection in the long cheval mirror. Her greensprigged muslin dress, one of several Robert had bought her, fit perfectly, showing her newly curved figure brought on by the good food and pure country air. Her auburn hair, tied back with a green velvet bow, held glints of gold. Satisfied that she looked her best she opened the door to the sitting room.

The service was already spread on the table before the small settee and their tea had been poured.

"Darling," Robert said, holding both hands out in greeting. "You grow more beautiful every day. I've never seen you look lovelier."

She smiled, pleased because she knew it made him happy to see her looking healthier and wearing the new clothes he had picked for her.

"Thank God this war was finally ended! If only we knew about Matthew, then we could get on with our lives here," he said.

"Yes," she answered, wondering as she had many times in the past few weeks why they had not heard anything.

As Robert picked up a cup of tea she walked to the row of windows overlooking the side yard. She wanted to tell him of her picnic with Woody, but as usual she hesitated, knowing his antipathy toward the boy. She stopped and glanced out at the many songbirds flitting in the branches of the trees.

"Robert," she said, "this is the loveliest, most beautiful place. I am glad I came."

She heard a sound from Robert and turned to see an odd, almost puzzled look on his face as he clutched at his throat. The teacup and saucer fell from his hands, clattering loudly on the floor.

"Robert!" she said, rushing to his side.

"I . . . I feel so ill. I can't . . . breathe. Help me Kathryn . . ."

Frightened, she ran to the hallway, calling loudly for help. Soon she was joined by Sula and Thursa, with Mrs. Spencer following behind them.

"Where's Joseph?" Kathryn cried. "Here, help me carry him to his bed!"

The four women carried Robert through the sitting room to his bedroom. Thursa was in near hysteria as they laid her semiconscious son on the bed. His labored breathing filled the room. His eyes were open but unseeing, and Kathryn knew then . . . her feelings of fright, the almost frantic worry over Matthew, this was what it had been about all along. Robert was dying and Matthew had felt it too—a premonition. For Kathryn, it had been a feeling that something was wrong or some terrible thing was going to happen. She had sensed that same concern in Matthew that night at the overlook.

Kathryn knelt beside the bed. There was nothing she could do as she waited, hands clasped as if in prayer, rocking wordlessly in sorrow. No one spoke; there was only the sound of Thursa's quiet pleading prayers and Robert's heavy breathing. Then silence.

When Joseph returned with Dr. Logan, Kathryn knew what he would tell them. She had seen it too many times at the hospital not to know. But it had all happened so suddenly that they were numb, speechless with shock at Robert's death by an apparent heart attack.

Kathryn Kincaid stood apart from the others at the small, isolated cemetery. Her dark cinnamon-colored hair was tousled about her face by the gusting spring winds. At least the rain had stopped in time for the funeral. She felt grateful for that, at least.

When she arose this morning the ever-present winds that buffeted the mountain plateau seemed louder, more mournful somehow, as if in sympathy with the grieving family within the walls of Foxfire Manor.

It seemed years ago, rather than days, that she had ventured here with Woody to stand in this cemetery, admiring the green sprouts of spring flowers. Now some of them were strewn haphazardly about in the freshly dug black earth. She watched, her green eyes glistening with tears, as the plain wooden coffin was lowered into the grave. The yellow blossoms of the daffodil would now cover the remains of her husband, Robert.

Gray clouds hung low over the mountain and the forest surrounding the small cemetery was dark and shadowy. Nothing seemed real about this day. Kathryn felt as if she were in the middle of a horrible dream. She shivered. As the pastor droned on she tried to recapture reality by remembering Robert as he was at the hospital when he was so sweetly tender to her, so loving. As often happens when one is confronted by death, she had already forgotten his moodiness and the strange remarks about Eugene and Woody. She remembered only the good, and she was painfully saddened.

The sound of Kathryn's name returned her to the scene before her. Pastor Morgan was reciting the virtues of a good wife.

"Wife," she thought in disbelief. There had

scarcely been time for her to grow accustomed to the sound of that. Now it was another name she must be called—widow.

The thud of dirt against wood shook Kathryn from her thoughts. Guiltily she realized she had not heard much of the service.

Thunder rumbled threateningly above them, causing the birds to become still and silent. The other members of the party were turning to leave the cemetery. Across from her she saw Joseph reach to place his hand underneath Cynthia's elbow to steady her as they walked away. The girl jerked away from him almost angrily, making Kathryn realize how hard Robert's death had struck Cynthia.

"Come, my dear, we must get back to the house before the rain starts again," a quiet masculine voice spoke beside her.

Kathryn looked up into Eugene's sympathetic hazel eyes. She supposed he had been standing there beside her during the service but she had been too deep in thought to notice.

She took his arm and leaned slightly against him, allowing him to lead her from the stone-fenced area of the Kincaid family plot.

She turned once to look anxiously back at the open grave. The men shoveling dirt did not glance up at the slim young widow.

Eugene patted her hand compassionately and led her to the waiting carriage, helping her up into the seat beside her mother-in-law.

Kathryn was worried about Thursa. Today she had stood numbly at the graveyard, emotionless and dry-eyed. Kathryn knew that she had not cried for Robert since the day he died. The fact that they had heard nothing from Matthew only made her sorrow deeper.

Kathryn knew there was an unspoken fear in Thursa's mind that she might have lost her other son as well. If that were true Kathryn did not know how the petite woman could survive.

As if reading her mind, Thursa reached out to take Kathryn's hand. Her fingers felt cold as she clasped Kathryn's. "Are you all right, Kathryn?" she murmured softly.

"Thursa, you must not worry about me. I'm concerned about you. Are *you* all right?"

"I'm fine, dear," she answered.

Eugene climbed up into the front seat beside Joseph, who clucked his tongue at the horses, causing the carriage to move smoothly away through the forest, back toward the house.

As they rode, Kathryn thought of the day she first saw Foxfire, the same day she had met Eugene. Had it been only four months ago?

The carriage bounced over a large rock, the motion jostling Kathryn against the cushioned seat as they rolled on toward the imposing house and away from the cemetery. She hardly noticed.

Regrets, she thought . . . so many regrets. How she had regretted her decision to marry Robert . . . so many times. She had lain awake nights wishing things could have been different, deriding herself for making such an impulsive, foolish decision. She felt guilty about everything—but most of all that she had never been able to tell Robert she loved him. How she wished now she had lied. And there was Matthew, whose touch had caused an overpowering sense of guilt within her. Thankfully, Robert never knew, and now she would have to be content knowing she had made the best of it, that she had given Robert no reason to doubt her, and that he'd had a few months of happiness.

Her first frightening, uncertain day at Foxfire—when she'd imagined the gruesome face and felt such overpowering feelings of danger—had been terrible. But for all that she never imagined it would end this way, so abruptly and so painfully. Now she must face the truth; Robert was gone—and with him her reason for being here at Foxfire. She wasn't sure what would happen next, what she should do. It was something she had not let herself think about yet.

They were almost upon the house now, its lights flickered dimly in the foggy, rain-induced twilight. The lights seemed to hang in the air, ghostly and wavering. Each time Kathryn saw the house from afar she felt no easier about it, and she was not sure if it were any more welcoming now than it had been that cold December day when she first arrived.

Joseph pulled the carriage up to the front steps of the house.

Kathryn couldn't wait to get to her room and change into something cooler and more comfortable. More than that she longed to be away from the oppressiveness of the house and the sadness of its occupants.

The thought now of being alone at the overlook was overpowering. It was all she could think of. She hardly remembered telling Eugene goodbye as he looked at her with tenderness and concern. She needed to be away from his ever-present looks of longing, away from Thursa's silent anguish and

Sula's constant mothering.

She ran past all of them, quickly going up to her room. They attributed her anxiety to grief and did not try to stop her.

Glancing at the cheval mirror by the windows she looked solemnly at her reflection. She hardly recognized the pale, wan face that looked back at her. Today the green eyes no longer sparkled and the thick mass of unruly auburn hair seemed to overwhelm her features.

Turning toward the fireplace she ran her hand across the back of the delicate love seat, enjoying the feel of the dark green velvet upholstery.

She still had not grown completely used to the luxuries and comforts here, with a servant always nearby to do her bidding. That was something she'd never experienced, even at McClary house before the war. Still, there was an anxiety within her that she could not explain. Only here in her room did she feel secure. Only here she did not feel the eyes of Foxfire watching her.

Hurriedly she slipped out of the hot black bombazin gown and changed into a yellow gauze day dress. She crept quietly down the hall toward the stairs, hoping to get away unnoticed. As she reached the front door a voice behind her caused her to stop.

"Jes where are you goin', missy?" Sula asked in her most motherly voice. "You know it's rainin'? Well, course you do—that's most likely why you're goin' out anyway," she said, answering her own question.

Taking Sula by the hand, Kathryn pulled her toward the door.

"Come outside Sula, where we can talk without being heard," Kathryn said.

Seated on the front porch away from the curious eyes of anyone else, Kathryn began to pour out the feelings she'd kept hidden within her for so long.

"Sula, I don't know what's wrong with me. I just feel so lost all of a sudden, but it has nothing to do with Robert and that only makes me feel worse. I should never have come here. Last night I had a terrible feeling that this is some horrible dream. How could I ever have thought I could marry a man I didn't love and move into a house with strangers? And now this horrible thing . . . Robert's death. I don't know what to do . . . I don't really belong here."

Sula had feared all along this might happen—not that Mister Robert would die—none of them ever guessed that, but that one day Kathryn would come to herself and realize she had made the mistake of her life. And now it had happened.

Well, that didn't matter now. All Sula wanted was to get Kathryn out of this place, away from that Miz Spencer and her daughter and that strange little woman Teresa. She didn't care if Teresa *was* Miz Thursa's twin sister—she didn't trust her, no sir, not one bit.

"Everything's gonna be all right, honey." Her round face softened as she reassured Kathryn. "You don't have to worry about it right now. Miz Thursa ain't likely to put you out with no place to go. You know that. You jes go on now, out to your place, and try to enjoy this miserable weather you seem to like so much!" Sula's eyes were teasing and affectionate.

Kathryn kissed Sula's cheek and promised to return in time for tea with Thursa.

The walk outdoors in the light mist did help to clear Kathryn's head. She knew Sula was right. She would enjoy whatever small pleasures she could and take the rest one day at a time. Her surroundings would help her to put aside her doubts and questions at least for awhile. She could only be grateful that spring was here at last.

But spring in the mountains was a teasing lady—one day sweet and warm, the next all ice and evasion. And this spring was no different. The crocuses bloomed, only to be enveloped in a late snow; birds sang and flew wildly about, only to return the next day to a frozen puddle where the birdbath once had been. But if winter was tenacious so were the creatures and the flowers, waiting, ever watchful for their time to come.

Kathryn could feel spring winning the waiting battle as she surveyed the landscape from high upon her mountain. She felt strangely alive and vibrant, a somehow irreverent feeling in this time of grief. She delighted in this place that she had shared with no one until she discovered the boy.

Woody, her delightful little Woody. What would she have done without him?

As Kathryn stood at the overlook thinking of Woody and the day they met, she felt some of the coldness of her grief for Robert dissipate just a bit and she caught a glimpse of a future that might one day be happier. At least she still had Woody.

"Kat . . . Kat," Woody's voice called. He bounded across the lawn toward the ledge and she caught him to her, her heart pounding at the thought of his tripping and tumbling over the cliff.

"Woody!" she said. "You must be more careful when you come out here. We've talked about this before. This is a very dangerous place and you must always walk, not run."

Her palms were moist with fear as she picked him up in her arms and glanced down at the rock-strewn mountainside and tree-covered slope far below them.

"I'm sorry, I forgot," he said innocently, patting her face with his chubby little hands. Nothing ever seemed to dampen his spirits, she thought, as she smiled indulgently at him.

"Want to see the flowers, Kat? Sula says they're real pretty." His blue eyes were wide and questioning.

"Yes, I think that would be nice, Woody," she declared. She was unable to remain gloomy for very long in his sunny presence.

The yard in back of the house curved around and up to the edge of the forest. They walked the graveled path through Thursa's small English garden. It had been americanized with wildflowers, some of which Woody ran to pick.

Kathryn could see the old ice house at the edge of the forest and the road through the trees that led to the barn. She didn't allow herself to dwell on thoughts of the cemetery there in the depths of the forest, so dark and still.

Spring flowers were blooming, purple violets and glistening white bloodroot. White and yellow trilliums bloomed *en masse* around the rock gardens. Curling up through the leaves were fragile green shoots of mountain fern.

It was somehow reassuring to see life beginning again. Being outside took away some of the dark frightening thoughts she had had earlier.

Woody laughed and jumped about, running ahead and coaxing Kathryn to hurry. They stopped once to gaze into the ice house at the far edge of the woods. It was dark, filled with an aged musty smell, and had not been used during the past few years. For a moment Kathryn felt an alarming sense of suffocation, but she didn't want to spoil Woody's sense of adventure and so said nothing.

Inside the ice house, access to the deep pit was protected by a small, wooden fencelike structure. The actual pit was about ten feet wide and twelve feet deep, with a wooden ladder propped up against it.

In better times, large blocks of ice were cut from the river in winter and hauled up to the mountain to be stored in this pit. Protected in the earth, the ice would last all summer, making lemonade and iced sherbets a lovely addition to hot summer meals or leisurely lawn parties. Together, Kathryn and Robert had envisioned spectacular parties and elegant dinners once again as everything returned to some semblance of normalcy.

Thinking of Robert was a mistake. Quietly she coaxed Woody away and back toward the house.

The boy ran ahead past the English garden. When Kathryn first spotted the dead sparrow lying in the garden she thought nothing of it, except to hide it from Woody, for she didn't want him to be upset. He was especially fond of animals and birds and she knew he would be alarmed. She sent him on to the house and found a shovel with which to dispose of the bird.

With a small gasp she saw what had happened: its head had been severed from its body. It seemed to have been twisted off. She couldn't imagine what kind of animal could have done it.

Picking up the bird with the shovel, she noticed something bright on the ground beneath the scattered feathers—a tiny, red ribbon tied neatly into a bow.

Kathryn's skin prickled uneasily and she felt the sharp return of that terrible sick feeling. She imagined eyes watching her from some hidden spot. Had the ribbon been left there deliberately? If so, was it left for her to see? She turned about, half expecting Teresa to appear wild-eyed beside her, laughing at her discomfort. But there was no one, only the hushed murmur of the wind through the trees.

With a shudder, she quickly buried the bird, throwing the ribbon in with it and covering it with dirt. She told herself it was simply a strange coincidence that the red bow was there on the ground. Surely not even Teresa would kill a helpless sparrow. But if not Teresa, then who?

The day that had begun with the funeral of her husband now took on a bizarre twist.

She felt more alone than ever. . . .

The web of our life is of a mingled yarn, good and ill together.

Wm. Shakespeare

Chapter Seven

Kathryn thought it best that she not bring up the subject of the dead sparrow to anyone except Sula. Sometimes she felt as if all she'd done since coming here was to question and criticize. There was probably nothing to this whole thing, and if there were, she would simply handle it herself.

It was days after the funeral, but the house was quiet, still filled with a silent mournfulness. As Kathryn dressed for breakfast she thought she heard sounds from the entryway downstairs. She slipped quietly to the landing to see Eugene entering the parlor.

She could not imagine why he was here so early, and so went quickly down to the parlor.

Thursa sat beside Eugene on the sofa. She was sobbing uncontrollably. Eugene looked confused, as if he did not know how to comfort her. Kathryn's heart lurched painfully with a sudden stab of alarm. Not Matthew, she wanted to scream. Please God, not Matthew.

"Thursa, what is it?" Kathryn asked. "Is it Matthew?"

"No, no . . ." Thursa answered, but she was so distraught that she could not explain.

Eugene poured a cup of tea for her and sat back down on the sofa helplessly.

"I'm sorry," he said. "If I had known how upset she would be, I'd never have brought the news."

"What news?" Kathryn asked anxiously.

"President Lincoln has been assassinated."

"No!" Kathryn said in disbelief.

"I had no idea this would upset her so. Why it's practically news for celebration throughout the South," Eugene said.

Kathryn looked at him and shook her head in disbelief. "I can't believe you feel that way Eugene. Anyone who would not mourn such a tragedy, especially now, would have to be demented!"

"Yes, well, evidently the shock of it and the recent funeral . . . it's just been too much for Mrs. Kincaid." Eugene turned to Thursa. "Dear lady, let us take you up to your room. Perhaps you should take some medication so you can rest," he added.

"This news could have waited, Eugene," Kathryn said to him under her breath. Eugene's thoughtlessness was always irritating, but she felt really angry with him now.

"No, I'm better now," Thursa insisted. "I'm all right. I haven't been able to cry since Robert . . . and now . . . I can't seem to stop."

Kathryn sat in a chair close to Thursa. Her knees were shaky and she felt ill.

"Life is just so cruel," she muttered helplessly.

"Aye, it is that."

Kathryn had not even seen Lila Spencer enter the room until she spoke. But as Kathryn glanced up and across the tea cart into the catlike eyes of the woman, she wondered what Mrs. Spencer meant by her agreement with Kathryn's statement. For a moment she thought she saw pure hatred in those eyes, but then the woman looked away and Kathryn wasn't sure she'd seen anything at all.

Thursa was now more composed and spoke quietly. "In a way I'm not surprised. You know all my life I've noticed that some people carry the aura of death with them. It's in their eyes; I can sense it. Mr. Lincoln did have that sad, melancholy look, now that I think of it. No, I'm not at all surprised. But poor Mrs. Lincoln, I wonder what she will do now . . . they say she enjoyed his power more than he did, but poor thing, I know she must truly have loved him."

She grew silent and thoughtful for a moment. "It's odd, I never thought Robert had the look of a person destined to die young. I think that's why I took the news of his injury so well . . . I simply knew he would be all right—that he would survive. . . ." Her thoughts seemed to wander. "Oh, I wish Matthew were here . . . if I could just see him for myself . . ."

Tears began to run slowly down her cheeks as Kathryn went to her and held her small body, letting her finally cry out her pent-up grief. The pain of the news about the president had broken that barrier and had at last allowed her to cry for her dead son.

Kathryn felt like crying too, and the words about Matthew tugged at her emotions. She wanted him home, but only for Thursa's sake, she told herself.

Teresa appeared and helped her sister from the room. The care reflected on the woman's face surprised Kathryn. At times like this Teresa appeared almost normal.

Kathryn sat back down tiredly, afraid to think of what this latest news would mean to the already torn country. She'd almost forgotten Eugene until she felt his eyes upon her.

Mrs. Spencer still stood by the tea cart as if she had every intention of staying. Today her arrogance irritated Kathryn more than usual.

"That will be all, Mrs. Spencer, thank you," Kathryn said coldly.

The woman's cool sand-colored eyes flicked toward Kathryn for a second as if she might challenge her, then she slowly glided through the door, the rustle of her dress the only sound in the room.

"Are you all right, Kathryn? Shall I get you something to drink?" Eugene asked.

"No," Kathryn said, knowing she should be touched rather than irritated at his kindness. "But thank you for being such a good friend, Eugene." At least he tried hard to be that.

"Yes, well, I hope you know that I truly am your friend. I've grown fond of you since your arrival here, more than fond I should say."

Kathryn frowned and her eyes flashed a warning to the tall, sandy-haired man who sat beside her.

Even before Robert had mentioned it, Kathryn had known of Eugene's admiration for her, and it had become even more apparent lately. Still, he had always conducted himself as a gentleman and she hoped he would continue to do so. The thought of the look on Robert's face that day he had asked her about Eugene made her feel ill even now.

But Eugene did not miss the meaning in her look and promptly changed the subject.

"What will you do now, Kathryn, do you know?" he asked.

"I really haven't had time to decide. As soon as Thursa is able, we'll discuss it. I've had so many changes recently, I just don't know." She frowned, not wanting to talk about it just now.

"Yes . . . It seems only days ago that I was best man for my friend Robert, right here in this room," he said, glancing toward the windows where they said their vows.

"Not so very long ago," she said quietly.

"I can still see it," he reminisced. "You in your mother's wedding gown. You were the most beautiful bride I've ever seen," he said longingly, forgetting himself as he recalled the day of the wedding.

"Eugene, please," she said, rising to flee his persistent attention.

"I'm sorry, Kathryn, truly I am. I should not be speaking to you in such a manner, certainly not so soon. Please, say you will forgive me and I promise to be more careful in the future," he pleaded.

Kathryn sighed. "Of course I forgive you, Eugene. Let's not speak of it again."

"Then I'll leave you to your breakfast, but I'll be back in a few days to see if you or Mrs. Kincaid should need anything."

"Thank you, Eugene."

"By the way I suppose Robert left a will, didn't he? So you'll be well fixed financially at least. I mean, I'd like to think you will be properly taken care of."

"Why, I . . . really, I had not thought about it. I don't believe so, but that's the last thing on my mind at the moment," she replied.

As she escorted him to the door, Kathryn thought what an odd thing that was for him to say.

She took a deep breath and closed her eyes for a moment. She was grateful to be alone for awhile. She looked distractedly about the parlor and through the double windows that faced the front lawn, watching Eugene as he rode off down the hill. The wind had died down and the large trees and evergreens stood motionless.

She thought again of the dead swallow and the neatly bowed red ribbon. She shuddered and quickly rose to return to the security of her room. There she found Sula briskly putting away Kathryn's clothes and arranging the bed covers.

"You don't have to do that, Sula . . . I can do it," Kathryn said.

"I want to do it. It keeps me busy. Besides, I don't want you to be alone right now," Sula stated.

"You heard about the president?" Kathryn asked.

Sula shook her head sorrowfully. "Miz Spencer told us. Jes like I told Joseph, I don't know what's gonna happen next to this poor old world. And little Miz Thursa, well, I just feel so sorry for her, losin' her boy and worryin' herself to death about the other one."

Kathryn sat at the dresser, absentmindedly brushing her hair as she told Sula the story of the dead sparrow.

The black woman's eyes grew large and expressive. "Voodoo!" she said with a certainty that made Kathryn wince. "I don't like it! I don't like it one bit!" she repeated vehemently. "They's somethin' mightly strange goin' on round this house! I think you best tell Miz Thursa about this."

"No, Sula," Kathryn replied, wishing she had kept the story to herself. "She has enough worries without my telling her some silly story about voodoo. And don't you tell her either!"

"Well . . . you jes be careful . . . wanderin' about all over this mountain by yourself!" She looked at Kathryn reproachfully. "They're somethin' funny about that Cynthia, with them big eyes astarin' at you so strange like. Ain't natural! And that Miz Teresa—sneakin' around, always appearin' out of nowhere. She makes my blood run cold! Some days I wish we was back in town at the house—burned or not!"

"Yes . . . I know, Sula. So do I. But I didn't mean

to upset you. Let's just try and forget it. As you said, we'll just have to make the best of it here until I can decide what to do."

Sula's fright and her confession that she wished they were back home worried Kathryn. It was not like her to run from anything, and that frightened Kathryn.

But on this morning, after Eugene's reminiscences about the wedding, Kathryn could not dwell on the ribbon or the dead sparrow. She could think of nothing, no one, except Robert. Her dear friend, the man she had married, was dead. She felt so alone at Foxfire now without him. He had been her one assurance that she belonged. Only now, days after he was buried, the finality of it all hit her and she allowed all her anguish to pour out, mourning both for Robert and herself.

Sula pulled her close and began to hum an old spiritual, comforting her as she had since she was a little girl. Kathryn sobbed out all her anger and frustration against Sula's motherly shoulder. She cried for the Kincaids, for her papa, and for a man she dared not mention, not even to Sula. Soon there were no tears left and she felt drained, but strangely calm and at peace.

"I'm sorry," she muttered, pulling away from Sula. "I didn't mean to do that."

"It's jes natural, child . . . it's jes natural."

"Well, I'm going down and eat a nice breakfast, then I need to get busy with the spring cleaning."

Even after a hard day of cleaning and supervising the rolling up of some of the carpets for storage, Kathryn still felt restless and full of energy.

She slept poorly, tossing and turning, waking many times to the ever-present knowledge of Robert's death. Her sleep was interrupted by strange dreams of small frightened birds with red-ribboned bows about their necks . . . and of Robert. She dreamed she and Robert danced together and laughed gaily, that someone was beside her bed watching her, always watching. "Matthew?" She sat up, drenched in perspiration and trembling with fear.

She did not want to close her eyes again to be confronted by the hateful visions. So she waited for the light of day, steeling herself against the fact that she would never see Robert alive again and afraid she would never again sleep peacefully in this house.

In the days that followed, Foxfire Manor was quiet and subdued. Melancholy hung in the atmosphere like an approaching storm. Voices murmured and whispered. Even Woody's chatter and clatter was repressed. Cynthia, with red and swollen eyes, looked as if she had been crying endlessly, causing surprise in Kathryn at the intensity of the strange girl's grief.

As for Kathryn, it was her nature to grieve alone, letting down only in the privacy of her room or when she was with Sula. She knew it made her seem cold and unfeeling to the others but there was nothing she could do to change that.

Thursa continued her litany of prayers for Matthew, yet there was still no word from him. It was sad that he did not even know of his brother's death.

But it was not only Foxfire but the whole country that was in mourning for the slain president as well as for the young men who would not be coming home. There was still great bitterness and division because of the war, and many wondered if the country could survive. In Washington there was uncertainty about the new president. It was a time of near panic.

Sula, at least, never failed to try and reconcile all of them to the inevitable. Kathryn thought she'd never seen Sula so happy and content as she was with her gardening.

"Strawberries is gettin' ripe," she would declare. "The orchard's full of blossoms. If it don't frost, we gonna' have a fine crop of cherries and peaches, apples and pears. Oh, it's gonna be so good having fresh fruit again and makin' preserves. It's a real blessin', yessir, a real blessin'."

Then there was that one final rain that seemed to turn the trees green overnight. Down in the valley and along the river trees were beginning to leaf, looking as if the branches had been sprinkled with bright green confetti.

It was a time of healing for Kathryn, and with each passing day she became more hopeful, more alive. Even that she felt she had to suppress somewhat, for somehow it seemed a betrayal of Robert that she was young and so vibrantly alive.

And she had the visit of Tilda and her mother to look forward to. She hoped it would also be good for Thursa.

Then one afternoon they heard the carriage coming up the drive. Both she and Thursa met the Simmonses at the door.

Mrs. Simmons came forward first, arms outstretched to gather Kathryn to her ample bosom. "Kathryn, sweetheart . . . Thursa, we're all so sorry about Robert."

Tilda stepped forward, and for once her face was solemn, not filled with its usual mischief and fun.

"Kathryn, Mrs. Kincaid, I'm so sorry." It was the only time Kathryn had ever seen the girl cry. She was touched to know her friend cared so much.

"Thursa," Mrs. Simmons said. "Thank you so much for having us. I know it cannot be a good time for guests now, but Tilda missed the wedding and she was so looking forward to this visit . . . well, we both were."

"Evelyn," Thursa said, calling Mrs. Simmons by her first name. "It's always a good time for you to visit with us and I'm sure we've looked forward to it as much as you have."

Mrs. Spencer came into the hallway and stood waiting to take Tilda and her mother upstairs. She was as stone-faced as ever, with her cold amber eyes staring straight ahead.

"This is Mrs. Spencer; she will take you to your rooms. After you're rested we'll have tea in the parlor," Thursa said.

Kathryn hugged Tilda, who had by now wiped her eyes and seemed to be feeling more herself.

"I'm glad you've come, Tilda," Kathryn said. "I've missed you."

In fact, Kathryn had not realized just how much she missed Tilda until the girl actually arrived, filling the hallway with a lighter atmosphere.

By the time Tilda and Mrs. Simmons came back down for tea, Eugene and his mother had also joined them, and Kathryn was filled with a warm, pleasant feeling.

"Evelyn, Tilda, have you met Mrs. Davenport and her son Eugene?" Thursa asked as the Simmonses entered the room.

Eugene stood to greet them and Kathryn almost laughed aloud at the spark of life that leapt into Tilda's brown eyes upon finding a man in the parlor.

"How do you do," Mrs. Simmons said, stepping forward to nod politely toward the two newcomers.

It was a comfortable gathering, almost like the times before the war when friends visited daily. Kathryn noticed that Thursa carefully skirted the issue of the war, not wanting to give Eugene the opportunity to express his views. Kathryn and Tilda sat quietly listening to the others as they busied their hands with pieces of embroidery. Kathryn had been afraid at first that Eugene might feel uncomfortable in the feminine atmosphere of a ladies' afternoon tea, but she soon had no need to wonder as Tilda immediately involved him in every conversation.

"Did you serve in the war, Mr. Davenport?" she asked, coyly fluttering her eyelashes toward him.

Eugene sat forward as if to speak, but before he could his mother answered the question for him, as she often did.

"Eugene was needed on the farm with us. Why we simply couldn't run the place without him . . . so much to do! We have over three hundred acres you know."

Thursa and Kathryn glanced quickly at each other, both of them trying to suppress their amusement.

It did not seem to bother Tilda that Eugene did not speak for himself, nor that he had not joined the war effort.

"My, I find that so admirable," Tilda murmured. "I just think that is so nice. You must be proud to have such a loving and responsible son, Mrs. Davenport."

Eugene blushed, but his eyes blinked in surprise and pleasure as he began to look at Tilda in a somewhat different light. Kathryn smiled as she wondered why she had never seen before what a perfect match the two would be. This visit was turning out to be even more interesting than she first thought.

Mrs. Davenport lowered her head and looked over her wire-rimmed glasses at Tilda, who sat contentedly sewing as if her voice had not so obviously simpered every time she spoke to Eugene.

From that afternoon Tilda never ceased talking about Eugene. Even the dark and mysterious Matthew Kincaid was forgotten in deference to Eugene.

For the few days that Tilda was at Foxfire it became a nightly ritual for her to steal into Kathryn's room, where they would laugh and talk and sometimes dream of the future. Tilda's presence renewed Kathryn and made her feel as if she had recaptured a bit of the carefree years they had both missed.

The day Tilda and her mother left, Kathryn thought she had never hated to see anyone leave quite so much.

"Promise you'll write, Tilda," Kathryn told her.

"Oh, I will . . . I have so much to talk about now and of course you'll have to keep me informed about my 'friend.' "

But for all Kathryn's happiness after Tilda's visit, she awoke the next morning with that familiar uneasy feeling that she was not alone in her bedroom.

She sat up in bed, her eyes drawn immediately to the mirror by the window. Hanging down from the carved niche on top of the mirror was a red ribbon—and tied to the ribbon were two small feathers.

Her hand went to her mouth in a gesture of horror. Without thinking, she jumped from her bed and ran to the mirror. She snatched the atrocious ribbon and flung it into the cold ashes of the fireplace.

She ran to the door and bolted it, then locked the other door to the sitting room, before collapsing on the loveseat. She sat shivering uncontrollably, sickened to think that someone had actually been in her room as she slept.

This time she could not so easily quell the fear that gripped her like a vice, for it left her weak and trembling and uncertain about what to do.

For now she knew that the bird she'd found in the garden had been killed and left deliberately for her to find. And this . . . this thing today was simply to make sure she realized it.

But who at Foxfire would do this . . . would want to frighten her this way? And why?

Perhaps it was her McClary temper returning, for she felt some of the fear being replaced by anger. She vowed that she would not give the perpetrator the satisfaction of knowing how well this little scheme had worked and how much it had unsettled her. She would mention it to no one this time, not even Sula. If someone expected her to go crying down the halls in alarm, they were sadly mistaken.

And from this morning on, she would make sure her doors were always locked when she was alone in her room.

When grief is fresh, any attempt to divert it only irritates.

Samuel Johnson

Chapter Eight

There was now a more stable weather pattern on the mountain, although the storms and winds still came unexpectedly. Sula continued to work in the new garden, and Joseph had turned and readied the black Carolina soil to begin another year of yielding. Sula had even managed to persuade Thursa to help in the garden, always mentioning Matthew's name and how he would enjoy fresh peas when he came home, or how he would like green beans. Before long the diminutive woman became totally immersed in the gardening chores.

One afternoon in late April Eugene and his mother came calling. Kathryn was happy to see him for she was busy indoors that day and felt the need of a break in the routine. She knew she and Eugene could sit and chat about local gossip. Sometimes he brought the latest magazines, and that was a small pleasure she increasingly looked forward to.

She was beginning to feel more comfortable with this shy man regardless of his sometimes outrageous opinions. For the most part she found him to be thoughtful and caring, and she looked forward to his visits. And since Tilda was now a mutual friend, Eugene's embarrassing admiration for Kathryn had lessened.

They were sitting in the parlor while Thursa and Mrs. Davenport went to the kitchen to talk with Sula. Today Eugene was in an especially happy mood, and his conversation was rich and buoyant in spirit. Eugene lapsed into funny stories about his and Robert's childhood, and Kathryn became caught up in his lively stories.

"We were about eight years old, I guess," Eugene was saying. "We weren't allowed to go to the river alone, but somehow we made an excuse to get away. We walked for miles it seemed to get to the river and we were pretty hot by the time we arrived. Robert looked at me and I looked at him and without a word both of us began to peel off our clothes. Ah, the water was glorious, as I recall. But the pleasure didn't last long," he laughed.

"Oh, no?" she said. "What happened?"

"Joshua Kincaid happened—that's what. They missed us at the house and Mr. Kincaid must have suspected all along where we were. He marched us out of that water with a hickory switch and made up start up the mountain as naked as the day we were born. He could be a stern man and we were scared to death. After awhile we heard him behind us chuckling with glee. We stood there dumbfounded while tears of laughter ran down the old man's face. Then Robert and I began to laugh. I can still see it now—him bent over laughing, the switch still in his hand, and Robert and I standing there in the middle of the road, stark naked. He gave us our clothes and we all went home. Oh, I'll never forget it." Eugene laughed.

Kathryn had not laughed so hard in years. Still laughing, she leaned forward and touched Eugene's arm in a companionable manner. At that moment a deep, drawling male voice came from the doorway behind them.

"Ah . . . the grieving widow." The voice fairly rippled with sarcasm.

Kathryn turned, startled to see a tall man leaning against the frame of the door. One arm was raised against the side of the entryway, while in his other hand he held a cane.

She did not recognize him at first, for he now wore a very short black beard, giving him an even more rugged look than she remembered, an almost demonic one.

Strangely, it was Matthew's eyes in the light of day that held her captive. They had appeared dark before, an indistinguishable gray color. Now she could see that they were a pale gray, a silvery color almost illuminated in his dark face as he looked at her ruthlessly. She had no idea what she had done to cause the anger she saw on his face, but then it seemed he was always angry when he was near her.

She sat staring at him; she could not tear her eyes away from his probing gaze. He would laugh if she knew the relief she felt within herself at seeing him alive. She thought she had never seen a man so strikingly handsome, nor one who affected her senses as he did. Yet she felt no kindness from him, no gentleness as she had the night he kissed her. He was not the sort of man one would ever want to have for an enemy and yet it seemed that he had made himself hers.

Thursa fluttered behind him. "Matthew is home everyone! Kathryn, my son is home—isn't it wonderful? Matthew, this is your sister-in-law, whom I've written so much about," she said.

"We met at the hospital before she and Robert were married," he drawled.

Matthew came slowly across the room toward her. Kathryn frowned as she noticed his slight limp, which caused him to lean heavily on the cane. She rose and held out her hand to him, trying to still the tremor inside her. Why should she be frightened of him . . . of Thursa's beloved Matthew?

"Welcome home, Matthew," she said forcing herself to meet the direct look he focused on her. For an instant the memory of his lips descending on hers came to mind and she glanced instinctively at his mouth. He smiled.

He took her hand in his long, brown fingers as he studied her face intently, only the glimmer of a smile flickering across his handsome face. She could feel her skin burning with embarrassment at his scrutiny. He looked slowly at her throat, then deliberately, mockingly, he let his eyes wander to the open neck of her gown.

"Kathryn," he said sardonically, as he raised her hand to his lips.

His deliberate sarcasm infuriated Kathryn. She could feel her eyes burn with what Sula called their "green fire." Why did he always deliberately taunt her in this manner? To think she had worried about him, wondered if she would ever see him alive again! She had imagined that somehow things would be different between them, but now she found herself disliking him as much as she had that first night they met.

She pulled her hand roughly from his, letting him know from the beginning that she would not be treated in such a manner.

Rather than being angry at her behavior, Matthew smiled, his teeth flashing behind the dark beard. He turned and growled, "Come, Mother, we must let Kathryn tell her guest goodbye." He had not even had the courtesy to acknowledge Eugene's presence until now!

Kathryn had never seen Eugene quite so discomfited as he rose to go. "I . . . I really should be leaving, Kathryn," he said.

"Eugene," Kathryn said firmly, "you need not go just yet. . . ." She looked defiantly at Matthew.

"Yes, I must be going. I'm sure Mother is anxious to get back home before dark." He nodded to Kathryn, and she thought she detected a look of sympathy for her reflected in his gray-green eyes.

Kathryn mumbled her goodbyes and thanked him for coming, but she was distracted and ill at ease and scarcely noticed his leaving.

Matthew turned to go, never looking back or seeming to care about the state in which he left her.

Thursa stayed after he had gone. She looked toward Kathryn with a note of apology. "Darling, I'm afraid he's being a bit moody. Please . . . pay him no mind. His leg is bothering him, I suspect, and I'm sure he's tired."

"I'm not at all offended, really," Kathryn smiled, trying to reassure Thursa. More than anything she wanted her to enjoy the moment of her son's arrival, after all the weeks of waiting and praying for his return. "I understand completely." Inwardly Kathryn was seething at Matthew's rude behavior.

As she had done many times since meeting Matthew Kincaid, Kathryn wondered about him. The tall, sullen man was actually still a stranger to her.

What exactly was on his mind? Had there always been ill feelings between him and Eugene or were they simply precipitated by what he had assumed to be an intimate conversation between her and Robert's friend?

She had almost forgotten Thursa until the woman spoke. "Matthew received a slight wound to his leg in the skirmish outside Richmond. He was with General Lee when he surrendered at Appomattox. His coming home was delayed until all his men were paroled by Grant and allowed to leave." She paused, her lip trembling slightly. "He only learned of Robert's death this morning as he came into Asheville. My last few letters never reached him."

Kathryn put an arm around Thursa's shoulder, comforting her as best she could. Her first thought was that she found it hard to believe anything could upset the cold-eyed man she'd just seen. But in her heart she knew that was not true. She'd seen his love for Robert. She would have to guard herself closely and not let her personal opinion of him blind her to the closeness he obviously felt for his family. She would never want to hurt Thursa by doing that.

Then, almost to herself, Thursa said, "Matthew has always been the strong one Kathryn. I depend on him and need him so much, especially now."

"Yes, Thursa, I know you do, of course. I'm happy for you that he's safely home," Kathryn said.

"Yes, and for you too. Oh, I just know you two will become close friends—brother and sister even."

Kathryn's eyes grew wide with surprise at her own reaction to Thursa's words. Of all the things she felt in Matthew Kincaid's present, *sisterly* was definitely not one of them.

"It's too wonderful for words," Thursa continued. "In any event, Sula is preparing a welcome home dinner tonight especially for Matthew. It will give us all an occasion to dress up and celebrate. Lord knows, we could use such a change, don't you agree?" She sounded happier than Kathryn had heard her in a long time.

"Yes," Kathryn agreed. "That will be grand . . . for all of us."

"But we shan't wear black, dear. Robert would not want it and neither do I. And you for one are far too young and beautiful to drag yourself down in those depressing widow's weeds. As I told you before, we don't have to worry about social graces here at Foxfire. So wear something bright, something pretty!"

"I shall," Kathryn said, smiling at her mother-in-law's enthusiasm.

Kathryn wondered about what she would wear that was bright and pretty. Most of her new clothes were informal cotton day dresses. The rest were bought when she was younger and her figure more immature. There was only one dress that might do.

Hurrying upstairs to her room, she found the dress hanging in the back of the wardrobe; it was one she and Sula had altered. Kathryn had always been fond of it, though it was much out of style now.

"Oh, well," she sighed, pulling the dress from the closet.

The cream-colored moire with its full, flaring skirt had rows of ecru lace sewn around the bottom. A wide chocolate-colored satin ribbon was tied at the waist, balancing the lace at the bottom. Kathryn knew that at least the colors complemented her hair and pale complexion. The round neckline, slightly off the shoulders, helped make it look not quite so old-fashioned. Overall, it had a look of simplicity that Kathryn had always favored.

She had done away with the worrisome corset and hoops while working at the hospital and did not intend to wear them again. Instead she stepped into a full, lacy crinoline that gave the skirt a bit of fullness.

She took the ribbon from her hair and brushed her hair til it shone, letting it fall loosely in a cloud about her shoulders. Then she turned about several times, observing herself in the oval mirror. She fastened a small cameo necklace about her neck, where it hung from its slender gold chain just above her breasts. She paused, looking at the woman before her, a beautiful woman she hardly recognized. There had been so little time in her life for reflecting on her looks that it came as a surprise to realize she had grown up.

As she left her room, the door across the hall opened and Matthew stepped out into the hallway. She could not help being struck by his devastating looks. Unbidden, the thought of his kiss and the taste of his mouth came rushing to her mind. She felt her cheeks sting with self-consciousness. He looked elegant in his dark cutaway coat and cream-colored silk waistcoat. He had not shaved his beard, unfashionable as it was now becoming. But then she suspected he was a man who cared little for fashion or for the opinion of his fellow man, either about his looks or anything else.

"Good evening, Kate," he said, his mouth set in a mocking smile.

"Good evening," she replied coolly. "I prefer to be

called Kathryn, if you don't mind."

His only response was a slight questioning lift of his eyebrows. She found herself on the defensive again, and uncomfortable as he scrutinized every detail of her appearance. She watched angrily as his eyes boldly took in the curves of her neck and shoulders above her gown. If smouldering looks could burn, she would have been aflame. It angered her, and yet she knew he only did it for the effect. He *wanted* to anger her.

Still smiling that disturbing little smile, he gave a small bow, indicating that she should go first. How easy it should be for her to despise the man, she thought.

Self-consciously she walked down the hallway in front of him, her dress and crinoline rustling faintly as she moved. She could feel his eyes following her. It was all she could do to walk slowly and appear unaware of his presence, for how far from the truth that was!

Dinner in the large dining room was more formal, not at all what they were used to. But Kathryn had to admit that she enjoyed it in spite of her discomfort with Matthew.

He expressed amazement at the sumptuous meal Sula set before them, prepared from practically nothing, and the woman fairly beamed at his every word. She told him of her spring garden, the pride of her life and the reason for the fresh salads and strawberries. There was also wild roast quail cooked with whole onions and tiny potatoes. There were pickled beets and cucumbers from the cellar and freshly baked hot bread. Kathryn wondered how she did it and where some of the ingredients came from, but she didn't ask. It was a delicious meal, and everyone seemed to enjoy the celebration.

"Sula, our meals have never been better since your arrival here," Thursa said.

"Well, I enjoy it, I surely do," Sula smiled.

The black woman glowed like a young girl at Matthew's continued praise of her cooking skills. Kathryn glared at Sula, wondering how she could be taken in by this man so obviously skilled at the use of flattery. Catching Kathryn's look, Sula only lifted her nose and gave a little sniff, indicating she would form her own opinion about the man.

Even Teresa honored them with her presence this evening, a rare occasion. She was clean at least, with her hair tied back into some semblance of order. She wore the same gown she had worn at the wedding, a gauze apricot-colored creation that was stylish thirty years ago. It was very young and gay looking, and it seemed odd on the older woman.

Kathryn watched as Teresa smiled and preened. No matter how much she had protested about Matthew, she was still trying to win his attention. Yet she also threw looks of distrust toward him when he wasn't looking, making Kathryn curious about the reason behind it. She smiled slightly as she recalled once hearing Teresa's dramatic nickname for him—"the dark one."

Mrs. Spencer and Cynthia joined them as they usually did. Cynthia looked very pretty, dressed in a pale blue cotton dress with her heavy dark hair tied back with a blue ribbon. Neither of them spoke much during the meal, although it was obvious that Cynthia was quite taken with Matthew and watched his every move.

After dinner the Spencers left the room, but not before Kathryn caught a wistful glance that Cynthia directed at Matthew, making Kathryn sure the girl wanted to stay in his presence. True to form, Teresa disappeared like a small shadowy ghost.

Thursa had been distracted all during dinner and it was obvious that she was anxious to speak more privately with Matthew. She insisted that Kathryn join them in the parlor as she told her son the whole story of Robert's injury, his apparent recovery, and then the sudden events of his death.

Sitting in the parlor before the fire, Thursa dabbed at her eyes as she spoke. Matthew leaned forward to take both her hands in his, comforting her with low, murmuring words. His gentleness with his mother touched and suprised Kathryn. He seemed a different person in his solicitude for her, no longer mocking or angry as he was when he was with her.

Kathryn sat quietly, feeling out of place. When Thursa regained her composure and sat back into the comfort of the chair, she began speaking softly, looking toward Kathryn as she spoke. "Kathryn took such good care of your brother—always seeing to it that he wanted for nothing. Its been a great comfort to me having her here. Robert's last few months had meaning and joy because of Kathryn and I'll always be grateful for that." As Thursa spoke she looked tenderly toward her daughter-in-law.

But Kathryn grew more and more uncomfortable with her profuse compliments and kept her eyes locked on the toe of her shoes.

When she finally looked up, it was to find Matthew studying her solemnly. She felt her cheeks burn with embarrassment at his gaze. She looked quickly away, wanting to get out of the over-warm room and away from his constant scrutiny. She had no idea what he was thinking, but she doubted if it was complimentary. Was he wondering about her marriage to his brother? About his warning to her that first night they met in Asheville? She was sure he knew she had not loved Robert. She only wanted at that moment to get away from those eyes and from the suffocating confines of the room.

"Thursa, would you please excuse me? I think I'll step outside for some fresh air and then go up to bed," Kathryn said, standing suddenly.

"Of course—you're not feeling ill, are you, dear?" Thursa questioned.

"No, I'm fine . . . just a little tired and sleepy after dinner," she replied, trying to hide her restlessness.

"All right then. Goodnight, dear," Thursa said.

She rose and kissed Kathryn lightly on the cheek. As always, her affection touched Kathryn, and she felt grateful for her continued acceptance at Foxfire.

Matthew stood slowly, and curtly nodded his goodnight. He continued leaning on his cane, watching her as she left the room.

The night air felt good. It was very warm, even for a late April evening. At once Kathryn began to relax. She couldn't understand why she was feeling so edgy and disconcerted. The first shocking effects of Robert's unexpected death had begun to dull. She felt she was better able to come to grips with the silly tricks being played on her by someone in this house. There was no valid reason now to feel such restlessness and confusion.

She looked up at the moon, heavy and haloed, shadowing the valley and mountains with its dim light. The moonglow touched the river, transforming it into a sparkling ribbon that wound through the countryside. The night was quiet, unlike summer, which would be abuzz with the noises of katydids and crickets chirping their loud choruses. Now there was only the sweet distant sounds of the tree frog, a harbinger of spring. She became lost in the sound, remembering how as a child she would wait for the first sound of the tree frog then run to her papa yelling, "Its spring, Papa, its spring!" He would laugh and hug her tightly. Her father loved the changes of the season as much as Kathryn. She missed him very much tonight.

She was so completely lost in thoughts of those happy yesterdays that she did not hear the footsteps behind her until the deep voice startled her and she jerked about suddenly.

"You shouldn't be out here alone at night," Matthew said.

Turning away from him, back toward the overlook, she answered him coolly, "I'm not afraid of the dark."

"No? Then perhaps you should be. There could still be dangerous renegades in the area, you know," he replied slowly. Something in his voice made her know he was referring sarcastically to that midnight not long ago.

"I'll be in soon," she said, turning to face him, determined that he would not intimidate her so easily.

His angular face in shadow was even more savage-looking than before. She shivered slightly as she looked up into his silvery gaze.

"You're shivering," he said, his voice deep and husky. He reached to pull the shawl around her shoulders. The slight brush of his hand caused a tingle where it had touched, causing her to pull away from him as if scorched, perplexed by her reaction to this bewildering man.

He smiled knowingly at her response. His hands caught her shoulders and pulled her toward him. His face was so close she could feel his soft breath on her lips. Knowing all the while she should resist, should deny his insulting advances, Kathryn could not; indeed, she had known all along that she would not. Instead she stood shakily, half against him, as if mesmerized by his touch and his look.

She saw the gleam of his smile and heard him laugh softly as he let her go. "I didn't want you to fall over the edge of the mountain," he taunted, his voice a low whisper.

She felt humiliated by his words and his smile. It was as if he knew exactly what her reaction to him would be, and was pleased by it. As arrogant and vile as she thought him to be, she had to admit it was true. At the moment he couldn't have thought less of her than she herself did. Had she actually wanted him to kiss her again? Yes, of course she had. But why was she so willing to be used by this rude, arrogant man?

She pushed past him and ran back toward the house. He did not try to stop her. She could imagine he was very pleased with himself, standing there, hands on hips, watching her as she fled his hateful laughter.

Silently she berated herself for her foolish reaction. She didn't understand what was happening to her. Her husband had been dead for only a few weeks and she was trembling at his brother's touch. She knew she must certainly have verified his low opinion of her.

As she ran into the house and up the stairs she

met Sula coming down the hall.

"Well, what the devil is wrong with you?" Sula's eyes were big with curiosity.

"Nothing, Sula!" Kathryn panted as she ran blindly up the stairway.

Sula stood watching Kathryn, looking from her to the open doorway. She could see Matthew as he limped slowly back toward the front porch. She muttered, "Now what do you make of that? Humph."

Kathryn couldn't get into her room fast enough. Quickly closing the door, she stood breathing heavily, the sound loud in the silent, darkened room. She was furious as much with herself as with Matthew. She had acted like a silly schoolgirl!

So, Matthew Kincaid was home, and as many times as Kathryn had dreaded his appearance, she never once thought she would feel such terrible rejection and humiliation. He had not wasted any time in establishing his authority, and something told her this would not be the last of their confrontations. But if he expected her to be a quiet mouse of a girl, awaiting his approval at every moment, then he was indeed in for a rude awakening.

Our todays and yesterdays are the blocks with which we build.

Henry Wadsworth Longfellow

Chapter Nine

Kathryn undressed and went straight to bed, as if there she could hide from her feelings. She lay restlessly awake as the bright moonlight streamed through the curtains, making tiny starlike patterns on the quilt. She stiffened as she heard footsteps coming down the hall, pausing at her door. For long moments she held her breath, waiting for him to move on. The soft knock startled her, though she had suspected it might happen.

So he was not finished punishing her. She was more angry than frightened as she threw on a robe and walked to the door.

She swung the door open angrily, unaware of the vision she presented there in the dim lights of the hallway, her long hair swirling about her face, her cheeks sparkling with color, and green eyes that defied him furiously.

Matthew arrogantly walked past her into the room.

"You . . . you can't come in here . . . like this," she sputtered.

Ignoring her words he said, "I just want you to

tell me exactly what happened the day my brother died."

His jaws were clenched and his gray eyes glittered dangerously. Kathryn could not be sure if it was from anger or sorrow.

"But . . . but your mother has already told you," Kathryn said.

"I want to hear it from you. You were the only one with him when he became ill, were you not?" he asked.

"Yes," she answered, "I was."

"Did he say anything, do anything . . . unusual?"

"I . . . no . . . I don't know what you mean" she said, his aggressiveness unnerving her.

Her hesitance seemed to anger him. "Did *you* say anything to him then? Farewell perhaps? Or declare your eternal love?" His sarcastic words were brutal and angry.

Tears came abruptly to Kathryn's eyes at the cruelty of his words. Did he know how it pained her knowing she had never said to Robert the words he most wanted to hear?

She stepped to the door, flinging it open. "Out! Get out of here, Mr. Kincaid. I will not sit quietly while you talk to me this way!"

Matthew was quickly at the door, his hand holding it closed. "Wait," he said. "I'm sorry . . . I should not have said that to you. Please, could we sit down and talk for a moment?" He rubbed his hand tiredly across his eyes, the spark of anger now gone.

Reluctantly she sat and agreed to tell him all she could remember about that day.

"What do you want to know?" she asked rather

stiffly.

"Just start at the beginning and tell me everything you can remember about that day," he said.

"Robert and I had tea together every afternoon in the sitting room between his room and mine. On that particular day, Woody and I had gone on a picnic." Kathryn's voice was low as she relived the anguish of that day.

"Where did you go?" he asked.

"Where? Why we went to the old log house, as Woody calls it—your parents' first home."

"Mine as well," he remarked wryly.

"Yes, well, then we walked to the cemetery. That was all. I got back in time for tea and Robert was already in the sitting room," she continued.

"Alone," he stated.

"Yes, alone. We . . . talked," she said remembering Robert's words to her that day.

"Then?" Matthew prompted.

"Then we had tea, that is, Robert had tea. I had just eaten. I was telling him about the picnic and about Woody. I walked to the windows and looked out." Her voice grew husky and emotional and she had to stop.

Matthew waited.

"I heard a moan and turned to see Robert. His face looked strange . . . puzzled, and he was in pain. He said he felt ill and could not breathe." Tears were streaming from Kathryn's eyes as she related the words to Matthew. "But I couldn't help him—none of us could." She lowered her face from his intense look, her hands in her lap nervously twisting the ribbons of her robe.

Matthew reached forward as if to touch her hair.

He felt an overwhelming desire to hold her, to comfort her, but he could not. He was too unsure of this woman. The one question that had haunted him since that night at the hospital was why someone as young and lovely as Kathryn would marry a man who was crippled, a man she barely knew. But Matthew learned years ago not to trust; it was a lesson he couldn't afford to forget. And something inside warned him not to trust her, for if he ever let himself become emotionally involved with his brother's widow, this beautiful girl with auburn hair and eyes like a sea nymph, he was afraid he would be lost. He withdrew his hand as she raised her eyes to his once more.

With no further prompting Kathryn continued. "When I ran to the stairway and cried for help, everyone came right away."

"Who came?" he asked.

"Mrs. Spencer, Sula and your mother. We couldn't find Joseph. We must have been outside, so the four of us carried Robert to his room. He was semiconscious; his breathing was labored; his pupils were fixed. I knew . . . I knew he was dying, but I could do nothing. We found Joseph and sent him to Asheville for a doctor. All we could do was try and make him comfortable." She stopped and looked at him.

"Tell me . . . tell me how he died." His voice was low and filled with an anguish that tore at her heart.

"Matthew, are you sure you want to hear this?" she said quietly.

"Yes . . . I need to know," he said.

"His breathing grew more and more shallow and

faint. He began having tremors, then his body grew tense and rigid. Finally his breathing . . . just stopped."

"God," he whispered.

She leaned forward toward him. "Matthew," she said.

He raised his hand and held it out toward her. "No, I'm all right," he said. Then he closed his eyes and took a deep breath. "And what did Dr. Logan say? What killed Robert?"

"Why, your mother told you . . . it was his heart," she said, frowning at Matthew.

"He didn't express any surprise that a man as young as my brother should become ill and die within such a short period of time?" he asked.

"Yes, he was shocked, but not unduly so, considering the condition Robert was in. He seemed more saddened than shocked," she said. "But having worked in the field hospital I can tell you it's not unusual for patients such as Robert to develop a blood clot that could be fatal."

"Really?" he said raising his eyebrows scornfully, as if he doubted she were capable of such knowledge.

"Yes, really!" she said, her green eyes sparkling with defiance. "And as to your earlier question—no, Robert never spoke another word after he asked for my help in the sitting room. And I had no time to tell him anything . . . not even goodbye." Her chin trembled, but she continued to look rebelliously at Matthew.

But he would not be put off by her manner. He met her eyes boldly, imperiously.

"One more question and then I shall leave you to

your rest. Did Robert ever mention a will to you?" he asked.

"A will? Why, no, he didn't," she said. He was the second person to mention a will, a possibility she had not even thought of. But then there was no reason to think Robert would make a will at his young age.

"Thank you, Kathryn," he said rising to go. "We need not mention our little talk to mother."

"Fine," she said, still smarting at his attitude toward her.

"Oh, and Kathryn, I'm glad you kept to our agreement that night at the Simmonses. Thank you for that at least."

She jumped to her feet. The arrogance in his voice infuriated her.

"You arrogant, self-righteous . . . For your information, the way I treated your brother had nothing to do with your threats! And I certainly made no such agreement with you because there was no need!" Her voice shook with anger and her green eyes sparked.

He smiled, his eyes as cold and unyielding as flint. She knew he did not believe her. Still, he said nothing, leaving her instead to flounder in her own anger and frustration.

After he had gone Kathryn paced the floor, too furious now to think of sleeping. She picked up a book, only to realize she had read the same paragraph over and over and was still not conscious of what she had read. She could not concentrate; her mind kept returning again and again to Matthew's accusatory tone and his insinuations that there was something mysterious about Robert's death.

Finally she put the book down. It was no use; she simply could not focus her thoughts on reading. She continued to pace the room and listen to the gradually quieting house as everyone prepared to retire for the night. She stood at the window, arms crossed before her as she scanned the shadowed yard below.

There was a sound behind her, somewhere in the room she thought, but she could not be sure from which direction it came. Turning quietly, she looked about the room. Perhaps a mouse had found its way in. She listened, hearing a small scratching sound. It was coming from the sitting room.

She took a deep breath, wondering if she should step across the hall for Matthew. But what if it was only a mouse? How ridiculous he would make her feel!

Softly she walked to the door of the sitting room. She picked a lamp from a nearby table and took another step toward the door. More than anything she wished the noise would stop, never to echo again through her room, for she did not want to open that door.

Her hand was outstretched, trembling as she reached to unbolt the lock. She held the lamp high in front of her to illuminate the small room, but she did not immediately step in.

At the other end of the room, where the door led to Robert's bedroom, she saw a flash of color. Someone *was* there.

"Stop!" Kathryn ordered. Her knees were so weak she could hardly make them carry her forward past the windows and the settee. The person stood still, making no effort to escape, and now Kathryn could make out the features of the intruder.

"Cynthia!" she said. "What are you doing here at this time of night?" Kathryn's voice was stern and angry, as much from fear as anything, but to the girl she supposed it might sound authoritative and even fearless.

Cynthia's eyes were bright as she stood in the light from the lamp, waiting like a trapped rabbit. But Kathryn could detect no real fear in the girl's manner.

She gave a nervous little laugh. "I was . . . cleaning in here this afternoon and I left some mending. I couldn't sleep so I came to get it," she stammered.

"Then where is it?" Kathryn asked.

The girl's hand, which was by her side, moved forward from beneath the folds of her dress. In it was a basket containing folds of material.

Something in her manner disturbed Kathryn. There was a smugness in the innocent smile she made, and her eyes were as flat and expressionless as ever.

"Do you have a key to the door between my room and this one?" Kathryn asked, knowing the girl carried a key ring containing keys to the various rooms she cleaned.

"Yes, ma'am," she said, still smiling her sly little smile.

"I would like to have it, please," Kathryn said.

"Yes ma'am," Cynthia said. She took the key ring and removed a key, which she placed in Kathryn's outstretched hand.

"That will be all then, Cynthia. Goodnight," Kathryn said, watching the girl closely.

"G'night ma'am," she said, leaving through the

other bedroom.

Kathryn went back toward her room and set the lamp on the floor. She inserted the key in the door and turned it. The lock clicked smoothly into place, assuring her that she had been given the correct key.

Once back inside her bedroom with the doors locked she surveyed the room for any disturbances. She had become obsessed with checking everything ever since the ribbon had been left on her mirror.

Once she was certain nothing was amiss, she searched the room for a hiding place for the key, finally wedging it into a small crack behind the mantlepiece.

The chilling remembrance of Robert's death in the room next door came back as vividly as if it had just happened and she sat down shaken and weak. She became aware of each noise in the house. Did she hear footsteps ascending the stairs? She thought of the malevolent face on the house's façade. Had it meant something—a portent of death? Had anyone else ever seen it?

She walked to the fire and stood warming her hands as she tried to banish the frightening thoughts from her mind. She must not allow this place and Robert's bizarre death to drive her mad.

But the feelings would not leave her. More trouble was coming; she could feel it. And the house held some of the secrets.

That night she dreamed again of Robert, of his hands outstretched to her, his eyes vacant and unseeing. She was afraid and could not waken herself. Then his face dissolved into the one she'd seen before, somehow enmeshed with Foxfire Manor.

She awoke, her heart pounding rapidly. She lay awake long into the night, until the clouds blocked the moonlight. The winds began to whistle around the house and she could hear sounds of twigs and debris being blown against the windows by the constantly changing winds.

It's going to rain, she thought, as she finally drifted toward an uneasy sleep. She heard the creaking as the house settled into the night; she felt the hostility . . . From Foxfire? From one of those who lived within?

By doubting we come at the truth.
Cicero

Chapter Ten

The changeable weather continued to plague the residents of Foxfire Manor, springlike one day and freezing cold the next. A few days after Matthew's disturbing visit to Kathryn's room she woke to the sound of the wind rushing furiously around the eaves of the house. She listened quietly as she heard another sound rising intermittently in and out of the wind's roar. It was the sound of a child's laughter—Woody. Smiling at the sound of his happy laughter, she left her bed and walked softly to the window.

Below in the yard, Cynthia and her son were struggling with a kite that they were preparing to launch into the furious wind. Matthew was on one knee, working on the tail of the kite as Woody came to him. With his dark head lowered toward the man, he watched and waited eagerly. He could hardly keep still. Kathryn laughed aloud at the excitement of his movements. Then his chubby little arm went up about Matthew's neck and the man turned and smiled at Woody as he hugged the boy close. Cynthia was laughing. It was the first time Kathryn had ever seen the girl laugh. The sweetness of the scene before her was to tug at her heart for days to come, disturbing her thoughts and her sleep.

As she continued to watch, she realized something else, something she should have seen before. How alike Woody and Matthew were! The same dark hair, the bright intensity of their eyes, the impatience of their actions.

"Of course," Kathryn whispered. She took a deep breath as that realization came to her, bringing with it for some unknown reason a sharp stab of pain in her heart.

She should have seen the resemblance before. Suddenly Cynthia's desperate looks of longing at Matthew became more understandable. All the comments Woody had attributed to his mother about Matthew . . . always Matthew.

She remembered when Woody had wanted to ride a horse. Kathryn had told him he was still too small. He had replied, "When Matthew comes home, he'll teach me to ride, just like he teached my mama."

He had once asked where his daddy was, and as Kathryn tried to think of an appropriate answer he had said. "Maybe when Matthew gets home, I can be his little boy." Had his mother told him that?

Kathryn found it almost impossible to imagine the hard, cynical Matthew Kincaid with a girl like Cynthia. But she could guess how it happened. Cynthia was a young, innocent girl, practically alone here, with no opportunity to meet people her own age. Matthew could simply have taken advantage of that. After all, it was not unknown for men of his position to seduce their servants, their slaves. Why should she expect he would be any different?

Kathryn found the thought very disturbing. She was not surprised, however, that a simple young girl might find the dark, handsome older man exciting, irresistible even. But how *could* he? she wondered. How could an intelligent, responsible man like Matthew take advantage of a simpleminded girl like Cynthia?

She herself could have no respect for men of such character. Matthew could at least have had the decency to marry the poor girl, if only to give that precious little boy his name. He was even more despicable than she previously thought.

Kathryn watched the scene below on the lawn and paced back and forth before the windows. It disturbed her to think she could have actually been attracted to this man. She didn't want to let herself continue to care for a man who treated people as callously as he did.

She needed to be out into the wind, to think, to chase the taunting thoughts from her mind. Turning from the window, she dressed hurriedly in a tan riding skirt and crisp white cotton blouse. She would go out to the view and wait for the coming storm to wash away all her cares and confusion.

Kathryn left the house unseen, not stopping to eat breakfast. She walked furiously, losing some of her frustration along the way. An hour later the wind raged on but the storm still had not come. She stopped to gather a fragrant bouquet of lilacs to take to Robert's grave. She found it comforting to go there and sit, thinking, sometimes even pretending to talk to Robert. Heavens! she chided herself, maybe she really *was* going mad. . . .

The wind was blustery, blowing first one way and

then another, flapping her long skirt against her legs as she walked out the road toward the barn.

As she drew nearer the clearing she could hear the sound of hammering. She stopped, looking about, then finally located the noise. It was Matthew. He was atop the barn roof nailing down loose shingles that the violent wind threatened to rip completely away.

From a distance she stood watching him as he worked. He wore tan pants tucked into knee-high leather boots. His white shirt billowed and whipped in the wind, accentuating the hard muscles of his chest and shoulders. Pausing a moment, he sat back, his forearm propped against his knee, seeming to enjoy the raging windstorm that howled about him. Suddenly, like a wild animal sensing the presence of an invader, he turned toward Kathryn, catching her standing there watching him.

His steel-colored eyes caught and held hers. As usual, she could not help being intimidated by his bold look, but this time she did not look away. Then with a dawning amazement she knew that the disgust she had sworn for him earlier had now vanished with the wind. She was lost in the look of him and the remembrance of his touch.

"Kat . . . Kat! Guess what?" Woody came running out of the barn. "Lady's got new puppies! Come see!" He tugged at Kathryn to follow him into the building.

In the dim interior of the barn, Woody proudly offered his new discoveries. She knelt on the hay-covered floor to see the wiggling, grunting little pups, laughing aloud at their antics.

"Woody, they're adorable," she said as she stroked

the tiny creatures softly with one finger. She had always loved small animals—who could resist them? Woody sat close to her as he began to think of names for each of the pups.

But sitting still was not an easy thing for Woody to do, and soon he could not contain himself any longer. "I'm going to go tell Sula—she's been looking for Lady for days!" He jumped up and ran out the entrance and toward the house.

Kathryn smiled at his retreating figure as she continued to sit, softly caressing the puppies. She felt rather than heard Matthew's approach. She looked up to find him standing silently in the doorway, a silhouette against the gray outside light.

"You continue to amaze me, Kate," he drawled.

"Don't call me that," she said without thinking. She stood quickly and brushed off her skirt. She did not want to become involved in another exchange with him.

Without speaking further she started to walk past him, but as she did he reached for her, grabbing her arm and pulling her against him.

"Let me go," she said, trying to hide the confusion she always felt in his presence.

"Where?" he asked, smiling grimly.

"I was on my way to the cemetery," she answered.

"Ah, yes, the heartbroken wife—how very noble you are . . . and I thought you came to see me," he said softly, his lips close to her ear.

"Matthew, please," she began. His underlying anger frightened her. Even his words of intimacy sounded like a threat.

"Please?" he laughed. "Please do . . . or please don't?"

"You are . . . why are you doing this?" she asked as she jerked away from him. He moved to bar her way outside, so that her back was against the wall of the barn.

"Why do you continue to treat me in this manner?" she asked again as he took a menacing step toward her, stopping only when she held out both hands to warn him off.

"And . . . how do I treat you, Kathryn?" he asked, stepping even closer. Daring her to protest, he reached one hand out and ran his finger down the collar of her shirtwaist toward the first button.

In an instant she knew that his intention was not to hurt her or even to seduce her. He wanted to bend her to his will, to humiliate her. She did not move but looked steadily into his eyes. Her heart turned cold at the raw anger she saw reflected there.

He studied her face too, looking deeply into her eyes. He seemed to be searching for some answer in their depths. Kathryn watched fascinated as his gray eyes darkened and his hand stopped its descent. Then unexpectedly his hand was behind her head, catching her unbound hair tightly in his fist.

"No, Matt . . ."

"Don't . . ." he growled. "Don't say a word . . . you know you want this as much as I do, I can see it in your green eyes," he whispered softly as he touched his lips to hers.

If she had expected savagery or brutality she was wrong. His beard was surprisingly soft against her skin as he teased her with kisses, lightly, gently. He left her leaning toward him breathlessly, seeking his lips, wanting to be closer, wanting more. In her innocence she wasn't sure exactly what she did want from him.

If Kathryn had been as experienced as Matthew suspected she might have known exactly what he was doing . . . the game he was playing. But, naively, she behaved just as he had expected, perhaps as many others had done at his expert touch.

She pulled away, her eyes burning with hunger for him. She did not know what to make of his tenderness and she was afraid he would laugh, mocking her again. Instead he pulled her closer and kissed her deeply, more passionately this time, as he whispered her name against her lips.

She moved closer, the fierce emotion of her response surprising even herself. A few schoolboy kisses and Robert's chaste ones had never prepared her for this man's intense assault on her senses.

So for that moment she returned his kisses with no holding back, no thought of regrets, no questions about his reasons. She had never known that desire between a man and woman could be so devastating a thing.

Kathryn knew, had known all along, that Matthew did not believe her to be an innocent but she did not stop to think how he would interpret her unsophisticated passion.

Later she was to doubt everything, believing only how easily he could turn away from her. She would see him as the man he really was, tempered like steel by the events of the war, a man who laughed at the tears of women, a man undaunted by sensual lips and passionate pleas. He could be as cold and unfeeling as his gray eyes turned to ice.

She discovered his motive all too soon as he

pulled away from her. She gazed up at him tenderly, lovingly. The last thing she expected to hear were the cruel words he spat at her.

"You're a witch, Kathryn!" he growled, pushing her away from him. "Your husband's memory has vanished all too soon, hasn't it?" He was so angry he trembled.

"What?" she gasped. She felt the blood drain from her face as she saw the fury in the look he directed at her.

"Don't play innocent, Kate, it doesn't become you! I suspected when I first saw you with poor, gullible Eugene that you weren't exactly the grieving widow, remember? Did you really think you could change my mind with a few passionate kisses?"

"Matthew, no . . . you don't understand . . . you're wrong." Tears began to dim her vision. She could not believe what he was saying to her.

"Oh, but I do understand . . . perfectly! You're a scheming little baggage who took advantage of Robert's attraction to you. But I must congratulate you on your performance. Mother thinks you're a princess. It makes me sick to think of Robert's complete trust in you." His anger was so intense that his gray eyes glittered with unshed tears. "Well, I'm fed up with the wonderful innocent Kathryn facade. Evidently Lila Spencer is the only one here able to see through you. You've only made one mistake, my dear Kate," he continued, unmindful of the tears that now flowed freely down her face. "Robert was a young and naive boy. I am not!"

She turned and ran from the barn, down the rocky path toward the log cabin. If she had thought the tragedies of the past few years had steeled her, then she was wrong . . . she was so very wrong. She ran on through the gathering storm toward the cemetery.

"Damn!" Matthew's expletive followed her as she ran. Moments later she heard his footsteps on the path behind her.

Blindly she ran past the cabin and through the trees toward the cemetery, where she flung herself past the stone fence and into the graveyard. There she fell on her knees beside Robert's grave. There among the fading blossoms of the daffodils she sobbed out her pain, her humiliation and her anger at Matthew.

"Oh, Robert," she cried. "Why did you have to leave me? I need you now . . . I need you to tell me everything will be all right." She cried forlornly, forgetting everything, heedless of Matthew's presence behind her. She ached for the injustice of it all, for her husband's short, unfinished life. And she cried for her inability to find peace and happiness.

The first fierce streak of lightning ripped through the sky, followed closely by the jarring crash of thunder.

She heard Matthew's muttered curse as he walked toward her and she recoiled from him as he knelt and clasped her trembling shoulders. "Kathryn, that's enough! We have to get inside, the rain will be here any moment."

"No!" she screamed, shaking away his hands. "Don't touch me." The violence of her reaction stunned him.

"Leave me alone!" she cried. "Don't pretend it matters to you. You only use people for your own amusement. I can't believe you're Robert's brother!

He was good and kind . . ."

"Enough!" he snarled through the roar of the storm. Moving swiftly he picked her up in his arms as if she were a child and carried her, kicking and fighting, back toward the cabin.

He stumbled through the doorway, dumping her onto the cold, bare floor. He seemed as anxious to be rid of her as she of him. By the time he had closed the door against the wind and rain, she had scurried to the other side of the room, where she sat, back against the log wall.

How she hated herself for shivering and making small hiccuping sounds like a child. Angrily she wiped away her tears and glared at him with pure hatred. He read her look, and his mirthless laughter rang in the small empty room.

Ignoring her, Matthew turned and began to place pieces of kindling into the fireplace. Soon the small fire began to chase the chill from the damp air as the storm continued to rage outside.

Matthew sat across the room from her, silently waiting for the deluge to pass. They were like two natural enemies, caught together in the same cave. As he looked at her wet, bedraggled appearance, she caught the slightest flicker of a smile on his face. She raised her chin defiantly, her look cold and contemptuous. How she yearned at that moment to be a man!

His smile faded as she challenged him, and a steely glitter sparkled in his eyes. How could she have believed his kisses or the momentary glint of compassion she thought she'd seen on his face before. Her heart and her imagination had gotten the best of her. She was a fool! Of course he believed only the worst of her. Why shouldn't he? She had married his brother for a home and security, just as he believed all along. Lila Spencer's stories could only have confirmed it.

They continued to sit, waiting out the storm, each lost in thought. Kathryn wanted to shout at him: What did he know of her? How dare he judge her?

But if Matthew Kincaid had any doubts about his cruelty toward her his cool gray eyes did not betray him. Kathryn had no reason to doubt that he despised her as much as she despised him.

When the pounding rain finally let up Kathryn stalked silently out of the cabin, slamming the door behind her. She charged breathlessly toward the barn, oblivious to the soggy bushes and tree limbs that blocked her path.

In the cabin behind her Matthew sat silently staring into the dying embers of the fire.

Kathryn dashed into the barn and looked quickly about, making sure she was alone before allowing her tears free rein. It felt good to be able to cry without trying to pretend she wasn't hurt, without needing to show Matthew how immune she was to his words.

On impulse she reached for saddle gear and opened the door to the stall where Bitsy, a small gentle mare, stood watching her with soulful eyes.

She threw the saddle across the horse and tightened the girth, then led her out of the barn. Kathryn lifted her damp skirts, slipping easily into the saddle.

Bitsy could smell the rain and sulphurous lightning in the air and pranced sideways until Kathryn pulled firmly on the reins and nudged the mare's sides, urging her forward. Then she guided the mare down the road toward the house. After they reached the edge of the yard, Kathryn pulled the mare to the left, skirting the lawn just at the boundary of the forest, and headed off the mountain, away from Foxfire. She looked quickly over her shoulder, half expecting to see Matthew behind her. She shrugged her shoulders, knowing he would not approve of her riding out alone. But his approval meant nothing to her.

She nudged the horse into a trot, feeling with exuberance the storm-washed wind against her face as she rode. She pulled the mare into the woods where laurel and rhododendron grew densely, their limbs pulling at Kathryn's hair and clothing as she passed. She had to slow the mare to a walk to get through the tangled bushes, but as they proceeded down the slope the thick clumps of shrubbery gave way to hardwood stands of towering beech and hickory and the forest floor became clearer. She rode for at least a mile, coming finally alongside a stream where clear sparkling waters tumbled and cascaded over moss-covered rocks.

The ride had freed her somewhat from the frustrations she felt earlier. She pulled Bitsy to a stop at the stream and dismounted, allowing the mare to drink her fill while Kathryn walked beneath the huge old trees.

She brushed aside twigs and leaves and sat on the ground beside the bubbling water. The ground was covered with small, thorny beechnuts, which she picked up and threw absentmindedly into the stream.

"Well, lookee here! What have we got here, boys?"

Kathryn jumped to her feet and turned to face the man. His voice sent chills through her body. She saw there were three of them on horseback, the one in front seeming to be in charge. It was he who had spoken.

The men were dressed in filthy clothes that looked as if they might once have been military uniforms. But the mixture of blue and gray material and unkempt appearance identified them as scavengers. She could smell their nauseating scent from where she stood.

The bearded man in front sat on his horse watching her, a wide leering grin covering his face.

Kathryn made a slow, deliberate move toward Bitsy.

"Don't you move, girl!" the man ordered. "I'd rather have you alive, but right now . . . we ain't too particular!"

Their laughter filled the forest around her and Kathryn felt a sick, sinking feeling come over her at the look on their faces.

"My husband is just behind me," she said. "You had better leave before he comes."

Once again they laughed, and the spokesman scowled as he stepped down from his horse.

"Now what do we look like, girl? One of your dandified southern aristocrats who will believe anything you say?" He took a step toward her, his mud-covered boots pointed outward as he walked in a crude, swaggering manner.

"If that's the kind of man you're used to, why honey . . . you're in for a real treat!" Again he laughed, showing the ugliness of his brown tobacco-stained teeth.

She spun around quickly and grabbed Bitsy's bridle. She knew he might shoot her but in that split second she had made her decision—she preferred death to having such an animal touch her.

The sound of a gunshot exploded through the forest, echoing down the mountain. Kathryn screamed and clung to Bitsy's bridle as her ears began to ring loudly and her heart beat hard at her throat.

"I'd climb back on that horse if I were you." Matthew sat astride the big horse Blackjack. He had followed Kathryn's trail down the mountain and was now about fifty feet from the men. In his right hand was a long-barreled revolver, which was leveled at the chest of the man standing on the ground.

Their surprise was evident as they stared at Matthew. Kathryn was afraid to move or make a sound. More than that, she was afraid the men would simply overpower Matthew and kill them both.

"We just stopped to rest. Now you ain't gonna deny us poor soldiers that and a little something to eat, are you, mister?" one of them sneered.

"The war's over, friend, and if you ever were soldiers, you're not now. I'd advise you to move out of here . . . *now.* This is Kincaid land . . . shooting three trespassers would hardly cause a stir in these mountains—if anyone found your bodies, that is." Matthew's voice was as cold as steel and his piercing gaze left no mistake as to his intention.

One of the men cleared his throat and looked about, his eyes darting nervously to the man who still stood in front of them.

"Let's go, Nate. I ain't aimin' to die here on this God-forsaken mountain!"

"This man ain't gonna shoot us," Nate said, spitting tobacco juice on the ground.

Matthew cocked the revolver, the click of the hammer making a bone-chilling noise in the silence.

"We're goin', mister, we're goin," the two riders said. "You won't see us back in these parts again!"

Matthew said nothing as the two rode down the long slope toward the foothills, but his eyes never shifted from the man in his gunsight.

"And how about you, Nate?" he drawled.

"Yeah," the man said. "I reckon I'll be goin' too." His angry eyes darted toward Kathryn and he wiped a hand across his mouth.

"Good," Matthew said. "And Nate . . . if I ever see your ugly face anywhere in the state of North Carolina, I'll kill you—do you understand?"

Kathryn shivered at the intensity of his words. She knew he meant it. She could see by Nate's ashen face that he knew it too. The renegade pulled himself into the saddle and cantered quickly through the trees after his partners.

Kathryn leaned her head against the mare's side and took a long slow breath. She reins she had been grasping were stuck to her hand. Now that the men were gone she felt an overwhelming sense of weakness in her limbs. Matthew's rescue only made her feel awkward . . . not that she wasn't grateful. She was, more than she could express, but then that was the problem, for after their bitter words, earlier, how could she thank him?

Matthew stuck the revolver into the belt of his

trousers and dismounted, leading his horse behind him as he walked toward her.

"Girl, you do sorely try my patience," he said.

"I know," she murmured.

Matthew looked at her standing there before the stream, her hair still wet and tangled, her eyes unable to meet his. He found it impossible to be angry with her, and that disturbed him more than he'd ever have thought possible.

"Damn," he muttered under his breath. "Are you all right?" he asked.

"Yes," she said. "I guess I should thank you." Her words were an almost inaudible whisper.

"What?" he said, annoyance at himself making his tone of voice more irritable than it should have been.

Kathryn's chin lifted and her nostrils flared slightly. He knew how much it cost her to thank him and how he wanted to further humiliate her by demanding she repeat it!

"I said thank you!" she snapped.

Matthew grinned, his silver eyes sparkling down at her as he raked his fingers through his hair.

He pulled Blackjack forward and gracefully mounted him. "God forbid you should have to be grateful to me for anything," he muttered.

She flushed, aware of how ungrateful she must have sounded. She knew she was behaving like a little girl, but somehow he always goaded her into saying the wrong things.

"Here, get on your horse," he said moving closer to help her up.

As they turned their horses homeward she pulled beside him and placed her hand on his arm.

"Matthew wait . . . please wait. I am grateful to you, and I do thank you, sincerely. Those men probably would have killed me."

His hands were folded casually over the pommel of his saddle, his head slightly lowered. He glanced at her from the corner of his eyes and his lips quirked crookedly beneath his beard, causing a long groove beside his mouth.

"Don't worry Kathryn, I won't tell any one you actually had to say those words to me."

She watched with a puzzled, exasperated look as he rode away. She didn't know if he was teasing her or if he was serious.

The horses made the trek slowly back up the mountain and finally emerged from the forest onto the lawn of Foxfire Manor. It was growing late and Kathryn knew Thursa would be wondering where they were.

"I'll let you off at the house while I put the horses in the barn," Matthew said.

"Matthew . . . please don't mention this to your mother or Sula. I don't want to worry them." Kathryn got down from the horse at the front porch.

"I had not intended to," he said, his look impersonal as he watched her from his saddle.

She couldn't wait to get upstairs and change into something warm. If only she could do so without running into Mom Sula.

But love is blind and cannot see the petty follies that themselves commit.

Wm. Shakespeare

Chapter Eleven

Kathryn slipped unnoticed to her room and changed into dry clothes. She sat exhausted, staring out the windows as she brushed out her wet, tangled hair. Her thinking was confused, remembering not only Matthew's fierce anger but his passionate kisses as well. Had his anger at her cooled when he found her there with those men?

She laid the hairbrush down with a clatter, angry with herself for trying to wish away his resentment so easily. And where was her cherished pride and independence, that one man could so quickly alter her feelings? She didn't understand what was happening to her lately.

She must be more careful. Perhaps she would never know why Matthew treated her with such bitterness, but neither must he know how deeply he affected her, how deeply he had hurt her.

Her thoughts were interrupted as Woody came running into her room, throwing himself across her knees. He hugged her tightly, his small body trembling.

"Woody, sweetheart, whatever is the matter?" she asked. She had never seen him like this; Woody rarely cried.

She stroked his back and his tangled black hair until he stopped crying. He raised his head and she gasped as she saw the dark, ugly bruise on the side of his face.

"What happened honey . . . did you fall?" she asked.

He shook his head, not speaking . . . his blue eyes large and expressive.

"What then?" she asked.

From the doorway came a voice as cold and pitiless as any Kathryn had ever heard. "It's nothing! He only tripped and fell. He doesn't need anyone to baby him! Come with me, Woody," Lila Spencer said.

Woody looked at Kathryn with pleading eyes, making no move to go with his grandmother. There in his eyes she saw something she'd not seen before—fear. Woody was afraid of his grandmother.

"It's quite all right, Mrs. Spencer," she said, all the while knowing she had no right to be defiant where the woman's own grandson was involved. "He may stay here with me for awhile. Please have some tea sent up and a few cookies that Woody likes."

Lila Spencer hesitated for only a fraction of a second before she whirled and left the room, but not before Kathryn had seen the anger and resentment in her eyes.

But Kathryn was not as calm, as authoritative as

she appeared. Inside she was shaken by the woman's open hostility. Still, she preferred the woman's wrath to letting Woody go with her, at least until she found out exactly what had happened to him. Her eyes glinted with fury to think that his injury could be the result of that woman's hateful treatment, and like a mother tigress she felt her protective instincts spark to life.

Woody obviously did not want to talk about what had happened so she did not question him further. She would have to wait patiently until he wished to tell her. She held him to her, knowing that somehow she would find the strength to protect him from the ugliness that lurked so mysteriously in this household.

Even as she made that vow she knew there was another thing which she must find the strength to do. It was time for Matthew Kincaid to take full responsibility for his son, and Kathryn intended to see that he did just that.

She carried the boy to the love seat, where they snuggled together in the corner. Soon the trauma of the day took its toll and they both fell sound asleep.

When Sula came with the tea she smiled at the picture of them there together. Her beautiful little Kat should have children of her own. Gently she set the tray down, leaving it where they could find it, and tiptoed from the room.

As Sula left she met Matthew coming up the stairs. His black hair was wet, curling crisply about his head; his clothes were also wet. He did not see her at first, but she had time to observe him, wondering as she did at the closed look on his face and the tight clench of his jaw.

"Afternoon, Mister Matthew," Sula said as she passed him in the hall.

He looked up distractedly and she realized he had not even been aware of her presence until she spoke.

"Hello, Sula," he said.

She went downstairs and did not look back, so she did not see him pause outside Kathryn's room.

Matthew hesitated a moment with his hand on the doorknob. When Kathryn had ridden away from the barn so angrily this afternoon he had almost let her go, let her do as she so stubbornly pleased. But his conscience would not permit it. And when he'd seen her there alone in the woods, her green eyes sick with fear . . . the looks on those men's faces as they watched her . . . God! he'd wanted to kill them. All of them. It shocked him that as sick as he was of killing, it had taken every ounce of his will not to pull that trigger. The thought of what might have happened to her if he'd stubbornly allowed her to go kept running through his mind and would not leave him alone. It shook him to his very soul to think of it.

Matthew opened her door quietly and stepped into the room. He had no idea what it was he would say to Kathryn. He only knew that something was not right, either in his first impression of her or in his judgement. And he was not used to being wrong.

He saw the two of them sleeping on the small settee, Kathryn's face slightly flushed and her hair still damp from the rain. Her dark lashes rested against creamy ivory skin and a small wrinkle creased her brow, as if even in sleep she worried. She cradled the child lovingly in her arms. At the sight of them, a deep ache blossomed within his chest.

He frowned and shook his head as if to clear his thoughts then quietly turned and left them sleeping.

Kathryn woke to a tingling sensation in her arm. She moved Woody so that he lay next to her on the seat. He continued to sleep, his warm little body totally relaxed. The rush of tenderness she felt for him was powerful; she thought she could not love a child of her own any more than she did this little boy.

When he roused from his nap they ate the cookies and drank the lukewarm tea. He seemed more like himself now, but she was not happy sending him away. She did so with the caution that he come directly to her or Sula if anything or anyone caused him to be afraid again. Eyes downcast, he promised her that he would.

Mrs. Spencer obviously knew that Kathryn suspected her, and for that reason she felt it was unlikely she would punish him further. In any case, Kathryn knew Matthew was the only person with any influence over Lila Spencer. She would tell him about the incident, and no matter what

Matthew felt toward her, she knew in her heart that he would never allow anything to happen to Woody. She had seen the great love he felt for his family. Even though he despised her she knew he could never turn his back on his own son.

It was imperative that Kathryn tell Matthew about Woody, but she did not want to face him tonight. She simply could not bear to sit at the same table, pretending indifference while he silently accused her with his eyes. The memory of his hateful words were still too fresh and painful. She sent word to Thursa that she was not feeling well and would take her dinner in her room.

Kathryn had just dressed for bed as dusk fell over the mountains when a knock sounded at her door. Holding her robe tightly about her she cautiously opened the door.

Matthew stood there, poised like an animal ready to spring. She was not surprised to see that the distrust he felt toward her earlier had returned, and she had to admit she was disappointed by this.

"I would like you to come down to dinner," he said, his voice deceptively quiet. "Mother has worried enough, and I don't want her upset any more by our private disagreements."

"I have no intention of coming downstairs. I . . ."

"Don't say another word. You either get dressed and stop behaving like a coddled child or I'll come in and dress you myself!" His quietly spoken words were made through clenched teeth.

"You . . . you . . . wouldn't!" she sputtered, almost speechless at his overbearing behavior.

A smile played about the corner of his mouth as he sarcastically laughed. "You know I would."

He turned on his heel and walked casually down the hall as if they'd only been discussing the weather. Kathryn didn't know who disgusted her most—the hateful overbearing devil she watched walking away from her or herself for putting up with his dominating attitude. But she knew he meant every word of his nasty little threat and would like nothing better than to cause her further humiliation.

Moments later she was dressed and walking down the stairway. Her cheeks were still bright with anger, but she didn't care. Somewhere deep inside she was looking forward to her next confrontation with the arrogant Mr. Kincaid.

As she entered the dining room the family was already being seated at the table. She came in behind Matthew, who was seated at the end of the table. Thursa was on his left and Lila and Cynthia beside her. Teresa sat on Matthew's right, focusing an all-knowing smirk on Kathryn. She had probably been lurking about spying on her again, Kathryn thought angrily; nevertheless, she ignored the look and sat down beside the spritely little woman.

Thursa was especially happy to see Kathryn. "Darling, I'm so glad you could join us after all. You make any gathering so much brighter. I do hope you're feeling better."

Matthew was watching Kathryn with a warning

smile that didn't quite reach to his wintry eyes.

Kathryn's voice was sweet as she answered. "Oh, much better . . . besides, who could resist such a charming personal invitation from a man like Matthew."

Thursa frowned, looking from Kathryn's tight little smile back to Matthew. Sula was coming into the room with a tureen full of steaming soup. She looked questioningly toward Thursa, who merely shook her head. Sula coughed lightly and glanced at Kathryn with a frown.

Matthew seemed momentarily taken aback by Kathryn's sarcasm, then he pursed his lips and tried to hide the involuntary grin on his dark face. One would almost think he delighted in these small battles with her. Kathryn did not find it amusing; she seemed, however, to be the only one at the table who did not.

The remainder of the meal was quiet and a little awkward. Just before they left the table, Thursa made an attempt to remedy the silence, reminding Matthew that he had spoken little of the war and of his friendship with General Lee. "Tell us about him," she coaxed.

A slight frown appeared between his brows. His eyes were hidden from them as he looked down at the table. He sat not speaking, drawing imaginary lines on the linen tablecloth with his butter knife until Kathryn began to wonder if he intended to answer his mother at all.

"General Lee . . . well, I've never met a man quite like him. I have no doubt he's a military genius, but he's much more than that. He is the kind of man we all wanted to be, I suppose—tough minded but fair, brilliant, compassionate. He genuinely cared about his soldiers and they knew it. I have been with him when the courageous efforts of his men actually brought tears to his eyes. He wouldn't speak of it, although it was felt by all of us close to him." Matthew's voice grew slightly hoarse and he paused for a moment.

Kathryn could only stare at him, surprised at the caring, the emotion she was beginning to see behind his tough facade. She could not believe this was the same man who had treated her so indifferently, who had spoken to her more cruelly than anyone ever had. She was a bit perplexed at this new insight. She had seen it toward the ones he cared for, but this was something new. She had to caution herself, for the last thing she wanted now was to feel compassion for him.

He continued more steadily. "He's quite a man. I hope someday you'll be able to meet him, Mother, and judge for yourself."

He sighed. "As for the war—battles began to merge with one another after awhile. They were never-ending—as was the suffering. When you thought you'd had all you could endure, it began all over again. I saw men march across open fields in a straight line, shoulder to shoulder, into the guns of the enemy. They did it to give another company the chance to advance, or to buy precious time. They knew they would die, yet they marched on—North and South alike. It was crazy."

Matthew's eyes looked as if he were elsewhere.

Thursa's face was stricken with pain as the nobility and high ideals of war were stripped away and the truth revealed by the words of her own son. Indeed, they all were touched by his words. Even Robert had never spoken of the war in quite this way. His version, like Eugene's ideas, had been much more glorified and idealistic.

Matthew took a deep breath and looked up, returning to the realm of Foxfire and the women sitting at the table. "Well . . . I suppose I've managed to dampen your evening quite enough. I'll be in the parlor, Mother . . . ladies." He did not look toward Kathryn.

Kathryn watched him as he walked, without his cane now, toward the door. His dark jacket fit snugly across his broad shoulders, tapering down to his narrow waist. She had to admit he was a most appealing figure. She would guess there had been many women in his life, yet at age thirty he was still unmarried.

Glancing across the table at Cynthia, Kathryn caught her in an unguarded moment. The blatant look of hunger on her face as she watched Matthew leave the room shocked Kathryn more than she could say. She'd never have guessed the girl was capable of such compelling emotions.

Sensing Kathryn's eyes on her, Cynthia turned slightly toward her and confronted her with a withering look. It was almost as if she dared Kathryn to say anything. For once the blank eyes were alive and Kathryn shuddered as she looked into their depths.

"Where's Woody?" Kathryn asked bluntly, her voice sharp from remembering him as he was that afternoon.

Cynthia looked toward her mother, who smiled rather slyly and said, "Don't worry, ma'am, he's fine. Miz Teresa's gone to read to him. She does that sometimes at night when he can't sleep."

Kathryn frowned. Woody with Teresa? Should she be alarmed? But she reminded herself that Woody loved Teresa and enjoyed being with her. Whatever was wrong with her? She was becoming suspicious and guarded of everyone in the house.

She hated to think about the unpleasant task that faced her regarding Woody. Although she felt a twinge of reluctance at bringing it to Matthew's attention right now, she knew that for the boy's sake it could not be delayed.

"Thursa, would you excuse me? I need to speak to Matthew . . . privately," she murmured.

"Of course dear, I'm going to make it an early night anyway."

Kathryn could feel the dark, resentful glances of Mrs. Spencer and her daughter, but she did not acknowledge them in any way. As Sula had suggested, it was best to avoid both of them if she could.

The door to the parlor was slightly ajar so she did not bother to knock. Instead she stepped quietly but purposefully into the room. The fire burning in the grate warmed the room and chased away the chill and dampness of the spring storm.

Matthew stood with his arm resting on the mantle as he stared thoughtfully into the flames.

"Matthew . . ." she whispered tentatively.

As he looked up his pensive gaze met hers with a force that left her breathless and shaken. Neither of them spoke. She could not guess what thought had been in his mind when she walked in, but he looked troubled and alone. If she had not known what a hard and unyielding man he was she'd have thought he looked apologetic and very vulnerable.

He took a deep breath as if to clear his thoughts, and the spellbinding moment was gone.

She walked toward him, "Are you all right?"

"You came here to inquire about my well-being? How very kind of you." His eyes were once again cold and hard.

So, she thought, we are back to this. Well, at least she knew what to expect from his antagonistic manner, and she had to admit that the vulnerable one she had just glimpsed troubled her.

"There's something I need to discuss with you. But yes, I am concerned about you, whether you choose to believe it or not," she said.

"Don't be!" he said abruptly. "I don't need the pity of anyone." His face twisted angrily. "Especially not yours, Kathryn."

He always seemed to know just how to keep her angry and off balance. Despite her earlier vow that he would not hurt her again, he had. That was something, she was beginning to realize, that she simply could not control.

"I don't believe you," she said, suddenly seeing

the hurt and anger in him for what it was. "You sounded like your brother. He didn't want to be pitied either," she said. "Perhaps the two of you were not so different after all."

"Don't count on that," he said. "I'm sure you didn't come here to discuss similarities."

"No, I didn't," she said. "I'll get straight to the point."

"And that is . . . ?" he drawled, still leaning against the fireplace.

His sarcastic indifference so irritated her that she blurted out what she had come to say more abruptly than she had intended to. "I suspect that Woody has been physically abused by someone, most likely his grandmother . . ." She paused at the frown of doubt that appeared on his face, then continued rapidly, "And I think, as his father, its your responsibility to see that it never happens again! I want you to make sure that he has a safe and secure home, if nothing else!" She stopped, breathless, almost wincing as she waited for his reply.

He had grown deathly quiet. Dropping his arm from the mantle he placed his fists on his lean hips and stood facing her. He took a deep breath and fixed his eyes upon her face in a cold, furious stare, his jaws clenched beneath the dark beard. "His father? You believe I'm Woody's father?" His anger was barely contained and his voice was a low, menacing growl.

Determined not to be intimidated by his attitude, she lifted her chin and replied, "I'm certain of it! I've seen you with the boy! The resemblance is not a coincidence, and it's quite obvious how much he adores you. Besides, when Cynthia looks at you . . ." She stopped at the sardonic lift of his eyebrows.

"Oh?" He smiled coolly at her blushing reluctance to continue. "And why don't you tell me exactly how Cynthia looks at me." His voice had turned quiet and he stepped toward her. "What would a sweet, innocent girl like yourself know of lustful looks?"

"I . . . she . . ." Kathryn stammered, flushing deeply at his pointed remarks. "You're trying to confuse the real issue and I mean to have my say about this!" Her lips trembled as she faced him.

His eyes opened wide, shining with real amusement at her discomfort. "Ah, good. This is the Kathryn I've come to know!"

She took a deep breath, wanting to turn and run, to get away from his mockery and his derisive smile. But she could not. She withstood his attempt to unsettle her and waited. This was too important to have it end in another argument.

Seeing that he could not intimidate her he said lightly, "All right, Kathryn, go ahead. Say what's on your mind."

His movements had brought him uncomfortably close to her. She found it hard to think clearly when he was so near. She turned and walked to the window to watch the rain still dripping from the trees and the house.

With her back to him she tried to speak quietly,

calmly. "I didn't come here to accuse or condemn anyone, Matthew . . . not even you. I'm sorry if I made it sound that way. My concern, whether you believe it or not, is for that little boy," she said.

"All right, I believe that. I have seen how you care for him." The vision of her asleep with the boy cradled lovingly in her arms flashed into his mind.

Kathryn turned to him and told him how Woody had come to her and of his obvious fright. She spoke of Mrs. Spencer's rude behavior, both today and in the past, and of her fear that it was his grandmother who had hit him. But she stopped short of telling him about the red ribbons or the other things that had frightened her since she came here.

Matthew seemed troubled by her words and he stroked his beared chin thoughtfully. "Perhaps he did fall. He's a very active little boy. . . ."

"No, Matthew! I know that's not it. If you could have seen his eyes, he was so frightened." She had to stop at the thought of his little bruised face and his shining blue eyes filled with tears.

Matthew frowned and said soberly. "You really believe someone here would hurt Woody?"

"Yes, I do," she said. "Can I be the only one who sees something peculiar in the Spencers? Mrs. Spencer is so cold and hateful, while Cynthia . . . well, she seems to be adrift in a dream world most of the time, seldom speaking. Most of the time she's withdrawn and lifeless, yet there are times when I think I see something in her eyes almost

. . . almost evil." She was afraid she had said too much, not knowing if she should continue in this way, or how Matthew would react to it. This was more than she had confided to anyone, even Sula, and she felt self-conscious that Matthew should be the one she would go to.

Her words seemed to have struck a response in Matthew. She saw a flicker of something hidden in his eyes, a memory perhaps. He nodded his head in agreement, silently, thoughtfully.

"I'm only interested in Woody's welfare. . . ."

He looked down at her distractedly, almost as if he'd forgotten she was there. "I know Kathryn . . . I believe you. You and I may have our differences, but I hope you know that I wouldn't let it keep me from doing the right thing where Woody is concerned. I can see that you care about him, and I promise you I will see that this does not happen again." He voice was authoritative and certain as he spoke.

"Thank you," she said, the relief evident in her words. As much as she disliked him, she had to admit that both his words and his manner were reassuring. She did feel safer now that he was at Foxfire, and that was something she never thought she'd feel.

To her surprise he reached out and touched her face gently, his fingers warm and caressing. "Go to bed, Kate," he whispered. "I'll take care of this."

Even after the vicious words he had said to her today she was again totally disarmed by him and by what his touch could do to her. Before he could see the response in her eyes she turned and walked away from him, her heart hammering from an emotional reaction she did not want to acknowledge.

They did not know how hate can burn
In hearts once changed from soft to stern.
Lord Byron

Chapter Twelve

The night held only confusion for Kathryn as jumbled thoughts ran through her head, pushing sleep further and further away. She could not explain these sudden changes in her feelings toward Matthew . . . one moment despising him and the other . . . But one thing she knew for certain, she could no longer deny that he was in her thoughts much more than she wanted him to be.

She rose from the love seat and paced the room, pausing in the glow from the fireplace to look at the clock. Two A.M. She sighed and started back toward the bed. As she passed the windows she caught the flicker of a light near the edge of the woods. Stepping closer to the window, she looked out to see the outline of someone standing in the dim glow of a lantern.

Could this be the person who was trying to frighten her—the phantom with the red ribbons? Anger stirred within her and she felt a burning determination to discover once and for all who it was. She would start by finding out who lurked there in the woods, watching the house.

She threw on a heavy cloak over her nightgown and quickly slipped into her shoes. Peeking out the window again, she could see the shadow still there in the glow of the light. She shivered. Why was he standing so still, and why was he watching the house? The unpleasant thought came to her that perhaps it was Matthew, waiting for a rendezvous with Cynthia. Somehow she dismissed that from her mind. She had detected no interest from Matthew toward the girl, and she guessed that whatever was between them in the past was finished. It was only the boy that kept her here at Foxfire under Matthew's protection.

Quietly she slipped out the back door and around toward the woods. She wan't sure she'd have enough nerve to actually confront the intruder, but at least she might get close enough to find out who was trying to terrorize her.

Ahead of her the light moved, swinging around in her direction! She stopped, sheltering herself underneath a huge hemlock. She could hear nothing . . . then suddenly the light was gone. Perhaps it was the foxfire lights, she thought. But she was sure she had seen clearly the outline of a person there in the glow of the lantern.

She stood frozen, fearful that she had been seen, scarcely breathing. She could see nothing in the blackness of the forest. There was only the darkness and the rich pungent scent of the decaying leaves beneath her feet. Again she had the horrifying feeling of being watched. It was as if the person waiting there in the woods wanted her to see them, had even lured her there. In that instant she knew something was terribly wrong and that she had to get back to the safety of the house.

She gasped, for suddenly the light was there again, before her . . . so near she could almost touch it! Crazed laughter shattered the silence of the night around her and she jumped. She had to get away! The person hidden behind the lantern cackled loudly in a wild frenzy. She couldn't tell if the voice was that of a man or a woman.

Kathryn began to run, terror filling her. The watcher threw the lantern on the ground, where its flame was quickly extinguished by the dampness of the dense forest floor. She felt him tear at her cloak, and then long, bony fingers clutched at her neck. Horrible, cold, frenzied fingers!

She screamed hysterically as he continued to laugh. His hands tightened about her throat, causing her breath to rasp painfully as she struggled for air. Blackness crept over her as she sank slowly toward the ground, helpless to defend herself, knowing she was going to die. In those last minutes she never managed to see the face of the intruder, though she tried desperately to do so.

The next thing she felt was a sensation of warmth. She realized through a hazy fog that someone's arms were holding her. Frightened, she began to struggle anew, knowing it was the person who had attacked her that held her now.

Then she heard Matthew's voice soothing her,

"Shhh, Kate, its all right. It's Matthew . . . you're all right now.

"Oh, Matthew!" she cried, relaxing as he picked her up and carried her across the lawn toward the house. She could hear the rumble of his deep voice soothing her as she lay against his chest. She felt only relief, not wondering how he came to be there so quickly to rescue her.

Then Thursa and Sula were there, following Matthew, fluttering about them like two mother hens. Kathryn was beginning to remember the sound of crazed laughter, the feel of those cold fingers about her throat. She was shivering as Matthew removed her cloak and placed her carefully on her bed. Lamps were lit and the coals from the fire nudged into flame.

Everyone was talking at once, asking questions. Her head throbbed painfully and she felt dizzy. She raised a hand to her aching head and said wearily, "I . . . I don't know . . . please, don't everyone ask me at once."

Thursa soothed, "There, darling, we're just worried about you, that's all. Sula and I will go down and make you something hot to drink. You must tell Matthew everything that happened."

Kathryn nodded as they left and was thankful for the silence.

Matthew sat beside the bed, waiting for her to speak. The look on his face reflected only his concern, and she wondered if this was another charade, yet another side of this perplexing man. It was then that she wondered how he came to be near enough to rescue her there in the darkness of the forest.

"So, you've rescued me once again." Her voice cracked in the attempt to be humorous. "How did you find me?"

"I couldn't sleep. I had gone out to the overlook when I heard you screaming. It's lucky I did, no?"

"Yes, very lucky indeed," she said, watching him carefully.

"Kathryn, what happened. Have you lost all your senses? What on earth were you doing out there alone at this time of night, especially after what happened today?"

He probably thought her totally mad. After all, why did these things keep happening only to her? But she had no choice but to tell him all of it now.

"It's all so crazy," she began. "I don't know where to start, but I had to find out." Her words sounded confused and she knew she was making no sense at all. She was trembling uncontrollably. "Oh, Matthew," she cried. "I've never been so scared in my life!"

"It's all right . . . you're safe now," he assured her. He felt a small tug of emotion that she would let go of her stubborn independence long enough to admit her fear, especially to him. "Would you rather wait 'til morning to talk about it?"

"No!" she said desperately, reaching out toward him. "Please . . . don't go. I need to tell someone about this. This is not the first time someone has tried to frighten me since I came here." She watched his eyes warily to see if the expression on his face would give her a clue to his feelings. Could she trust him?

"Dammit, Kathryn! This is more than just someone trying to frighten you! You were almost killed! I want you to tell me exactly what you are talking about." He pulled the quilts up about her chin, his look full of anger and frustration.

She told him about the dead sparrow and its red ribbon, of the time she was sure someone was in her room, and of the second ribbon she'd found on her mirror. She told him, in a rush, about the evil she'd felt and the feeling of being watched and of Teresa's vague warnings. Of course he already knew about Lila Spencer, but she reminded him once again of her hate-filled looks. Spoken aloud, it all sounded so ludicrous. She would not have been surprised to hear his mocking laughter, but he did not laugh.

She continued to talk, explaining about the figure she'd seen from her window and her certainty that it was the same person who had left the red ribbons. She told him she'd tried to find out who that person was and why he was doing this to her. Someone had never wanted her here at Foxfire and she wanted to know why.

When she told him of the maniacal laughter and the fingers about her throat his gray eyes darkened. He pulled the covers back from her chin, touching her neck gently with his fingers. Although he said nothing, she knew that he saw the evidence of those frightful hands.

"Your stubbornness almost got you killed this time. I can't believe you were foolish enough to go venturing about in the darkness." He left her bedside and walked thoughtfully to the fireplace. "Could it have been one of the marauders returning? Did you recognize his voice?"

She could not believe what he was saying! Not after all she had told him.

She sat up in bed, her voice cracking with frustration. "No, Matthew, it was no marauder. It was the same person who's been trying to frighten me ever since I came here!"

"Kathryn, you're not thinking straight. This was not just some mischievous trick! Who in this house would want to kill you? And why? How could this person have known you would be the one to spot him there at this time of morning? That was pure coincidence. And there were no red ribbons this time, were there?"

"I don't care what you say, Matthew! I know it was the same person," she insisted. "I can feel it!"

"All right," he said quietly. "Don't upset yourself further. I'll check into it. Do you think you can sleep? Shall I send Sula up?"

"Would you stay with me? Just for awhile . . ." Her voice trailed away and she could not believe she had actually said those words to him.

His eyes darkened as they raked across her bare arms and shoulders, then he raised them to meet her eyes. The sound of his expelled breath, like a small groan, was loud in the quiet room.

"I don't think . . . I know that's not a good idea

Kathryn." The look he gave her left no doubt as to his meaning.

"I'm sorry," she said. "I don't know what made me say that." Her teeth caught the edge of her lower lip and she looked away self-conciously. Yet inside, her heart soared at his intense burning look and all it implied. He did not hate her as much as he pretended. "I would like it if Sula came up," she said.

"Goodnight," he said.

As he walked back toward the bed, he absent-mindedly picked up her cloak from the floor where it had fallen when he carried her into the room. From its depths a bright object fluttered to the floor. Kathryn knew what it was before Matthew picked it up. . . . In his outstretched hand was a small red ribbon, neatly tied into a bow.

Kathryn gasped.

"Are you sure this is not yours? Or . . ." he asked.

"No, Matthew, it's just like the ones I've told you about," she said.

"Does anyone else know about this?"

"I told Sula about the first one in the garden, but she was so frightened that I didn't tell her about the other." It was actually a relief to see the ribbon there in his hand, knowing it was real and not some crazy nightmare. She was glad that someone else finally knew, and she felt safer that it was Matthew. In spite of their antagonism, he was the one she trusted and had turned to for help.

"We'll keep this between us for now. I don't want

to frighten Mother and Sula even more, and I don't want this character, whoever it is, to know that we're trying to find him. Agreed?" he asked.

"Yes, I agree," she said, just grateful that at last someone would help her get to the bottom of this nightmare.

"And, Kathryn, no more wandering about alone—not even in the daytime," he warned.

At that moment she was only too happy to heed his warning so she nodded her head in agreement. Matthew turned and left, the red ribbon still clutched in his fist.

The house was oddly quiet. Kathryn hoped Sula would come soon and help banish the vision that loomed before her. The monstrous face of the dark being seemed to be all around her. She clasped her hands over her eyes. Was it an illusion—or was it real?

The next morning Kathryn preferred to have breakfast with Sula in the kitchen, where she could sit on the tall stool by the work table and talk to her as she worked. Kathryn nibbled disinterestedly on a slice of freshly baked Sally Lunn bread and sipped hot tea, even though she was not hungry. She was only eating for Sula, for under her hawklike eyes, Kathryn had not much choice.

"What you thinkin' about, child?" Sula asked.

"I'm not thinking. Trying *not* to think, actually," Kathryn said.

"I don't like any of this . . . and I don't know

whatever possessed you to go out into those woods all by yourself that way. What in the world was you thinkin?"

"I'd rather not talk about it just now," Kathryn said, hiding her eyes as she concentrated on her cup of tea.

"Did something else happen yesterday? Something between you and Mister Matthew?"

Kathryn's green eyes flickered upward to where Sula stood working.

"Why do you ask that?"

"Well, you both was gone most of the day and when I came to your room he was just comin' in. His hair and clothes was wet and he acted kind of funny . . . like he got somethin' on his mind."

"So?" Kathryn said.

"So . . . you must have snuck in like a mouse—nobody saw you and when I came to your room you was curled up like a little girl asleep . . . and your hair was wet, too." Sula pummeled the dough she was working, turning it deftly over and over on the floured dough board. When Kathryn did not answer, she stopped and fixed her black eyes on the girl, lifting her eyebrows questioningly.

"Sula, you put too much into things."

The back door opened and Woody bounded in, followed more casually by Matthew. Kathryn's heart fluttered as she saw him standing there towering above them and looking at her so seriously. He brought a smell of the clean outdoor air into the warm fragrant kitchen, that and his own masculine scent of soap and spice.

"Look, Kat," Woody said, placing his small hands on her knees "We brought you a present."

It was only then that she noticed the small bundle that Matthew carried.

"Get that basket from the corner, son," Matthew said as Woody immediately went to do as he was asked.

Matthew walked to Kathryn and bent toward her. She could hear a quiet mewing noise from within the bundle he held. Her eyes grew larger with curiosity and she smiled shyly as he placed the bundle in her lap and folded back the material for her to see. Inside was a tiny, wriggling, feisty ball of yellow and white fur. A kitten. She looked up to where Matthew stood and her eyes met his. She saw in the steel gray depths a sweetness and gentleness he had never allowed her to see before, and she marveled at the transformation that had taken place.

"It's for me?" she asked, returning his smile sweetly.

"If you want it," he said. "I wasn't sure you liked cats."

"Oh, I do!" she said. "And I love this one." She stroked the kitten's soft fur as it curled into a ball in her lap and began to purr loudly.

"Good," was all he replied before opening the door to go back outside. Then as if on second thought he paused and turned back toward her. "Better be careful of its temper, though . . . if you will notice, it has green eyes."

She looked at him with a flash of surprise in her

eyes at the playfulness in his voice. The smile he gave her was warm and teasing and there was a reminder there of something only they had shared. The feeling it gave her warmed her to the very tips of her toes. She was smiling broadly when she looked up to catch Sula looking at her questioningly with a grin on her face and a knowing little nod of her head.

"Oh, Mom Sula, stop it," she said happily.

"Here, Kat," Woody said. "You can put it in this basket and it will have a bed all its own. You gonna keep it in the kitchen?" he asked.

"No, Woody, I think I'll put it in my room by the fireplace where it's warm. It will keep me company."

Sula smiled indulgently at the two of them as they cuddled and stroked the kitten. A frown came to her face, however, as the door from the main house opened and Teresa stepped into the room.

"What's in the basket?" she asked, stepping forward on her quiet slippers to look inside.

"Oh, a kitten!" she exclaimed. "Teresa likes kittens too," She reached out with her hand to touch the small animal.

"Matthew brought it to me, Teresa. Wasn't that nice? Shall I ask him to bring one for you?" Kathryn asked.

Immediately the woman pulled her hand away from the basket as if she'd been burned.

"No . . . No. Don't want him to bring me a kitten." Then she shuffled away as quickly and quietly as she had come.

Sula shook her head and gave Kathryn a look as if this proved what she was always saying about the small, secretive woman.

Is there ev'n a happiness
That makes the heart afraid?
Thomas Hood

Chapter Thirteen

Life for Kathryn seemed to return almost to normal after that horrifying attack. She felt not quite so alone now that Matthew had given her the kitten, which scampered and climbed all over her bedroom. She could not keep from laughing aloud at its antics, and Woody was often there with her, enjoying the kitten too. And even though they were no closer to finding out who was hiding the secret red ribbons, she felt more secure knowing that Matthew had promised to help.

Somehow with the beautiful weather and her unspoken truce with Matthew, the frightening events seemed far away and unimportant. Sometimes she almost convinced herself her attacker had been a lone straggler looking for food, or even that she had dreamed it.

But at least Sula and Thursa had stopped pampering her and watching her every move. She knew she could also thank Matthew for that. Then again, they were all excited about the coming of the spring concert and ball to be held in Asheville, the first one since the beginning of the war. Most of North Carolina's soldiers were home for good now, so not only would the event be a much needed return to normalcy, it would also serve as a celebration and a homecoming.

Matthew had already made the arrangements for their stay overnight at the Swannanoa Hotel, so they would not need to make the long trip up the mountain afterward in the middle of the night.

They arrived in town in midafternoon and found the hotel stirring with many people, most of them like the Kincaid family, anxiously awaiting the evening festivities.

Kathryn and Sula were in one room with an adjoining suite that was occupied by Thursa, Cynthia and Woody. Matthew was across the hall. When Thursa had insisted on bringing Cynthia and allowing her to experience her first night of dancing and musical entertainment Kathryn thought it a little odd. But then she supposed Thursa considered the Spencers to be a part of the family. Kathryn would not hear of leaving Woody alone at Foxfire with Mrs. Spencer, although it didn't seem to bother Cynthia. Of course, Teresa had remained behind, but Kathryn feared that the woman was no match for the uncompromising housekeeper. She was greatly relieved when Matthew agreed that the boy should join them, and then Sula had said she would come too and stay with Woody while they attended the dance.

They all enjoyed a late tea in the dining room of the hotel, foregoing dinner since refreshments would be served later at the ball. They returned to their rooms, all eagerly ready to dress for the dance.

Kathryn knew her black mourning dress somewhat dampened the spirit of excitement, but she insisted on wearing it, if for no other reason than to show respect. Thursa had already assured her it would be perfectly understood if she wore something slightly less somber, but Kathryn steadfastly declined. Even with Thursa's assurance, Kathryn could feel her relief when she insisted on wearing the traditional black.

Kathryn pushed aside the corset that Sula handed her. "I'm not wearing a corset, Sula, scandalous or not," she declared.

Sula chuckled. "Don't worry 'bout that. Your waist is so tiny, no one will even notice!"

Sula helped slip the rustling dress over Kathryn's head. Kathryn could not help feeling pleased at the fit and the look of the dress. The black summer satin complemented her hair and creamy skin, causing her eyes to shine a bright emerald green.

The bodice draped gracefully just below her shoulders, with elbow-length puffed sleeves caught at the top by small clusters of white roses. The full, delicately ruffled underskirt was also sprinkled here and there with the same clustering of roses, while the shorter overskirt of black satin was caught up in scallops edged with fine lace.

"Are you sure this is not too . . . elegant for a widow?" Kathryn asked with a small frown as she turned around slowly before the mirror.

Sula's eyes twinkled and she smiled widely as she patted down the skirt and smoothed imaginary wrinkles.

"It's jes fine!" Sula assured her. "Miz Thursa said when you picked it out that it's perfectly suited for a beautiful young widow. So don't go borrowin' trouble!"

"It is lovely, isn't it?" Kathryn smiled. "I've never

owned a dressed so beautiful."

"Well, you deserve to finally have a dress like this, and you never looked prettier than you do tonight!" Sula looked at her proudly. "You've grown up into a fine young woman. I can't help thinkin' how proud your mama and papa would be . . ." She stopped, careful not to spoil the happy moment for Kathryn.

"Yes," Kathryn said wistfully while Sula pinned a lace-trimmed black satin ribbon at the back of her unswept hair.

"And tonight those young men are gonna notice you and be askin' who you are, and before long Foxfire's driveway will be lined with carriages on Sunday afternoon!" Sula declared.

"Oh, no," Kathryn said. "I don't want to think about that. I've learned my lesson. I don't think I'll ever be interested in anyone again."

"No?" Sula asked slyly. "Couldn't be you've already met someone? Remember when I warned you about a man who'd come along and capture your heart quick as a wink?"

"What do you mean? Of course I've not met anyone—why I haven't been anywhere. . . .

"You know very well who I'm talkin' about . . . that handsome Matthew Kincaid, that's who! Now there's a man to make a woman pay attention!"

"What about Matthew?" Thursa asked, entering the sitting room from behind them.

Kathryn kept her back turned to Thursa, pretending to look at the back of her dress over her shoulder. Never would she want Thursa to know how the very mention of her son's name could cause her limbs to tremble and her cheeks to flame with color.

"Sula was only wondering if Matthew had arrived yet," Kathryn answered quickly.

"He should be here any moment. My dear, you look absolutely stunning. The dress becomes you splendidly." Thursa, like Sula, fussed with the dress as she talked. "Now, I want you to relax tonight and enjoy yourself for a change. You've been working much too hard at home and I want tonight to be a very special night for you."

"It will be Thursa. In fact, it's already special, thanks to you . . . having this dress made for me. I know you planned this night as much for me as anyone and I love you for it."

"Pish, it's nothing," Thursa said waving her small hand in the air before turning to go back to her suite. "Besides, you deserve it!" she said gaily.

Cynthia joined them in the sitting room as they waited for Matthew. She seemed even more nervous than Kathryn, but she looked very pretty in her pale yellow muslin gown with its wide green satin sash. More of Thursa's handiwork, Kathryn knew. The girl looked very young and innocent with her dark hair tied back sweetly. Kathryn felt both a sadness and a kinship for her. They both had missed the best part of their youth, although for different reasons, and Cynthia already had a four-year-old child to raise alone.

Woody was very excited seeing his mama dressed so differently than she was at home. But it was Kathryn whom he sat with on the sofa, counting the number of roses sprinkled about on her dress.

A knock sounded at the door and Sula opened it, making a funny little curtsy to Matthew as he came in. All he had to do was smile at her and she was almost purring with pleasure.

"Sula, you should have on your ball gown and go with us," he declared. "You and I would dance the night away."

"La, Mister Matthew," she chortled. "You jes won't do."

"Ladies, you all look beautiful," he murmured politely.

Matthew had to force himself to look away from Kathryn. He thought she was the most stunning vision he had ever seen, and he frowned slightly at the ripple of longing that went through him. He remembered her as she looked that night at the hospital, with her unkempt hair and worn clothes—her work-worn hands. She looked little more than a scullery maid, although her speech betrayed her genteel upbringing. Tonight she looked like a different person.

"Ladies, shall we go?" he said. As Matthew followed them down the hallway he watched the proud way Kathryn carried herself and the slight but sensuous sway of her hips as she walked.

Matthew knew of the circumstances of her family, but he also had heard of the circumstances of her home life and of the zealots and radicals who were welcomed at the judge's home for so-called intellectual debates. Some of them had less-than-sterling reputations. It could not have been a healthy environment for a young, motherless girl. He guessed that when her father died she was penniless and desperate to find a man to take care of her, preferably one with money. Robert had fallen right into her web of honeyed deception. Still, perhaps he should not have judged her so harshly, and indeed he might not have were it not for Robert's sudden and mysterious death. There were still too many questions that needed answering, and he only hoped he could find the solutions with a clear head. That was becoming harder to do each day he was near the spirited girl.

They all walked the short distance to the concert hall, enjoying the renewed hustle and bustle of the busy gaslit street and the warm air of the May evening.

The Kincaid family's seats were in a spacious box on the upper level of the hall. The chairs were arranged in a semicircle so that when they were seated, with Matthew on one end beside his mother and Kathryn on the other end next to Cynthia, she and Matthew sat almost opposite one another.

The hall was noisy with the chatter and laughter of friends and relatives talking and mingling. The scent of flowery perfumes and fragrant tobaccos drifted up to their box, and Kathryn smiled with remembered pleasure at the familiarity of it all. She looked across at Matthew, whose dark head was bent low so that he could catch his mother's softly spoken words.

His black hair glinted in the dimly lit box, and his thick black eyelashes were lowered against his dark cheeks. His blue evening coat fit superbly across his broad shoulders and smoothly down his chest, the tucked shirtfront beneath it appearing a sparkling white. Kathryn looked at his hands, one fist against his slim hips, the other resting loosely across his thigh as he bent forward. His fingers were long and tapered—graceful hands for such a muscular man.

The look of him made her heart skitter crazily in her throat, threatening even to stop its beating at the sight of him. He was the most splendid looking man she'd ever seen. Indeed, masculine though he definitely was, he could only be described as beautiful.

She pulled her eyes away and saw Cynthia watching her closely. *She knows,* Kathryn thought. But how could anyone not know it when she looked at him with her heart in her eyes the way she was doing tonight. She must learn to be more discreet.

"You're very quiet this evening, Cynthia," she said. "How do you like it so far?"

"It's very nice, ma'am," she replied, her face blank and expressionless.

"Cynthia," Kathryn laughed. "I'm not much older than you. Surely you need not call me ma'am."

The girl did not reply, and Kathryn blamed her reluctance on nerves and shyness. After all, this was a whole new experience for the girl—probably a frightening one.

The hall grew silent as the orchestra entered, followed by the concertmaster, to a warm welcoming applause. Then the conductor came on stage and quickly the music began, the sweet haunting sounds of the violins filling the large room with their beauty.

The majestic, lilting strands of Scottish rhapsodies surrounded them, the soaring composition from the homeland of many North Carolina residents being a special favorite. Throughout the evening they heard several works of the masters—Beethoven and Mozzart as well as some of the new American composers.

Kathryn had always loved music, and by the end was swept away in the beauty of the melodies that soared around her. She sat misty-eyed with emotion on the edge of her seat, clutching her black lace fan to her breast as she became lost in the perfect beauty of the moment.

She was so intent that she did not see Matthew's dark glances at her, or the way he watched the emotion flicker across her beautiful features, the soft whispered sigh from her lips. He shook his head imperceptibly, afraid that he was drunk with the music and the magic of the evening.

The program ended with a beautiful haunting waltz, heralding the beginning of the ball. By concert's end the appreciative audience was on its feet with much applauding and shouting of compliments.

They all went downstairs, where a long table of refreshments had been set up in the entry hall. Just as they came down the stairs they were joined by Mr. and Mrs. Simmons and Tilda. The girl came forward in her rather tomboyish way and embraced Kathryn with a fierce hug, whispering in her ear as she did so.

"Lord, Kathryn, that Matthew Kincaid is the handsomest man here!"

"Tilda," Kathryn laughed. "It's so good to see you, too."

They stood for awhile snacking on *hors d'oeuvres* and talking with neighbors they had not seen in a while. Even Cynthia's color seemed bright, her eyes shining with life.

They were soon joined by Eugene and his parents, who followed them next door to the large ballroom. Tilda's attention was immediately drawn from Matthew, who seemed to find her amusing, to the tall, slender Eugene. The musicians had moved to the front of the room and already several couples danced around the shining wood floors.

Kathryn sat with Thursa and Mrs. Davenport, for it was not considered proper for a widow to dance more than a few polite numbers during the evening. She watched as Cynthia was asked to dance by several young men. She did so, but with a reluctance and an uncertain awkwardness that discouraged many from returning for a second dance. Matthew had disappeared, probably to the smoking room where the men would discuss politics and the war. The thought of it made Kathryn fairly ache to join them—it had been so long since she'd participated in such stimulating conversation. But out of respect for Thursa's conventional standards she did not.

She danced a slow, almost somber dance with Eugene, who held her stiffly away from him. His hand felt cold and his pale, grayish-green eyes blinked rapidly as he attempted to make conversation.

As the dancers began to leave the floor she saw Eugene's glance scan the crowd.

"Why don't you find Tilda, Eugene, and ask her to dance?" Kathryn suggested.

"Oh, I . . . I don't want to leave you alone."

"Nonsense. I'm hardly alone. You go ahead," she urged.

"Well, I don't actually know her very well . . . I hate to appear too forward."

Kathryn laughed. "Eugene, believe me, Tilda will not think you too forward."

"All right, then, if you're sure you don't mind . . . then I think I shall."

"I don't mind, Eugene, I don't mind at all," she said.

"She *is* a jolly sort of girl, isn't she?" Eugene commented as they walked from the dance area.

Kathryn found it very amusing that he could hardly stay long enough to be civil before going to Tilda, who was obviously pleased as she winked at Kathryn.

She watched as Matthew walked back into the ballroom and crossed it to stand by his mother's side. Kathryn's was not the only female glance in the room to watch his graceful long-legged walk around the edge of the floor. And although she knew he could have his pick of the single young ladies at the dance, she had seen him dance with no one.

Eugene escorted Tilda back to her seat and stood for a moment, politely chatting with the others.

"Did you enjoy the concert, Eugene?" Thursa asked.

"Yes, it was quite nice, although I was disappointed that they did not end the evening with a rousing rendition of "Dixie," he said.

Kathryn frowned at him. "I don't think that would really have been appropriate, Eugene, do you?"

"Appropriate? Whyever not? It has practically become the South's national anthem," he snorted.

"I know there was talk that the orchestra might do something foolish, such as play a political piece, but I for one thought it very wise of the conductor not to spoil the lovely evening by doing so," she said. "After all, this is a homecoming, not a continuation of a war we have already lost." Her eyes sparkled with fire.

"Kathryn has some rather unusual ideas about the war," Eugene said rather condescendingly.

"Then mine are also unusual, for I agree." Matthew's voice was deep and slightly amused. He stepped toward Kathryn and extended his hand to her. "Do you think it will be permissible for you to dance with your brother-in-law?"

"Yes . . . quite," she whispered, placing her hand in his and rising from her chair. Eugene, Tilda, and the rest became only a distant blur, and there were no sounds except the music, no people in the room other than she and the tall handsome man who pulled her into his arms.

He held her apart from him the proper distance, but it made little difference, for she could feel his hand at her waist as hot as a branding iron. And tonight she knew beyond the shadow of a doubt that he was feeling the same pull of emotion. Kathryn found herself almost dizzy with delight as his silver gray eyes studied her intently. His look was probing, as if there was something there that puzzled him. Yet she knew instinctively that this fragile feeling between them was something best not spoken of.

"I didn't have a chance to tell you earlier how beautiful you look tonight," he said, his voice low and intimate.

"Thank you," she answered, blushing only the slightest bit. "So do you . . . handsome, I mean."

Matthew smiled crookedly at her awkwardness, even as some small voice within warned him. Is this how she bewitched Robert, casting a spell with her gentle shyness and beautiful smile . . . a sensuous approach with the promise of everything, then a coy retreat? He had to admit that even he was in danger of falling prey to her charms. His entire masculine instinct was urging him on.

"Kathryn," he said. "I've wanted to apologize for . . . that day at the barn. Some of the things I said were cruel and I should not have said them. But I was not myself that day. Robert's death was a great shock to me."

She was silent for a moment, not knowing how to answer him for she could never forget some of the things he said to her that day. "I understand how you felt about your brother."

She was afraid to let herself believe even for one moment that he was truly sorry. But she could not deny the pain in his voice when he spoke of Robert. The grief that was now visible in his eyes tore at her heart. The feelings of tenderness that swept over her unbidden were there in her eyes for him to see, and she did not even care.

Seeing her look, Matthew took a deep breath and stepped back away from her just as the music ended. But the disappointment in her green eyes was not hidden, and he knew she did not want to leave his arms any more than he wanted to relinquish her. But if his instincts told him to reach out for her once more, his head warned him not to. How could he commit his heart to his brother's widow under the circumstances, especially with all the unanswered questions between them? He had never been one to let his heart get in the way of duty, and he knew he could not let himself forget that now. And his duty was to his brother's memory. . .

He walked slowly with her back to her seat, and without another word moved on to another group of acquaintances.

Kathryn could still feel the imprint of his hand at her waist, and she did not keep her eyes from wandering over his stately physique as he stood casually talking. She was beginning to see that he was not the unfeeling, coldhearted man she'd thought in the beginning. If there was one thing she would wish for at this moment it would be to take away the pain she saw in his gray eyes every time he said Robert's name.

It had been a wonderful evening, and now that it was nearing an end, Kathryn smiled as she noticed Eugene and Tilda still on the floor. They had danced almost every dance together. They seemed to be the object of several conversations around the room, including Mrs. Davenport and Mrs. Simmons, who stood together even now whispering coyly behind their fans. As the two women watched their precious children glide about the room, Kathryn wondered whether or not they approved.

Kathryn accepted one more dance with a boy who had been a patient at the hospital. She was happy to see him looking so well, and in her enthusiasm she did not see Matthew leave the ballroom.

Later, when the last waltz began and he had not returned, she tried to hide her disappointment by chatting happily with Thursa. But she had hoped in the most secret part of her heart that he would come to claim her for the traditional dance of love, and that perhaps he would speak about the obvious attraction between them. Yet even as she dreamed, she knew it could not be, not yet. There was too much between them, and she felt she would have to prove herself to him.

She excused herself, and taking a cool cup of punch she walked slowly out onto the long colonnaded veranda. The sweet scent of lilac drifted on the warm spring air, and she leaned against a column to enjoy the quiet of the evening.

She noticed a couple dancing at the far end of the porch, and smiled at the romanticism of it—lovers who had stolen a few moments alone, away from the prying eyes of the staid matrons inside.

Then she straightened, straining for a better look at the strangely familiar man. She stood for seconds scarcely breathing as she watched the tall, ebony-haired man and the dark, petite girl in the lemon-colored dress. It was Matthew and Cynthia.

"No," she murmured, as every part of her seemed to ache with pain and longing at what she did not want to believe. Her heart wanted to deny what her eyes revealed, that there was still some sort of relationship between the two of them. Quickly she ran back inside before either of them saw her. That was a humiliation she could not bear.

Matthew swung Cynthia around and brought her to a sweeping, graceful stop as the music from inside ended.

"See, I knew you could do it," he said kindly. He could not help feeling sorry for Cynthia—he always had. And even though he halfway suspected she might be the person responsible for the not-so-childish stunts that had frightened Kathryn, he doubted she would ever try to seriously hurt her.

"Thank you, Matthew," she said, looking up at him with gratitude. "I never learned to dance . . . and the waltz—well! I knew I could never have done it in front of all those people."

"Then next time you will be able to," he said. "Shall we go in?"

Kathryn watched them walk in from the veranda, her heart in her throat. She noticed that they did not touch and stayed the proper distance apart. So this was why he was so distant, so careful not to allow any intimacy to develop with her. She found she could not even bear to think of Matthew kissing someone else.

Later, as they all prepared to leave, Kathryn said nothing. And if the others attributed her silence to a long, tiring evening then she would let them think as they would.

Thursa and Cynthia entered the suite first and Kathryn followed. Matthew stood in the hallway watching her. When she did not stop he reached for her arm, holding her back from entering the room.

"Kathryn," he said. "Is anything wrong? You've been awfully quiet."

She did not turn to face him; she dared not, for he would wonder at the tears in her eyes. She gently pulled her arm away and glanced back at him.

"No, nothing. I'm just tired. Goodnight."

She could not even bring herself to speak his name. Thankfully Sula was already asleep, for she would surely want to know what was wrong. She could hide nothing from the woman for very long.

Quietly she undressed, running her hand lovingly over the beautiful gown before hanging it back in the clothes wardrobe.

She sat at the window for what seemed like hours, until most of the lights of the city were extinguished and the streets below were silent and empty.

She could never forget the look in Matthew's eyes as he tried to apologize, and the anguish she saw there still tore at her heart. But she was confused with conflicting emotions. She could not bear seeing him in Cynthia's, in anyone's, arms. She confessed, if only to herself and to Heaven, how much she wanted him for her own.

And yet she felt a great surge of longing that he be happy, for she'd never known before tonight how deeply she cared. And there was little Woody—she must be happy for Woody. If Cynthia made Matthew happy, then she would pray that she had the strength to accept it both for Matthew's and Woody's sake. And if her only happiness could be from being near him at Foxfire, then that was how it would have to be.

With that decision made, as painful as it was for her, she felt a certain small peace wash over her, and she knew she would sleep. . . .

Man's love is of man's life a thing apart;
It is woman's whole existence.

Lord Byron

Chapter Fourteen

The drive home the next day was quiet. It seemed everyone had talked and laughed their fill and was ready again for the isolation and peace of the country. It was a very warm day, and by the time they neared Foxfire a bank of thick gray clouds could be seen far away to the west.

"Gonna storm," Sula declared, looking at the sky. "We need to find Joseph when we get home and cover those new bean plants."

"Yes, we'll do that, Sula," Thursa agreed, patting the black woman's arm in a companionable manner.

Kathryn smiled. At least Sula was happy with their new life here at Foxfire. She could never regret that. It gave her total joy to see Sula and Thursa form such a warm friendship.

It was good to be back in the comfort of their own home. Cynthia took Woody upstairs while Sula and Thursa quickly tended the garden.

Later Kathryn joined the two women in the parlor, where they passed the late afternoon and evening sewing and chatting quietly about the dance and concert and the old friends they had seen. Outside the thunder rumbled closer as night fell.

Matthew had gone to the barn to see to the horses. He did not return until the ladies had eaten their cold supper. When he entered the parlor, Kathryn rose and excused herself on the pretext of being tired from the trip.

She lay on the bed reading until the sound of the storm lulled her into a deep sleep. She was dreaming of a voice, that same hoarse voice she'd heard in the forest that frightening night. But now it was whispering her name. "Kathryn . . . Kathryn." She knew she must be dreaming and fought desperately to waken herself.

Suddenly a great jarring crack of thunder shook the sky and rattled the windows in the house. Kathryn sat up with a start, her body moist with perspiration. Now she was wide awake, and to her horror she saw before her bed the black-clad figure of someone, arms outstretched toward her. Kathryn blinked, hoping it was only a shadow or a dream from which she might awaken.

Lightning flashed again, seeming to illuminate the entire earth, bathing her room in its powerful light. In that split second she saw that it was no illusion, and as the thunder rumbled over the mountains she saw before her the same hooded figure who had tried to kill her in the woods.

She screamed then, her voice piercing the air in the now silent room. She screamed again and again, closing her eyes so that she could not see the person who would surely murder her this time.

She was aware of the sound of the door as it crashed open, its lock splintering from the pressure. She did not know as she struggled that the powerful hands that caught her flailing arms were Matthew's.

Her eyes were tightly closed and her hands fought to cover her ears. She could still hear the sound of the rain falling heavily on the roof and blowing against the windows. Then she became aware of Matthew and the light that filled her room. She opened her eyes to see Sula and Thursa watching her anxiously from the foot of her bed.

"That must have been some nightmare," Matthew said, "to frighten you so badly."

"Nightmare?" she whispered. Then she remembered the flash of light that revealed the hooded figure coming toward her, remembered that horrible feeling of impending death as she waited helplessly.

"But there was someone here," she said clutching at his arm. "It was no dream . . . there *was* someone here!"

"It's all right," he said watching her closely. "I'm here now."

"You don't believe me!" she said, her eyes full of disbelief.

"Darling," Thursa said, coming around to the side of the bed. "It's not that we don't believe you—I'm sure it seemed very real and terrifying, but your door was locked, you can see where Matthew broke through, and the door to the sitting room was still locked when we came in. There was no one here." She spoke gently, as if speaking to a child.

Kathryn looked at Thursa with growing alarm. She frowned and placed her hands on each side of her face, shaking her head in confusion and disbelief.

"That can't be . . . I know there was someone. What's happening to me?" she murmured, more to herself than to the others.

"Would you like Sula to stay with you the rest of the night?" Matthew asked.

"No. . . . I'll be all right," she said. But she felt so much confusion. She was sure it could not have been a dream.

"I'll stay," Sula declared.

"Let me get you something warm to drink," Thursa offered.

"My door will be open, Sula," Matthew said quietly. "If you need me, just call. I'll have her door repaired first thing tomorrow morning."

After they had left Sula came quickly to the bed.

"You sure you're all right?" she asked.

"I don't know . . . I've never felt so foolish or so confused. I know there was someone in this room. I couldn't have dreamed it!"

"Well, I don't like it. Maybe we should leave here—go back to town." Sula suggested.

"I know you love it here, Sula . . . and besides, where would we go? I couldn't bear to move back in with the Simmonses. If only we could find out who's doing these things."

"I know you ain't gonna like what I'm about to say," Sula began, "but I'd give a pretty penny to know where that little bit of a woman was tonight and where she is right now!"

"Teresa? Oh, no . . . I don't think . . ."

"I know, I know. But it sounds so much like her—sneakin' about tryin' to scare people. . . . Why, there might even be a hidden panel in the room somewhere." Sula looked questioningly about the room.

Kathryn recalled her first day here, when she'd felt as if someone were watching her and Teresa had boasted that it was she. Kathryn had not believed her then. But there *were* no panels in the room, and just as Thursa said earlier, the only way in was from the hallway or the sitting room, and both doors were locked.

Kathryn slid back down in bed. "I just don't know anymore," she sighed. "Maybe I did dream the whole thing. Maybe I'm losing my mind."

"They ain't nothin' wrong with your mind! Now, you just try to go to sleep. I'll keep a watch out," Sula said.

"I don't want you to sit up all night Mom Sula—you need your rest as much as anyone else—at least lie here in bed with me. We'll leave a lamp burning."

"If I get tired, I'll do that very thing. You jes go to sleep, little girl," she said firmly.

Kathryn slept later than usual the next morning. When she woke Sula was already gone. She lay in bed looking out at the refreshing rain-washed green of the treetops swaying gently back and forth. The sun was shining and she could almost imagine that last night had really been only a bad dream.

She let her mind wander, thinking of nothing important, trying to picture herself in the top of one of the gigantic old trees, swaying back and forth, watching layers of clouds drift by. It was a game she had played when she was a little girl. Soon she began to feel her tension easing, and if her fears were not completely gone, at least they were quieted.

Her daydreams were interrupted by a pounding at her splintered door. Before she could think about what was happening Woody came bouncing in. He scrambled onto the bed, crawling across her, laughing and clumsy. He obviously did not know about last night's events. His happiness as usual was so infectious she couldn't keep from laughing.

"Woody . . . what in the world? What are you doing?"

"Get up, Kat, c'mon, I need you," he giggled.

"Sweetheart, calm down," she said, still laughing.

"All right," he said in mock seriousness. Sitting back on the bed he clasped his hands before him and sat, lips pursed, his blue eyes twinkling with mischief.

Kathryn hugged him and said. "Tell me now—what has you so excited this morning?"

"Matthew is going to take me down to the river! He said we can fish and he's going to let me ride on Blackjack with him! Sula's making a picnic, too!" He could hardly contain his excitement at the prospect.

She felt a little tug deep inside her chest. What she was feeling toward Matthew now was gratitude, she told herself. If she had not accomplished another thing here, perhaps she at least had something to do with this. Matthew was trying to spend more time with his son, and Woody was fairly blossoming from the attention.

"That's wonderful, Woody. I hope you catch a great big fish! I'm sure you can persuade Sula to cook it just for you. You be careful though, all right?"

Matthew's deep voice from the doorway startled her. "Why don't you come with us, Kate . . . then you can be sure he's safe." He stood just inside her door, propped against the doorframe. Her heart jumped so quickly that she was certain he must see it pulsing at her throat.

"Please, Kat, please! That's why I came to wake you. It will be ever so much fun if you go!" Woody pleaded.

The thought of a day on the river sounded good to her, perhaps just the thing to banish the terrors of the night. The sights, sounds, and smells of summer were all about them. Suddenly she couldn't wait to be outside.

"I think I'd like that, Woody. In fact, I'd love it!" She gave the boy a little nudge. "Now scoot, so I can get dressed."

"Oh, boy!" he shouted as he jumped down and ran to Matthew.

"You run along to the kitchen, Woody. I'll be

down in a minute," Matthew said.

Kathryn waited until Woody had gone. "I'm not fooled by your invitation, you know," she said.

"Oh? And what do you think my ulterior motive is?" he smiled.

"You can take Woody fishing and still keep an eye on me," she said.

"Are you sure you're feeling well enough to go?" he asked, not denying what she had said.

"Yes, I'm sure." She smiled hesitantly, not wanting to reveal just how happy his invitation had made her.

"Good. We'll be downstairs whenever you're ready. And by the way—you're right . . . I do intend to keep an eye on you. I promised I wouldn't let anything happen to you and I meant it."

So she was only an obligation along with everything else that belonged to Foxfire. She told herself it didn't matter, as long as she could be with him she didn't care what the reason.

Soon they were slowly making their way down the mountain. Kathryn gloried more than ever in the clear, crisp air and the look of blue mist on the surrounding hills. She watched the two riding the black horse in front of her. Woody chattered and laughed all the way to the river. At times she could hear Matthew's deep answering chuckle.

She cautioned herself about feeling such happiness, as she often had since Robert's death. She could not forget that it was just before that horrifying event that she had felt the happiest. Yet when

Matthew looked at her with such tenderness and care, as if to assure himself she was all right, she simply could not stop the joy that arose within her.

Even the smallest things brought renewed hope to her, yet she knew she was probably behaving in a totally irrational manner.

As they were leaving the house she had stumbled slightly as he helped her onto her horse. "Be careful," he'd said, his touch warm on her arm. She'd had to force herself to think of Cynthia and the sight of them dancing together on the veranda.

The morning passed in a bright glow for her . . . one she would store in her memory. When they arrived at the river Woody became so excited he could not focus his attention on just one thing and instead bounced from one place to another. After lunch Kathryn insisted they go for a walk along the river to help use some of his energy. Then, she promised, he could settle down and fish.

Matthew leaned back against a large sycamore tree, his long legs stretched out before him. When Kathryn and Woody teased him about being lazy he only nodded and laughed good naturedly, waving them away. She knew he probably needed the relaxation . . . after all, the war was not that far behind him. But as they left, Kathryn could feel his eyes watching her.

"Don't go too far, Kathryn," he cautioned.

She turned and waved to him. She soon discovered she was not at all afraid, for here along the river in the bright light of day, the events of the night and the storm seemed far away and easily forgotten.

Wildflowers and ferns covered the riverbanks, and in some places the overhanging trees, still wet with rain, formed a dark tunnel. The moss and damp greenery made it seem like a warm and exotic jungle.

Woody discovered a salamander under a rock, and from then on he turned over every rock by the river in search of more of the slithery creatures.

"Are you ready to fish now, Woody?" Kathryn asked.

"Yep." He ran back toward the clearing. Matthew was still in the same spot, his eyes closed. "Shhh," Woody whispered, placing his finger across his lips.

Woody took his bait and fishing pole and walked down to the edge of the river. Matthew had deliberately chosen this spot because it was shallow enough to allow for the boy's exuberance.

Kathryn sat down quietly beside Matthew, keeping an eye on Woody. She glanced over at Matthew. He looked so young and vulnerable, different somehow from the hardened soldier she'd met in Asheville. For once she could get her fill of looking at him. She allowed her eyes to wander over him, from the tips of his fine leather boots to his long legs. His shirt was partially unbuttoned, showing a glimpse of his smooth, muscled chest. Her eyes traveled upward to his closely trimmed beard and sensuous lips, his straight nose, and high, prominent cheekbones. She almost jumped when she found his eyes open and twinkling with amusement as he watched her.

Quickly she looked away and began to chatter about the discoveries she and Woody had made on their walk. But she didn't fool him. He continued to watch her, his eyes filled with mischief.

"Matthew, please . . ." she finally pleaded. "Stop it."

"Turn about's fair play, isn't it?" he laughed.

"I don't know what you mean," she said demurely.

He laughed, then his face turned thoughtful and his frank look was admiring as he looked into her eyes and at the pinkness he had brought to her cheeks with his appraisal.

"I can see why Robert was so taken with you . . . you're very beautiful. But then I suppose you've heard that often." His words were spoken simply, but they took her by surprise.

"No . . ." she mumbled.

"No?" he repeated. "I think you really mean that. You don't realize the power your beauty has, do you?" He spoke as if something had just been made clear to him.

She shrugged her shoulders and would not look at him. She didn't know what he wanted her to say.

"Kate . . . come here," he said quietly but with unmistakable authority.

Her eyes flashed upwards at the command in his voice, given so softly and with such sweet tenderness. She could not resist. She leaned toward him slowly, cautiously, watching his eyes as they grew dark and serious.

Suddenly the air was shattered by childish screams from the river.

They both jumped up and ran toward Woody. They found him thrashing about in the ankle-deep water, screaming because his fishing pole was being dragged out into the rippling waters of the stream by a fish on the end of the line.

Kathryn stood on the bank shaking with laughter and relief as Matthew quickly took off his boots and waded out into the river to bring the pole back. Woody was soaked from head to toe after his struggle to bring the large fish onto the bank. Matthew stood grinning, shaking his head at the mutterings of the boy, but he let him do it himself. His clothes were also wet, and Kathryn watched them, still laughing. Matthew, hands on hips, looked toward her with a gleam in his eye.

"Laugh at us will you?" he warned. "How would you like a dip in the river too? Its very refreshing."

"No!" she yelled as he started toward her. "You wouldn't!"

Matthew quickly slipped behind her and put his arms around her, holding her arms crossed in front of her as he gently pushed her forward. "What do you say, Woody?" Matthew asked the giggling boy.

"Hummmmm." Woody pretended to be thinking it over, one finger tapping the side of his cheek.

"Woody!" Kathryn said in mock surprise.

He laughed. "No, I guess not. It wouldn't be gent'mon'ly to dunk a pretty lady as nice as our Kat," he said.

"Indeed, it would not, Woody," Matthew agreed.

But his arms did not release her immediately and she turned to find his eyes alive with pleasure.

The day was perfect, or would have been if they had not returned to Foxfire.

As the horses clip-clopped slowly up the mountain and they rounded the last long curve toward home, Kathryn could see the overlook far ahead of them. Standing there were Eugene and Cynthia, so deep in conversation that they did not seem to hear the approaching horses until they were almost upon them.

Kathryn glanced at Matthew. The smile was gone from his lips and the change in him was so visible she could see it. Once again the cold, hard look came onto his face—just like that day in the parlor when he first returned from the war.

"I wonder what that's all about?" Kathryn said.

"I'm sure I don't know," Matthew answered curtly. "Are you jealous?"

She looked at him oddly. "No, of course I'm not jealous. I'm just surprised that they would be talking so . . . . so . . ." She searched for the right words to express herself.

"Intimately?" Matthew suggested.

"Kathryn!" Eugene called as he first spotted them, and walked to stand beside her horse. "I'm glad I caught you. I was just leaving. Mrs. Kincaid said she didn't know when you'd be back."

Cynthia glowered, then turned and walked back toward the house. She had not even acknowledged her son's presence.

"We took Woody fishing down at the river,"

Kathryn said.

"Look, Mr. Davenport," Woody said, holding up the fish he'd wrangled to shore. He, at least, did not seem to notice his mother's coldness.

"That's a nice one, boy," Eugene replied. Then to Matthew he nodded. "Afternoon, Matthew."

"Eugene," Matthew replied coolly.

Kathryn didn't understand the look she saw exchanged between the two men. She tried to ignore the small voice within her that warned that Cynthia was the reason for their antagonism.

Eugene looked up at Kathryn. "Kathryn, why don't you climb down and walk with me for a way," he suggested.

"Well, Matthew and I . . ." she began.

"Yes, Kathryn, why don't you do that?" Matthew said, the old sarcasm back in his voice. "I'll tell Mother you'll be in shortly for tea."

How quickly he had changed from the laughing, carefree man at the river, the charming man she had danced with. Now he was watching her, challenging her again as he had done at the beginning.

"Yes . . . I think I will, Eugene," she said as Matthew and Woody turned to go.

"Matthew . . ." she called after him, confused by his moodiness.

"Let him go, Kathryn. He's much too serious sometimes," Eugene said, helping her down from the horse.

Eugene wanted to talk about Tilda. He had received a letter from her that he wanted to share, but Kathryn paid little attention to his words. Her mind was still turned to Matthew and his changeable behavior. She wanted only to see him, cajole him somehow back into the mood of the afternoon. She was disappointed when Eugene slyly managed an invitation for tea.

Thursa and Sula were in the parlor, waiting for her. Sula had baked a plate of old-fashioned scones for Thursa and together they were enjoying a quiet domestic chat about the differences between America and England. Mrs. Spencer was also there and poured the tea.

"Kathryn, darling, come sit here between us," Thursa said. "How are you feeling?"

"Oh, have you been ill, Kathryn?" Eugene asked.

Kathryn looked at Eugene, but did not answer his question. "I'm just fine, Thursa," she answered. "Where's Matthew? I thought he was coming in too."

"I don't know where he went," Thursa said. "Is anything wrong? Did you have a nice time at the river?" She frowned at Kathryn as if she knew something was wrong between them.

"We had a lovely time," she answered, smiling at Thursa. "And nothing is wrong."

As Mrs. Spencer handed Kathryn her tea she had a little half smile on her face, as if she knew exactly where Kathryn's thoughts were.

But what had happened to change him so suddenly? And where could he have gone? One thing kept returning to her mind and she could not get it to leave her alone. Could it be *he* was the jealous one, that after seeing Eugene with Cynthia he had gone to seek her out?

"Would you all excuse me?" Kathryn said suddenly, standing to leave the room. "I've developed a terrible headache, too much sun, I suppose. I think I'll go lie down."

They all seemed so concerned that she felt guilty for telling the lie. But she didn't think she could endure one more minute of Mrs. Spencer's sneers or Eugene's mindless chatter.

As Kathryn closed the door to the parlor, Cynthia came running down the stairs. She looked as though she had been crying. Without acknowledging Kathryn's presence, she jerked open the front door and ran out and around the side of the house.

Kathryn walked to the stairs and placed one hand on the wood banister, looking out the door where Cynthia had just fled. As she slowly stepped onto the stairway and looked up she gasped to see Matthew standing at the top of the landing, silently looking down at her.

"Matthew . . . you startled me," she said awkwardly.

"Did you enjoy your walk?" he asked, baiting her again with the tone of his voice.

"Not particularly," she answered. "What was wrong with Cynthia?"

He raised his eyebrow. "Cynthia? I'm sure I don't know."

"Matthew . . ." she said in exasperation. She wanted to ask him what was wrong . . . what had happened to make him behave this way? And she knew he was lying about Cynthia.

Eugene stepped into the hallway from the parlor. "Why, Kathryn, my dear, I thought you had a headache and were going to lie down." He eyed Matthew suspiciously as he spoke.

Kathryn sighed. "I was, Eugene. I'm going right now." But she made no move to go upstairs.

Matthew did not offer to move from his position at the top of the stairs. He stood languidly, watching Eugene. His look was cool and appraising and not one to encourage further conversation.

"Yes, well . . ." Eugene said, "I'll be going then. I do hope you're feeling better soon. Perhaps you would like to go riding tomorrow?"

"I'm afraid Kathryn will be unable to go tomorrow. We have some family business to take care of." Matthew curtly dismissed the other man.

After Eugene left, Kathryn turned to Matthew. He looked at her defiantly, as if he were daring her to dispute him. She probably should be grateful to him for making an excuse not to see Eugene, but instead she found herself angered by his high-handed attitude.

"Why did you do that, Matthew? You had no right."

He sauntered down the stairs, glancing at her from the corner of his eye as he drew near her. "You'd better lie down, Kate. Your headache, remember?"

"Matthew . . . what is it? Why are you acting this way?" She could no longer refrain from confronting him with her feelings. She hated this pretense, this uneasy bantering.

"I don't know what you mean." His voice was cool.

"You know exactly what I mean. Today at the river . . . you were so different. I thought you enjoyed it, and now . . ."

"Now?" Again his eyebrows arched in the arrogant, disdainful manner that had so infuriated her before.

"Don't do this, Matthew!" she said. "Is it something I've done? Something I didn't do? Are you trying to punish me?" Her eyes glittered with tears at his coldness toward her. "I thought for awhile today . . . I thought . . . hoped we'd gotten beyond this point."

He sighed and ran his fingers through his hair, raking it to the side where short curling tendrils fell over his forehead. He stepped down one step below her until their eyes were on the same level.

"I'm sorry. I know you can't understand all the things I have on my mind, but I didn't mean to take it out on you. And you were right—I did enjoy today . . . more than you'll ever know . . . perhaps more than I should." His words were soft and tinged with regret.

A ripple of pleasure ran through her and she longed to reach forward to touch his face, to test the softness of his beard, his lips.

"I just think it might be a good idea if we don't spend so much time together alone." His voice was quiet and thoughtful and he watched her carefully, as if he could make her understand.

"But why?" she asked.

"Kathryn . . . dammit!" He turned from her to place both hands on the railing. She could see the whiteness of his knuckles as his hands tightened on the wood. "Robert has been dead a month. He was your husband, or have you forgotten?"

"No, Matthew, I haven't forgotten and I've not forgotten Robert!" Her eyes were burning with tears that threatened to overflow.

He turned to her again, his face only a breath away, and she could see the agony in his eyes. "And I *can't* forget Robert. I should have remembered that today."

Without another word he left her to feel the hot tears that spilled from her eyes.

So at least now she knew for sure: it was loyalty to his brother that kept him from allowing himself to care for her. But it was too late for her. She felt as if a knife had been plunged into her heart at the very thought of Matthew's rejection. For she wanted him more than she ever thought it possible to want anyone.

And what of Cynthia? He was as tied to her as he was to the memory of his dead brother, and there was nothing she could do about it.

She turned to go slowly up the stairs, her head now beginning to ache in earnest.

We are all born for love. It is the principle of existence, and its only end.

Benjamin Disraeli

Chapter Fifteen

Kathryn and Matthew had not been alone for the past few days, ever since that day at the river and their painful discussion on the stairs. Although there were times when she caught his looks of warmth and openness, she knew he was avoiding her. Sometimes he closed her out completely, maintaining a cool, aloof manner.

Kathryn began riding almost daily with Eugene. He was polite and charming and it took her mind off her problems with Matthew. Eugene was careful not to appear too familiar with her. She suspected that blessing was Tilda's doing and she rejoiced in it, much happier in Eugene's company now that he considered her only a friend.

One morning as they rode, Eugene mentioned a dinner party his parents were planning. "Mrs. Kincaid told me she will speak to Matthew about coming. I do hope he will allow you to come, Kathryn," Eugene said.

"*Allow* me?" she asked incredulously. Was that what Eugene thought? "Whatever makes you think I need Matthew's permission?"

Eugene's pale skin turned pink at the agitation in her voice. "I don't . . . I mean to say . . . Mrs. Kincaid was the one who suggested she must ask."

Kathryn looked at him for a long moment. She was sorry to make him uncomfortable and she knew she should not put him in the middle of her dispute with Matthew. "What do you know about Matthew, Eugene? How is it that you and Robert were friends, and yet not Matthew? There's not that much age difference between you."

"Oh, I don't know," he said, pausing to think about her question. "Matthew was always the serious one . . . always took his responsibilities to heart. Robert and I, in our younger days, you understand, just wanted to have a grand old time of it."

"Oh, I see. Lots of lady friends, I suppose?" Her voice was teasing as she smiled at him.

He smiled sheepishly. "Well, we tried, although they did seem to fall in love with Matthew more often. We never knew if it was his dark, romantic looks or his serious nature that appealed to women. Whatever it was, sometimes Robert hated him for it."

Immediately Eugene seemed to regret his choice of words. He looked at her oddly, as if he'd said something he shouldn't.

Kathryn frowned. "Robert hate Matthew? Or anyone? I'm afraid I find that hard to believe!"

"Well, perhaps *hate* is too strong a word. You know how rivalry between brothers can be," he said, passing it off as unimportant.

"Yes . . . I suppose," she said.

As Eugene left he said, "I do hope you will be at the dinner party Saturday evening Kathryn—Tilda is going to be there." His last words were almost an afterthought and were said with a slight degree of self-consciousness.

"Oh, Eugene, I'm glad. And I will be there, you can count on it," she promised. Not even Matthew Kincaid would keep her from it.

After he had left and Kathryn had stepped into the foyer she noticed that her gloves were missing. "Oh, no," she said aloud. "Where did I put them?" She turned about in the hallway, but they weren't there. Going back to the door she was surprised to see through the glass panes that Eugene's horse was still outside. At the corner of the house she saw a flash of color, a slight movement.

What was Eugene doing now, she wondered. Her curious smile was replaced by a puzzled frown when she saw Cynthia. The girl's face was scowling and angry as she stood before Eugene in the shelter of the large azalea bushes.

Kathryn knew she should not continue to stand and watch them. She felt as if she were spying. But for the life of her she couldn't imagine what the two of them could have to discuss, and so angrily at that. She could see Eugene gesturing at Cynthia and could hear the murmur of his voice, although she couldn't make out what was being said.

Eugene pointed his finger at Cynthia, his face close to hers as if he were warning her. Abruptly, he turned and walked back toward the front of the house.

Kathryn ducked away from the door and stood

with her back against the wall until she heard the sound of hooves leading away from the house. She peeked out again. Cynthia still stood near the corner of the house, her fists clenched tightly at her sides, her face glowering as she watched Eugene ride away.

Kathryn walked slowly up the stairs, puzzled and curious. She didn't see Matthew coming down the stairs until she almost collided into him.

"Whoa," he said. "You seem a million miles away."

"Matthew! I'm sorry. I was thinking, not watching my step," she said stiffly. Each time they met she hoped he would talk to her, perhaps say he'd changed his mind about spending time with her, but today, just as every other day, he did not.

"I thought I heard you go into your room a little while ago," he said.

"No . . . I've been riding with Eugene."

"He certainly is persistent, isn't he?" he said, his eyes once again cold and unsmiling.

"I don't know why you seem to resent him so. Eugene is just a good friend, and for you to imply . . ."

"I wasn't implying anything. But should I ask him what his intentions are, Kate?" he mocked.

"I don't believe, Matthew, that it is your duty to question my friends about me!" Her words were spoken between clenched teeth.

"I'm only trying to protect you. After all, you are my sister-in-law." He smiled coolly at her.

"Yes, as you so often remind me," she snapped, stepping around him. She was getting nowhere bantering with him.

His hand shot forward, clasping her arm in his hard, unyielding fingers.

"Let me go," she said.

When he behaved in this high-handed manner she found it hard to remember her more tender feelings for him. She could not abide being manhandled . . . by anyone.

"Eugene Davenport is not the man for you, Kate. You would squash his feeble spirit into nothing and turn him into a simpering idiot within weeks. He would bore you beyond tears and you would need look elsewhere for your pleasure." His voice was husky as he warned her.

Kathryn faced him, inches from his sparking eyes. He had made it plain he did not want her and yet it seemed he wanted no one else to have her either. "And what do you know about the kind of man I need?" she hissed.

"I think you and I both know the answer to that."

Kathryn was tired of his games, his insinuations, his constant change of emotions. Tears sprang to her eyes and she lowered her head, ashamed for him to see. "Yes, Matthew I think we both do . . . and that's the problem, isn't it?" she whispered.

Below them from the parlor door Thursa's voice called, "Matthew? Is that you?"

Matthew slowly released Kathryn and stepped away from her. But as he looked at her tear-streaked face she saw a look of sadness in his eyes. She thought he was about to say something to her but she pulled away and ran up the steps.

As she approached the door to her room, Kathryn thought she heard a noise from within.

She stopped and stood quietly for a moment, listening. As her hand reached for the doorknob, the thought of the red ribbon she found on the mirror flashed through her mind and she hesitated.

Matthew had not gone down the stairs, but still stood watching her. She did not want to talk with him again, so she quickly threw open the door. Stepping inside she stood against the closed door, waiting for her eyes to adjust to the dimness.

The room was quiet. Kathryn glanced about into the shadowy corners. A strong scent of spice pervaded the air, an aroma she could not immediately identify.

"He's right, you know," a voice rasped from the dimly lit room. "Eugene is weak."

Kathryn gasped in alarm.

A match flared; the smell of sulphur mingled with the spice-scented air. In the glow of the lamplight she could now make out the face, the unmistakable frizz of blonde hair.

"Teresa! My God, you almost frightened me to death," Kathryn gasped. "What are you doing here? How long have you been here?" Kathryn remembered Matthew's words about hearing someone go into her room.

Teresa's eyes were wide with feigned innocence. "I brought you a nice basket of potpourri for your room. Don't it smell sweet? There's cedar berries and cinnamon, and I dried the carnations myself." She was unusually chatty as she offered the basket to Kathryn.

"That's very nice of you, Teresa," she said. "And it is delightful; I could smell it as soon as I opened the door."

Kathryn moved to the love seat and collapsed wearily. It seemed that everything in this house unnerved her lately.

"Kathryn's tired," Teresa crooned. "I could get you some tea, that's what I used to do for Robert when he was tired."

"No, thank you, Teresa. I'm fine now. I guess it's not been a good day."

"You see what I mean now? About the dark one? Born of the devil he was," she declared.

"Were you listening to us just now, Teresa?" Kathryn asked.

"Oh, yes!" Teresa smiled, nodding her head. "I always listen . . . and watch. Then I know what's going on."

"I can assure you nothing is going on," Kathryn said, snapping more than she intended. She only wanted to be alone and to forget the constant bickering and petty mysteries of Foxfire.

"No, you're wrong. There's always something going on here. You must stay away from the dark one, Miss Lady." The woman's smile had vanished and she looked genuinely frightened.

"I'm growing tired of these constant warnings," Kathryn said. "Tell me exactly what you mean Teresa—why must I stay away from Matthew?"

"He's a powerful man!" Teresa exclaimed. "And he always gets what he wants. If it's you he wants and you don't feel the same, then you best get away from here. Matthew Kincaid *always* gets what he wants."

"I'm not frightened of him, Teresa," Kathryn said.

If the attraction between her and Matthew was obvious even to this poor woman, then must it not be obvious to everyone else?

The door opened and they both turned toward it. "Teresa? Woody is ready for his story now," Cynthia called from the open doorway.

Teresa looked startled, spilling part of her spice-filled basket. "Oh! I'm sorry! I'm coming Miss Cynthia. I'm coming right away. Just let me clean this up. . . ." Her hands were trembling as she tried to sweep the bits and pieces back into the basket.

Kathryn's firm hands clasped the older woman's shaking ones. "It's all right, Teresa," she soothed. "Now go on. I'll clean this up. Thank you for bringing it to me. It was very sweet of you to do so."

Teresa smiled tremulously at Kathryn and walked toward Cynthia. The girl stood looking coldly at both of them. Cynthia's behavior seemed odd to Kathryn, almost as if she were the head of the house and Teresa a servant. That disturbed Kathryn, for she had never noticed before how fragile the woman was and how easily frightened.

She raked the spice scented particles back into the basket. Placing the basket on a table, she noticed a piece of paper sticking up through the potpourri. Dumping the basket's contents into a large crystal bowl, she carefully extracted the paper from the bottom of the basket. It was an envelope, addressed simply. "To Kathryn."

She opened it quickly and found inside another envelope. "It's a will," she said, surprise reflected in her face. "It's Robert's will." But why did Teresa have it, and why had she tried to smuggle it to Kathryn like this? Where had it been all this time?

She was not sure she should unseal the envelope so she placed it back into the one with her name on it. She would give it to Matthew tonight at dinner.

Kathryn dressed in a new, emerald green satin skirt and a white, lace-trimmed Garibaldi blouse, one of Robert's Christmas gifts to her. It was the most stylish outfit she possessed. She pinned a small emerald brooch at the neck of her blouse. Robert had given it to her when they married, saying it matched her eyes. She smiled wistfully at the thought of his many kindnesses.

With the envelope and will clasped tightly in her hand, she stepped into the dining room. Matthew stood talking with his mother. He did not turn to face Kathryn but she could see him looking at her from the corner of his eye, his head slightly lowered.

"You look lovely, my dear," Thursa told her.

Kathryn could feel Matthew's appraisal of her as his eyes drifted slowly from her face to encompass every inch of her. Deep within it pleased her that she could capture his attention so thoroughly. But tonight there was no measure of teasing in his look, only one of sadness and regret.

Teresa stood across the room, watching Kathryn anxiously. Her bright eyes flickered toward the envelope in Kathryn's hand and she looked pleased. Kathryn smiled at her.

After they were seated she handed the envelope to Matthew. He looked at her in surprise as he saw the second envelope and realized what it was.

"Where did you get this, Kathryn?" he asked.

Kathryn glanced at Teresa. Something had made Teresa give the will to her in such a secretive manner and she decided to say nothing. "I found it in some of Robert's belongings."

The answer seemed to satisfy Teresa, who sat waiting almost breathlessly for Matthew to speak.

For moments he was silent, gazing at the envelope in his hand. A look of pain flashed across his face.

"I was surprised that Robert's lawyer, Mr. Mason, didn't have a will for Robert. Mother and I were sure he had made one after he came home. When we didn't find one I assumed he didn't have a chance. Well, I'll get this to Mason first thing tomorrow morning."

Almost imperceptibly Teresa nodded toward Kathryn as she breathed a sigh of relief. With an approving look on her face she turned to her meal and ate hungrily and with obvious enjoyment. Kathryn, watching her, knew she had made the right choice in not involving the woman.

"Matthew, you seem so quiet. Are you all right?" Thursa asked softly.

He reached out to clasp his mother's hand. "I'm fine, Mother. It's just the discovery of this will, I suppose. It doesn't seem possible . . ."

"I know . . . I know." she said, patting his hand sympathetically.

Kathryn could not stand seeing the anguish in Matthew's eyes as he spoke of Robert. She had never wanted to comfort anyone as much as she did him.

They finished the meal in silence and seemed content to retire to their own rooms. The discovery of the will had brought renewed thoughts of Robert's death and had cast a dark cloud on the evening.

When Matthew returned from Asheville the following day he told Kathryn and his mother, "Mr. Mason will be here Saturday for the reading of the will. He expects everyone to be present, including Lila and Cynthia."

Kathryn did not miss the look that passed between him and Thursa. Were they worried about something in the will?

Promptly at four on Saturday afternoon, Mr. Mason arrived and they all filed into the parlor.

The lawyer stood at the front of the room speaking quietly to Matthew. Seeing Matthew there, so obviously confident, so tall and masculine, Kathryn admitted to herself for the first time that she was in love with him. He had become so much a part of her that it did not come with a jolt of surprise but rather with a natural feeling of being right. Yet she knew he did not feel the same, would not allow himself to feel the same because of his brother. Oh, she knew that even he could not deny the spark that passed between them whenever they met or his gray eyes captured hers. But she had to face it—what he felt for her was not love. She didn't know what had changed since that day at the river, that day of sweetness that she'd never forgotten, but she did know that he had been carefully avoiding her ever since. And his message to her was clear.

Lila Spencer sat very erectly across from Kathryn, her chin held high in that rather proud, arrogant way. Cynthia sat beside her mother, looking down at her lap as she nervously twisted a handkerchief in her fingers. She seemed lost in her own world and did not glance up.

Thursa sat beside Kathryn on the sofa; Sula stood behind them. Teresa was late, sneaking quietly in the door to stand with her eyes riveted on Kathryn, an artless smile on her round face. Perhaps I have gained an ally, Kathryn thought. She was beginning to like the mysterious little woman in spite of her odd ways. At least she no longer felt afraid of her.

Matthew and the lawyer both took a seat at the front of the room; they were ready to begin.

Kathryn's mind wandered as the lawyer began to read the will. She became aware again of his words only when she heard him mention her name.

> "To my dearest wife, Kathryn, who has given unselfishly of her friendship, her loyalty, and her wisdom, I leave the entirety of my share of the Foxfire lands, consisting of 760 acres. She shall also receive $50,000 in gold bullion, which my brother Matthew has secured for me for safekeeping. Upon the event of my death, it is my wish that she remain at Foxfire and allow the share of land that she will receive to be overseen by my brother. However, the land is hers to dispose of as she wishes and she shall not be bound legally to

keep the land, nor to remain at Foxfire if it be against her wishes. Thank you, Kathryn, for your affection, for your companionship, and most of all, for your friendship."

Tears filled Kathryn's eyes. She heard his words just as clearly as if he were there before them. Thursa's eyes were also misty as she reached across and gripped Kathryn's hand in a squeeze of affection. Kathryn did not look up, but she could feel the eyes of everyone in the room upon her.

The lawyer continued.

"To my beloved mother and brother, I leave the remainder of the gold, also to use as they wish. I love you both very much. Further, I direct my lawyer to place $5000 cash in the hands of Lila and Cynthia Spencer, to be used in the upbringing of Cynthia's son."

Glancing up at Matthew, Kathryn saw his frown as a look of disbelief crossed his face. Kathryn could only assume that the look was one of surprise at Robert's generosity toward Matthew's son, but she also had the distinct feeling that he was not pleased by his brother's gesture and she wondered why.

The lawyer continued to read in his droning voice, indicating that Sula and Joseph be given small amounts of money. He provided a small trust for his Aunt Teresa, as well as a hope that she would be given a home at Foxfire for the remainder of her life.

Kathryn was dazed at the generous gift Robert had left her. She felt no joy, but instead a sick feeling of guilt, almost as if she had been paid for her marriage to Robert. Yet she knew that this was not what he had intended. She did not want the money, nor did she want the Kincaid land. She would keep only enough money to repair her home in Asheville. She had come to realize over the past few months that her marriage to Robert and the wish for a home and security had been an emotional one, born of loneliness and desperation. Now she knew she would be able to manage on her own. The girl she had been then seemed a stranger to her, and whatever it was she had felt and needed then was no longer a part of her. She intended to tell Matthew and his mother as soon as possible that she could not take Foxfire land.

Her time here in the comfort of their home had renewed her physically and emotionally. Lately she had been thinking of her home, wishing to see it returned to its former splendor. Now she would be able to do it. She knew she did not belong here, no matter how fond she had become of Thursa and of Foxfire Manor.

It would be hard leaving Woody, but she knew that she could not remain here, especially after today, when she finally admitted to herself that she loved Matthew.

Heaven alone knew how much she loved him, but if she stayed she would only be living for scraps of affection from a man who evidently would never let himself return those feelings. Knowing that, her pride would not let her stay. She had only been fooling herself before when she thought it would be enough just to be near him. No, it was time to make a new life for herself and Sula back in Asheville.

Thursa did not seem unduly surprised or upset at anything contained in Robert's will. But Kathryn could not help wondering about the resentment she thought she'd seen in Matthew's eyes.

She stood with Thursa in the entryway, seeing Mr. Mason out. Thursa had her arm lovingly about Kathryn's waist, her affection reminding Kathryn how difficult it would be to tell her of her decision to leave.

As they turned to go back into the parlor, Kathryn looked into the disquieting gray eyes of Matthew. What was the emotion she saw in their depths? Anger? Distrust? Resentment? She was so stunned by the renewed hostility there that she could not hide the hurt she felt. She was sure it was evident for him to see as he turned abruptly and walked into the parlor.

As she and Thursa entered the room, Matthew stood at the windows, hands in his pockets, looking broodingly out onto the coolness of the green lawn.

Thursa seemed ill at ease by his behavior. "Well, I think there no big surprises, do you Matthew?" she said.

As he turned and looked solemnly at his mother he avoided Kathryn's questioning look altogether. "Only a couple—but then we all know how unpredictable Robert could be."

"Yes, well . . . this is not the time . . . we're all tired now and I'm sure we can discuss this another day," Thursa said.

Something was wrong, but Kathryn could not quite grasp what it was. Whatever it was had made Matthew brooding and angry and Thursa uncharacteristically distant and nervous. Did they resent the fact that she had received the bulk of Robert's estate? She could not believe that of Thursa, for she had come to feel that the woman's welcome of her into the Kincaid family was sincere. And she was one of the most generous women she'd ever known. She had been almost like a mother to her.

As Thursa started to leave the room Kathryn said, "Thursa, wait . . . I must say something to you both." The petite woman stopped, looking at Kathryn oddly.

"Thursa, you know more than anyone the circumstances of my marriage to Robert," she said firmly. "Somehow I cannot feel right about receiving all that money, nor the land. It's not right that it should go to someone outside your family."

At her words, Thursa immediately came to Kathryn. "Darling . . . you *are* our family," she said firmly. "I love you as I would a daughter, and if you have even the slightest doubt that we want you to have what Robert left you legally, . . just put it out of your mind!" Kathryn felt the sincerity of her words, but that made her previous behavior all the more puzzling.

"Perhaps, Mother . . . Kathryn feels she did not fully earn it," Matthew drawled. Kathryn gasped aloud at the cruelty of his words.

"Matthew!" his mother exclaimed. "Apologize to Kathryn at once! Whatever do you mean by such a remark?" Kathryn had never seen the diminutive woman so angry.

Matthew made no move to answer or to apologize. Instead he turned his back on them once again and gazed out the window.

"No, Thursa, it's all right." Kathryn hoped her voice showed no sign of the hurt and burning anger she felt at his words. She had no intention of letting him get away with it. "Matthew will be happy to know that I have no desire for the Kincaid land. I intend to go immediately to Mr. Mason's office and inform him that I will not accept it."

He turned then to face her. "There is no question of acceptance—it's yours. The law is quite specific on that point, I believe, unless the will is contested . . . and it won't be." Matthew looked at her steadily as he spoke.

"Well, then, dear brother-in-law, I shall give it to you! The will says that it is mine to dispose of as I wish, does it not?" she asked, fury creeping into her voice.

"It does," he answered slowly, But . . ."

"Then it's yours! I shall see to the papers as soon as possible! Perhaps that will sweeten your disposition! I've tolerated your rudeness and resentment long enough. I have tried to understand the reason for it, but I cannot. I want nothing that is yours, Matthew Kincaid . . . *nothing!*" With that she left the room, skirt awhirl.

Kathryn stalked angrily up the stairs, ignoring Sula, who stood in the hallway, mouth agape, as she watched her storm by.

Sula could not help but worry about Kathryn.

The past few months had taken their toll on the girl and she didn't know how much more she could take. But today she suspected that the mysterious Matthew Kincaid was the cause of all this McClary fury. Hearing the slam of Kathryn's door, Sula could only shake her head in frustration. "When them two ever gonna learn?" she muttered.

A man's vanity tells him what is honor;
A man's conscience what is justice.
Walter Savage Landor

Chapter Sixteen

"Matthew Kincaid, I don't know what's come over you," Thursa snapped. "I have never seen you behave so rudely to any woman. And Kathryn, of all people! Why, she is the sweetest, kindest, most . . ."

"Mother, please, spare me the details of how wonderful you think Kathryn is," he said in annoyance.

"And I suppose you don't think so?" she asked icily. "You, son, could never fool me, and I've seen how the two of you look at one another, even if you are at odds most of the time. So please don't insult me by trying to tell me you're indifferent to her."

"Can you honestly tell me you haven't wondered why she married Robert?" Matthew asked.

"Is that what's bothering you? No, I don't wonder because I know why. And if you had asked her, I'm sure she would have had the honesty to tell you the truth. She needed Robert and he needed her. The circumstances of her life at the time made it seem like the only choice she had. And I'll tell you something else, even though she did not love him, and she never tried to fool anyone into thinking she did, that girl would have spent the rest of her life in devotion to him. Because that's the kind of person she is. If you can't see that about her then you don't know her at all, and you've changed from the perceptive son I thought I had raised."

Matthew sighed and made a small amused sound of surrender.

"All right, Mother, you've certainly made your point. I won't deny that I've been wrong about a lot of things where Kathryn is concerned. But I'm not the heartless man she thinks me to be." He walked to the window and stood silently looking out, his hands clasped behind his back.

Thursa went to him and put an arm around his waist. Her head barely came to his shoulder. She looked up at him, her eyes full of the love and pride she felt for him.

"I know that," she said. "I think I know you better than anyone, perhaps even better than you know yourself. That's why I think you're fooling yourself with this barrier you've put up between you and Kathryn. Personally, I think you've never met a woman who affects you the way she does and it frightens you," she added.

He looked down at her as she stood within the crook of his arm. A look of amazement crossed his face and he grinned at her.

"Oh, you do?" he asked.

"Yes, I do," she declared. Then her face turned more serious before she continued. "And son, as hard as it is to face, our Robert is gone . . . but you're alive. You can't stop living just because he's dead!" Then she patted his arm and turned to leave the parlor. "Think about it," she added.

Upstairs, Kathryn paced about her room, angry and confused. She was not in the mood now for Eugene's dinner party. She knew if she had any sense she would just stay home and forget it. But the words Eugene had spoken earlier haunted her—as if she needed Matthew's permission!

"Damn you, Matthew Kincaid!" she muttered. "I will not let you do this to me. And I will not sit here in this room and brood!"

She turned with a purposeful stride and began to rummage through her store of dresses.

She could wear the emerald green skirt again and with it the tiffany silk blouse of blue and emerald green plaid that she and Sula had made. She pinned her thick tumble of hair up and was ready an hour later.

Meeting Matthew downstairs in the foyer before departing, she became aware of the way in which he took in every detail of her appearance, from her trim figure and flattering hair style to the high color on her cheeks. Her emerald eyes still glinted with resentment and she stared defiantly at him.

Damnation! he thought. Why did the girl continue to challenge his every word and misinterpret his actions? And why did they both have such a hard time understanding each other?

She did not glance his way again, but stepped into the waiting carriage with Thursa. The two women sat side by side, each complimenting the other on her appearance. Tonight Thursa wore a new dress Kathryn had not seen. It was a magenta silk creation, the bodice beautifully decorated with jet beading. Kathryn had never seen her looking lovelier.

Matthew sat across from them, his profile solemn as he gazed out the side windows. Kathryn watched him through lowered lashes, noting his conservative but strikingly handsome appearance in his black frock coat and silver gray stock. He wore a small gold chain pinned across the stock and she watched as it glittered brightly with the sway of the carriage.

When they arrived at the Davenport house Kathryn was delighted to see Tilda standing behind Eugene as he greeted them at the door. She embraced the tall girl and they walked together arm in arm into the parlor to greet the others before dinner.

The Davenport home was lovely and spacious, if a bit austere in its furnishings, but Kathryn liked it. There was more a look of the country to it, for after all it was a working farm. She especially liked the wide expanses of bare, gleaming pine floors and the many long windows covered only by soft lacy curtains.

"Mrs. Davenport," Kathryn said as she walked with her into the dining room, "I love your home—it's really beautiful."

"Why, thank you, dear. It is a bit spare for most people's taste, but I like it that way. My mother was the same—probably because of her Dutch ancestry. They seem to prefer simple designs and styles."

The dinner of roast beef was accompanied by an enormous array of vegetable dishes and breads, and after the table was cleared a cart of various desserts was wheeled into the dining room. It was certainly impressive, especially in light of the fact that there still was a shortage of many foods, especially sugar and flour.

Kathryn was a little surprised at the pleasantness of the house and the generous dinner. Perhaps it was because she couldn't picture the sometimes pompous Eugene living here.

But it was most pleasant with everyone talking and laughing together in the warm, amiable atmosphere. After the desserts had been cleared and coffee served Kathryn was pleased that the men stayed to smoke there, rather than separating themselves from the women. She for one heartily approved of this less formal country custom.

Tonight Kathryn was seeing Matthew in an entirely different way. It was obvious that Mr. Davenport enjoyed his company and respected his opinions as he sought his views about many aspects of the war and its consequences. Kathryn liked hearing Matthew's deep rumble of laughter and his warm, easy smile as he talked with Mr. Davenport.

"This blasted war just will not die!" Mr. Davenport said. "Here it is nearing the end of May and I just heard at the mill yesterday that General Johnston did not surrender his army until April twenty-sixth." Mr. Davenport was a big, blustery looking man, with thinning brown hair and bright rosy cheeks. His gray eyes were as soft and kind as a puppy's, but they were troubled now as he spoke.

Matthew nodded. He was holding a long thin cheroot between his fingers. "His army was here in North Carolina when Lee signed the surrender at Appomattox. He should have surrendered then."

"I disagree!" Eugene snapped. "We could have

won this bloody war if all of our generals were as persistent as Johnston!"

Matthew flashed a look of disdain toward Eugene, his gray eyes dark and alive. "At what cost? Thousands more dead? Five thousand more wounded or maimed to come home to burned and ravaged land that will grow nothing . . . or homes that no longer exist? Believe me, most places have not fared as well as we have here in the mountains. The South was beaten a year ago!"

Eugene's face flamed and he looked away from Matthew's steely glance.

"But from the account I read in the paper it was not Johnston's decision. It was Jefferson Davis who was unwilling to surrender," Kathryn said.

Matthew looked at her silently for a moment, squinting his eyes through the smoke of his cigar. She thought he might rebuke her for entering into a conversation that normally was restricted to gentlemen.

"I think that's probably true. And it's a shame, after all these years of slaughter, that he could not just let it go. Don't you agree?" There was a touch of mischief in Matthew's eyes as he watched her.

When he looked at her like that, she could not resist the slight smile that came to her lips. "Yes, I agree," she replied.

"Well, I for one never expected to hear such words from either of you!" Eugene said, obviously still stung by Matthew's previous words.

Matthew clamped the brown cigar between his teeth and smiled faintly as he shrugged his broad shoulders.

Nothing more was said, but Kathryn hid a smile as she looked toward Tilda and saw her unabashed gaze of affection at Eugene. It was obvious that she had finally found her very own hero.

Mr. Davenport spoke again to Matthew. "There's much speculation now about what will happen to our Southern states. They say that throughout the North there is a disposition to beat a fallen foe. I'm afraid we disobedient Southerners are in for a good deal of punishment from our neighbors to the north."

"I'm afraid you're right," Matthew said thoughtfully. "I don't believe we'll be able to depend on the sale of cotton any more to fill empty coffers. It will sit and rot on the docks before a penny goes into the pockets of Southern planters."

"What do you plan on doing with Foxfire, Matthew?" Mrs. Davenport asked.

"I believe there's another possibility for us here in North Carolina. We've grown it on a small scale before and I believe it will do well if we expand. I'm speaking of tobacco."

"I think you may be right," Eugene agreed, the anger lost in his enthusiasm for the subject. "Father and I had discussed the same thing."

"I've been thinking of visiting Mr. Reynolds in Salem next week," Matthew said. "He's gaining quite a reputation as a pioneer in the tobacco business. If you'd like, I'll let you know what he suggests."

The evening passed quickly and Kathryn found herself surprised at the pleasantness of it. Her spirits lifted and she was glad she had not let her anger with Matthew keep her away. She said goodbye to Eugene and his family at the door and kissed Tilda on the cheek. "Write to me Tilda and let me know how it goes with you and Eugene." Kathryn whispered.

They rode home in silence. Kathryn thought about how much she enjoyed the evening and the neighborly atmosphere at the Davenport home. Strangely, despite her harsh words with Matthew over the will, tonight she had felt a genuine part of the Kincaid family. But she knew she could not let those warm feelings influence her decision to leave Foxfire, especially after today. She would leave Foxfire . . . she had to . . . and Matthew's trip to Salem would be the perfect opportunity.

Revenge is a confession of pain.
Seneca

Chapter Seventeen

"Leavin' Foxfire?" Sula asked. "You sure that's what you want?"

"I think it's best," was all Kathryn would say.

"But what about Mister Matthew? He ain't gonna' let you go."

"Matthew has nothing to do with it, Sula. We're going." Her tone of voice told Sula that the subject was closed.

"We can't live in the old house the way it is," Sula said.

"We'll live in the servant's quarters behind the house while the renovations are being done. It won't be disgraceful for a young widow to live alone . . . anyway, I have you. After all, there will be many young widows alone now," Kathryn added sadly.

Now that she had made the decision and told Sula, Kathryn was anxious to complete her plans. She would wait and tell Thursa at the last moment, for she knew the woman would plead with her to stay and Kathryn did not want to be persuaded by her kindness to change her mind. She knew Matthew would keep Woody safe, and perhaps he would allow him to visit her often in Asheville. She could not even let herself think of what her goodbye to Matthew meant.

So within a week she would leave Foxfire. She had been here less than six months, but in that short period her life had changed drastically. She had married, become widowed; she had been frightened, attacked . . . and she had fallen desperately in love for the first time in her life. So in love she knew she would never love anyone the way she loved Matthew Kincaid.

She had hoped it would be easier to leave with Matthew away. But as the day drew nearer for his departure, she found herself dreading it more and more.

Early on the morning he was to leave, Matthew stood in the hall saying his farewells, promising to bring the excited Woody a surprise from Salem. He also offered to bring precious kitchen items to Sula, items such as spices and flavorings . . . things she'd done without for a long time. Sula had a wistful look on her face and Kathryn noticed her hesitancy to say anything. It was obvious Sula did not approve of her going this way, without telling Matthew, but she would not let it slip that they would be gone when he returned.

As the others stood on the wide front porch talking to Matthew, Kathryn slipped away. She walked around the edge of the forest to the overlook, and stood back against the laurel and rhododendron, waiting for Matthew to pass.

The morning was clear, with a warm, honeysuckled breeze blowing across the mountain. The distant peaks rose and fell unendingly.

As Matthew approached, he slowed Blackjack and reined to a stop at the overlook. She knew she should already have disappeared into the surrounding forest, yet her heart had forced her to stay for one last glimpse of him. Now, to her embarrassment, he had seen her.

He swung his long legs off the horse and walked to her. "Kathryn, I wanted to talk to you."

His voice was deep and warm, more friendly than he'd been in a long while. "This is a beautiful place to begin the day, isn't it?" he said.

"I'm sure this must be one of the most beautiful views in the whole world," she said looking out at the mountains.

They both stood silently enjoying the pine-scented air and the muted sound of a hawk screaming high above them.

"I must have a bower built here when I return. Then you . . . or any of us . . . can sit here in weather fair or foul and enjoy the view," he said.

"That would be nice," she said, still lacking the courage to tell him that she would not be here to enjoy it.

He looked at Kathryn, his eyes warm and caring, devoid of the resentment she'd seen there before. He puzzled her with his changing emotions. Did he know what his silvery eyes did to her when he looked at her that way? And she could not get enough of looking at him. At this moment she wanted to etch his face into her mind for the times she would be alone and without him.

How she had despised him in the beginning! She

didn't know when, but slowly and surely her opinion of him had changed. Now she saw his quiet strength and courage, his patience with Woody, his love for his neighbors and his family. He was much admired, she had learned, by everyone who knew him. As it turned out, he was the kind of man she'd always dreamed of.

She wondered why it took her so long to see that and why, even now, Teresa seem so frightened of him. She probably would never have the answer to that.

Still, she did not want her feelings for him to be known, for she was convinced now that he would never return her love. Yet she could not be totally dishonest with him. "Matthew, I'm not sure how long I'll be here. You see, I plan to return to Asheville, to the McClary house. I've a great deal of work to do on the house before we can move back in."

"You had not intended to tell me this," he said. His hands were on his hips and he looked down at the ground as he spoke.

"No," she whispered.

"Why?" He looked at her in disbelief and a hint of his old anger.

"I . . . I didn't think it would matter to you, and I want to see my home," she said.

"Didn't think it would matter?" He shook his head and gave a disgusted sigh. "This is your home now, Kathryn! You belong here with us at Foxfire. Don't you think it's what Robert intended? And Mother?"

"But what about you, Matthew? What do you want?" She had become brave now that the time had come to say goodbye.

He gripped her arms and pulled her to him and with a soft moan covered her lips with his warm mouth. Her heart leapt as she felt an instant response to his touch. He kissed her hungrily as if he never wanted to let her go. And when he did they both were left shaken and breathless.

With his arms still around her he whispered, "I'm sorry you even had to ask what I want."

"Matthew, so much has happened here. I must do it now if ever I'm going to," she said.

"We won't argue . . . not now. I've been wrong about so many things. Just tell me you will stay, Kathryn! Give me a chance to begin again when I get home." His voice had that demanding ring of determination she knew so well, but this time there was also a degree of tenderness.

She could feel her determination slipping away at his plea, for she knew the price he paid with his stubborn pride.

"I want you here when I return. Promise me that you'll stay until then at least, until we can sit down and talk about this," he said with a touch of his old fierceness. "Please," he added.

"Matthew . . . I . . ."

"Wait . . . I know I treated you atrociously at times." He frowned, causing a small crease between his eyes. "But there were resentments . . . feelings within myself that I can't explain now, but I want to . . . I want to tell you everything when I get back." His voice was soft and his hand reached up to caress her face and lips . . . his eyes pleaded with her.

He still had not said the words she so longed to hear, but there was a renewed hope welling within her. She knew she could not resist him; the look of him and his touch were just too powerful for her to ignore.

"All right," she said softly. "I will wait, but only until you come home."

"And promise me you'll stay close to the house—no wandering off by yourself as you're apt to do . . . and certainly not in the middle of the night!" He looked at her sternly as he spoke, but he could not hide his real concern.

"I promise," she smiled.

"Stay inside with Mother and Sula. I know that's a lot to ask in this beautiful weather, but it won't be for long. Just think of my peace of mind," he grinned.

"All right," she laughed with him. "I said I promise."

He took her hands gently in his and stood for a moment looking down at her. Then he slowly lowered his head and touched his lips to hers in a kiss that was at once tender and fierce, gentle and bittersweet. Kathryn reached up to touch his face, tracing the outline of his beard and warm, sensitive lips until he turned his head and kissed the palm of her hand.

"I'll be back," he whispered. Quickly he moved away from her to his waiting horse. As he rode away he turned and smiled at her as she stood silently there against the background of his beloved Blue Ridge mountains.

Kathryn watched him go with both joy and fear

in her heart. She had lost so much; she did not think she could bear for anything to spoil this fragile hope that sprang up within her now.

How she adored this dark, ferocious, and sometimes infuriating man. She had loved him from the first tumultuous moment he had walked into her life. Only now could she see the tenderness behind his spirited nature, a nature so much like her own. So she would stay until he returned, and for now her love must remain locked away in her heart.

She was still standing, lost in thought, when a sound behind her caught her attention.

Someone was there in the density of the forest, watching. She knew somebody had been watching her and Matthew, had seen their intimate embraces. She was suddenly afraid, overcome with that same sense of fear she felt before when she'd seen the face on the house. "Who's there?" she called, turning to move toward the house.

"What's wrong with Kathryn now?" the voice sang.

"Teresa!" Kathryn said. She felt great relief at her presence, for at least she was harmless, but her impatience with the woman was hard to disguise. "What are you doing here?"

"I knew . . . I knew all along that you liked the dark one better. Robert was sweet and good, but they always like the dark one better," she said peevishly.

"You never told my why you don't like Matthew," Kathryn said.

Teresa looked blankly at Kathryn. "Oh, I like Matthew," she insisted meekly. "But he's not kind like our Robert. He was too hard on Robert—expected too much. Robert told him that everyone can't be as perfect, as high and mighty, as Matthew Kincaid. Some of us are not so strong—he should know that." She spoke like a child, as if she had been reprimanded and was defending herself.

Kathryn watched her closely. She was very nervous and agitated and seemed on the verge of hysteria.

"You should leave," Teresa told Kathryn. "Like you told Matthew. You should go. It's not good here. Foxfire doesn't want Kathryn."

"Why do you say that? It's not the first time you've said it—tell me what you mean." Kathryn was suddenly suspicious. What did she know? Was she involved with the red ribbons? Kathryn had not thought so before.

"I can't tell you why! Don't ask me things I can't tell!" She was becoming more agitated and upset.

She turned then and disappeared into the forest, a strange, shadowy little elf-woman.

"Teresa . . . wait!"

Kathryn's moment of hope and happiness was lost, snatched away by the strange warning of Teresa. She was beginning to think it was true, that Foxfire did not want her. Perhaps she had been wrong to tell Matthew she would stay.

In the two weeks following her confrontation with Teresa, Kathryn became more frightened than ever. She couldn't shake the feeling that something was wrong, and she didn't know why.

One morning Woody was in her room early. He wanted to play with the kitten. While Kathryn straightened the room, he sat on the floor watching the kitten's playful antics.

Kathryn's smile turned to horror as she saw what he bounced from hand to hand. "Where did you get that?" she demanded sharply, taking the red ribbon from his hand.

Woody looked up at her, surprise in his clear blue eyes. "It was on kitty's neck," he said innocently.

She looked at the red ribbon there in her hand. "Tied around her neck? Are you sure?"

"Yep," he said, a small frown appearing between his eyes. "It was tied in a pretty bow. Are you mad 'cause I took it off?"

"No, Woody . . . no, you did nothing wrong." An overwhelming rush of panic gripped her and she felt she couldn't breathe. The memory of that horrible night in the forest came back to her in an instant. She had felt so safe while Matthew was here. Now she felt terribly alone and vulnerable.

"Woody, sweetheart, will you go get Sula for me?"

Woody was back in a few minutes pulling a huffing Sula along behind him.

"If you'd like you can take kitty to see Teresa," she told Woody.

She waited until he was gone before turning to Sula. "I want you to get packed. I've decided to go home tomorrow rather than wait for Matthew's return," she said.

"But, honey, you done told him you'd wait. Things is gonna work out between you and him. I jes know it! Why you got to be so impatient, child?"

"It's not that, Sula . . ." Kathryn said, turning to pace the room.

"What's wrong? Has something else happened?" She asked, her face showing alarm.

"Nothing, Sula. Honestly, it's nothing. I need to get away from here. Its just a feeling . . . I know I'm probably being silly, but I can speak to Matthew when he gets back, even if I'm in Asheville. I just want to go home!"

"All right, all right!" Sula said. "Home we will go then!"

Kathryn sighed with relief. She knew she would be safe once she was away from here. Shc finally realized that Matthew was right. The person leaving the red ribbons was not playing tricks. This was much more serious than that.

Sula bustled out the door, shaking her head in consternation. "Lord, Lord, I'll be glad to be outta this place myself!"

Now that she had made the decision, Kathryn felt better. Surely she could make it through one more night. She went downstairs almost happily to join Thursa in the parlor.

They had not been seated long when Kathryn sensed that Thursa had something serious on her mind, something she wanted to tell her.

Finally she laid aside her needlework and turned to Kathryn with an unusually solemn look in her eyes. "Kathryn, dear, there's something I've wanted to tell you for some time now . . . and although Matthew asked me not to, I feel I must."

"What is it, Thursa?" Kathryn was puzzled. She

wondered how Matthew was involved in what Thursa wanted to tell her.

"I don't know quite how to begin. Let me say first that when men are young and immature . . . they sometimes do unpredictable and impetuous things. Some say it's the nature of a man. It doesn't necessarily mean he's bad or unworthy of our love. All of us are thoughtless and a bit selfish at times." She paused for a moment, seeming unsure of herself.

"I regret that my own son has caused shame to a young, innocent girl and her family . . . indeed, to our own family. We've managed to weather the storm because we are here in the mountains, in near isolation—still I cannot deny it has been hard at times."

Kathryn could feel the tension gathering in her as she froze before Thursa's words. She did not want to hear this, did not want to be reminded now that Cynthia and the man she loved were once lovers. Yet she knew she must. Wasn't it what she'd wanted, for them to bring their dark secret out into the open and be honest with her?

Thursa continued. "When it happened, I was furious. I didn't know what to do, but I knew we had to raise that child. After all, he is a Kincaid. Matthew, of course, insisted that Foxfire should be their home, and that's as it should be. Now, of course, we love the boy so much. I have wanted nothing more than to have the world know that he's my grandson."

"Thursa, I already guessed . . . about Woody. I even confronted Matthew with it, rather bluntly, I'm afraid. I became very angry with him when he refused to admit that Woody is his son."

Thursa looked at her blankly. "Matthew? Oh, no, no, dear . . . Woody is not Matthew's son!"

Kathryn was jolted by her words. "Not Matthew's?" She had been so convinced that he was Woody's father that she could not even imagine who else the father might be.

"Oh, dear, I'm making a terrible mess of this." Thursa paused, taking a deep breath. "Kathryn, dear . . . Woody was named for his father, Robert Wood Kincaid," she said slowly.

"Robert?" Kathryn asked. "Robert . . . and Cynthia?" She was clearly stunned by Thursa's revelation. "What must Matthew think of me? I was so sure! He must think I'm a total fool!" She raised her hands to her burning cheeks. "Why did he let me go on thinking that?"

Thursa looked sympathetically at her as she reached to take Kathryn's hands. "That's why I'm telling you now. I told Matthew all along we should. But you must remember that he has always protected his brother. Robert was young and, I must admit, more willful . . . he was never as strong or as responsible as Matthew.

"He was used to having his way in all things, I'm afraid. So we protected him, hoping some day he'd do the right thing and acknowledge the boy as his own. That's why Matthew was so upset when the will was read. He loves little Woody . . . and the idea that even after his death, Robert wouldn't claim him for his son, well, it simply infuriated Matthew. The boy should have been his heir;

Robert had promised us he would be. Then to leave him only five thousand . . ."

"That's why he was so angry at me!" Kathryn said.

"Well, he was angry to say the least; and I knew you thought it was directed at you, but it wasn't. He was angry at Robert and frustrated because he knew there was nothing to be done. I wanted him to tell you then, explain everything to you, but he felt it was not the right time."

"But why wouldn't he tell me?" Kathryn asked.

"You must understand, dear, that Matthew was never sure of your true feelings for Robert. You see, at first, please forgive me for saying so . . . he thought you only married his brother for money . . . and Foxfire. You are a strong woman—I could see that right away, and you took your grief privately, outwardly appearing calm and serene. Matthew mistook that as somehow unfeeling . . . uncaring."

"That isn't exactly untrue," Kathryn admitted.

"No, dear, it is untrue. You wanted to make Robert happy because you are a caring person . . . and you succeeded. He was happy because of you, and I will always love you for that." Kathryn could see that she meant it. "If you had cared only for power and possessions you could have taken everything, the lands, Foxfire . . ."

Kathryn said nothing but sat thinking about Thursa's words. Robert had been happy. There had not been the turbulent, bittersweet love she felt for Matthew, nonetheless, she had cared for Robert and loved him as one loves a friend.

Thursa continued, "Matthew came to see that you did care for Robert, perhaps even loved him, and I think that confused him. For on one hand, you see, he wanted you to care for his brother, while on the other, perhaps he became a little jealous at the memory you still held."

Kathryn closed her eyes, allowing the feeling of pure joy that came to her to rush over her. For the first time since coming to Foxfire she felt as if a great weight had been lifted. "Oh, Thursa, I'm so glad you told me. I mean . . . I was so angry and hurt at Matthew's rejection of me . . . but I was afraid he was right . . . I felt like such a fraud. But I don't feel that way any longer. I really did make Robert happy."

Thursa's eyes shone with understanding. "And despite Matthew's behavior toward you, you loved him anyway?" she asked.

Kathryn hesitated for a moment before she whispered, "Yes, oh, yes, I loved him anyway."

"I'm delighted Kathryn." Thursa reached over to kiss her cheek. "But I'm not so sure that my son will thank me for what I've done. I'm sure he wanted to tell you himself. I suppose I will just have to suffer the consequences when he comes home."

"I don't think you will have to worry, Thursa. Matthew adores you," Kathryn said with a smile.

Thursa shook her head and smiled. "Yes, I feel blessed to have a man like Matthew for my son."

Later, alone in her room with her thoughts and renewed hopes, Kathryn stood by the window hugging herself tightly. Everything was finally making sense. "Oh, Matthew, please hurry home," she prayed. She could now return to Asheville and wait for him there, feeling lighter and more carefree than she had in years.

Kathryn did not undress immediately but lay on the bed thinking and dreaming about what she and Matthew would say to each other when he came home. Soon she had drifted into a deep, relaxed sleep.

She was wakened by someone at her door. She looked at the clock and saw it was past midnight. Quickly going to the door she found Joseph standing in the hallway. "Excuse me, ma'am, but Mr. Matthew asked me to give you this. He says for you not to tell nobody else he's home."

"Matthew's home?" she asked, her eyes shining with joy.

"Yes'm," he said, handing her an envelope. Her heart leapt at the prospect of finally seeing him. She drew the short note from the envelop.

"Dearest Kathryn, I have arrived home and wish to speak to you alone. Meet me at the old ice house. Matthew."

What a strange, enigmatic request. He wanted to see her alone, yet there was no hint of affection in the short missive.

Kathryn wondered briefly how he had managed to arrive unseen and unheard, but that thought was quickly forgotten in her haste to see him.

Hurriedly she brushed her hair and straightened her rumpled gown. Checking the mirror, she smiled at the heightened color in her cheeks and her sparkling eyes. She eased down the stairs and out the back door without being heard.

She made her way through the gathering darkness, walking quickly past the aromatic gardens toward the ice house. It was a dark, quiet evening with light mists covering the ground, swirling about her feet as she walked.

When she arrived at the ice house she saw no one.

"Matthew?" she whispered.

She heard a noise from inside. Carefully pushing the door open, she entered quietly and was met by the musty smell of disuse. Inside was as black as a tomb. She reached out to locate the protective railing around the pit, wishing she'd thought to bring a light. "Matthew . . . where are you?"

She suddenly sensed the presence of someone behind her. As she started to turn she felt a violent blow against her shoulders and the side of her head and found herself being hurled through the brittle board into the the black empty space of the pit. The breath was expelled from her lungs in a great rush as she hit the hard-packed earth at the bottom of the hole.

She was surprised to find she was still alive, but the pain in her head and shoulders was excruciating. Her fall had been partially broken by the wall of the ice pit; she had slid most of the way down. Now she lay at the bottom, stunned, unable to see, and trying to comprehend what had just happened to her.

Not Matt, she prayed, please, it can't be. Yet Joseph had said the message was given to him by Matthew . . . The dim images before her seemed to swirl. She could not believe this was happening; she could not believe what her mind was telling her must be true.

Above in the darkness she saw a flash of white and heard a voice speaking hysterically, as if to no one in particular . . .

"Now, I have killed you . . . at last! Robert never loved you—he loved me! Only me—always me!" The voice was a hysterical scream. "He only said those hateful things to me after you came. He loved me before!"

It was Cynthia. How could she have thought it was anyone *but* Cynthia, with her blank eyes and cold bizarre ways?

She knew the girl standing above her thought she had accomplished her goal, so Kathryn dared not move or make a sound. Cynthia began to whimper so quietly that Kathryn had to listen intently to catch all her words. "Oh, Robert . . . I didn't mean to kill you, my love. I wanted *her* to drink the tea. Foolish Robert. Did you really think I would let her stay here? She tried to take my little boy from me too, but I punished him for that. He was a bad boy! Now Matthew is mad at me . . . dark, beautiful Matthew." Kathryn shivered as the girl's voice rambled on, telling all the evil things she'd done. Her voice changed, becoming harsh, frenzied, and there was no doubt it was the same voice Kathryn had heard there in the forest that night.

It had been Cynthia's cold thin fingers clasped about her throat, Cynthia's crazed laughter ringing through the dark forest. It was all so clear now. Why had she not seen it before?

Cynthia's voice continued to echo about the

empty walls. "Matthew could have been mine too . . . until you came . . . you with your proper ways. You fooled them all, but you couldn't fool me!"

Kathryn's terror grew as Cynthia's voice became louder. What was she going to do? In her sickened rage she screamed down into the pit, "I hated you . . . you green-eyed bitch! You spoiled everything at Foxfire! Now your lover will find the note I left telling him you've gone away. They won't find your beautiful body, and even if they do it will be too late—he'll be *mine*, and Foxfire too!" Again the horrible maniacal laughter reverberated through the emptiness. Kathryn shivered, praying that the girl would leave.

Kathryn pressed her hands tightly over her lips to muffle the frightened sobs that threatened to come. She heard the sound of the door being closed and bolted. Only then did she relax against the cold hard earth. Then she remembered nothing more.

Hours later she woke, her body cold and stiff. She shuddered at the scurrying sounds of mice in the building above. Dear God, she thought, I've been here all night. She knew it would be later in the morning before she was missed, and even then they would not think of looking for her here. Cynthia said she had left a note . . . everyone would think she'd left—perhaps they would not even bother to look for her. But Sula would know, she reasoned . . . Sula would know, she kept whispering over and over again.

But each minute seemed like an hour and in her despair she imagined Matthew finding her lifeless body. Her one regret was that she would never be able to tell him how much she loved him. She began to cry quietly and hopelessly. When Matthew returned she would be dead. Her head was throbbing painfully as darkness surrounded her and carried her away.

The silent hours steal on, and flaky darkness breaks within the east.

Shakespeare

Chapter Eighteen

Kathryn thought she was dreaming. Far away she could hear voices, agitated and excited. She knew then she must wake up, must hide, but the fog continued to drift before her eyes and she could not make her body respond.

"Kathryn! Kathryn!" Someone was calling her name from a great distance. It sounded like Matthew but she knew that could not be. He was not here. No one knew she was here except Cynthia, poor sick demented Cynthia. Kathryn began to cry hopelessly.

"Kathryn, don't cry love. I'm here now. Everything will be all right," Was it Matthew's voice that kept reassuring her, comforting her? No, she knew it couldn't be. She must be dying and this was the end of it.

"Matthew?" She tried to open her eyes, but it was dark, so dark, and she was cold and afraid. Again the blackness washed over her.

For two days and nights Kathryn drifted in and out of consciousness, burning with fever, and tossing about through fitful dreams. At times she could feel the evil of Foxfire Manor and hear Cynthia's crazed laughter ringing in her ears. She thought she felt cool hands on her forehead and the sound of Sula's quiet melodies. She asked for Matthew, sometimes imagining she saw silver eyes, full of pain and anguish. But why was he upset? She wanted to ask him, but the darkness was always there and she could not speak.

Sometimes Kathryn cried for Robert and asked for his understanding. "I should not have loved Matthew . . . not so soon, Robert . . . I tried not to." She wanted Robert to understand. She had not felt his presence so near since his death. Great love and warmth flowed around her as Robert seemed to be pushing her back toward Foxfire. But it hurt so badly. She did not want to go. She longed to stay with him, surrounded by the beautiful warm glow of light and affection.

But Matthew was calling her, begging her to stay with him. "Don't leave me, Kathryn . . . don't you dare leave me now!" His words were a fierce demand.

And it was then that Kathryn knew she could battle the pain, the tiredness, anything, as long as he wanted her with him.

It took every ounce of strength she had, but she pulled herself away from the light and warmth. When she opened her eyes Matthew sat by her bed, his eyes dark and full of anguish. Her heart ached at the tenderness she saw reflected there and she reached out to touch him.

"Kathryn!" he exclaimed. "Oh, Kate," he whispered, his lips against her fingers. "I'm going to get

Sula and Mother now. Don't move . . . I'll be right back!"

Kathryn smiled as he rushed from her side shouting. "Sula! Mother!"

They both came bustling into the room, alternately laughing and crying. Kathryn was so weak she kept drifting away, but she would waken again with a smile on her lips at their joy. She couldn't get enough of seeing their faces as she exulted in being alive and warm and cozy in her own room. She knew now she would not die.

She was drenched in perspiration and tried weakly to kick the heavy quilts off. Her throat was so dry she could barely speak above a whisper.

Sula and Thursa went about gathering up the quilts and brought her hot broth and tea. Matthew stood at the foot of the bed watching her as if someone would suddenly come and tear her from him. Never before had she seen this intensity in his eyes nor felt such an overwhelming flood of emotions from him.

"Matthew," his mother said firmly. "We're going to bathe Kathryn and change her bed. Then I'm sure she'll be exhausted and ready for a normal night's sleep."

"All right," he said, his gaze still clinging to the slim form lying so still beneath the covers.

"Son," Thursa said tenderly. "You must get some rest. You haven't slept for two days. Please," she added.

"Yes . . . Matthew," Kathryn whispered, urging him to rest.

He came to the side of the bed. Kneeling beside

it, he took Kathryn's hand in his. "I'll be back in the morning, Kate." Even a simple statement from him could be a command, an order for her to be there, safe and sound, when he returned.

Kathryn smiled at the familiar authoritative tone and said, "Yes, I'll be waiting."

The hot broth soothed her tired body and the sweet sun-drenched fragrance of fresh linens was like an opiate. She grew languid and weightless, her eyes heavy with sleep. Fear had vanished, for even without asking she knew that Matthew would take care of everything.

She slept then, a deep and healing sleep, waking early the next morning feeling more like herself. Breakfast seemed the most delicious meal she'd ever eaten.

Now that she was rested and awake, her mind turned more and more to Cynthia. What had happened to her? Where was she? But her euphoria would not let her worry long. She wanted only to revel in the safety and security she felt.

She closed her eyes and dozed peacefully. She became aware of a movement somewhere in her room and opened her eyes to find Teresa standing at the foot of the bed.

"Teresa," Kathryn said softly.

To Kathryn's surprise the woman's elfin features collapsed into a look of anguish. She came rushing to Kathryn's side, tears spilling down her cheeks, her shaking hands outstretched in supplication.

"I'm sorry, Katie, I'm sorry," she cried. "I didn't know what she wanted with the musquash. I didn't know she would kill our Robert!" Her voice rose into a hysterical wail so loud that Kathryn was sure it could be heard down the hallways. The little woman poured out her grief and guilt. "I didn't mean to hurt you!"

"Teresa," Kathryn said, sitting up in bed. "Whatever are you talking about? Is it Cynthia?"

The woman nodded.

"Here, sit down. Tell me what happened."

The door burst open and Matthew walked into the room, followed by Sula, anxiously looking past him.

"What is going on up here?" he demanded. "What's all the shouting about Aunt Teresa?"

Sula looked at Teresa as if she would strangle her.

"It's all right, Matthew . . . Sula. It's all right. Teresa is just a little upset." Kathryn looked at them pointedly. "She has something to tell us about Cynthia."

"Is that true, Aunt Teresa?" Matthew asked, walking slowly toward her as one would approach a small wounded animal. "Don't be upset now, we're going to sit and talk quietly—all right?"

Teresa nodded. Her breath came in little hiccuping sobs. Slowly, soothed by Matthew, she quieted.

"Tell us what happened, Teresa," Kathryn coaxed.

Matthew watched Kathryn as she gently persuaded his aunt to continue. She was sitting up in bed, large pillows at her back. Her auburn hair had been brushed into a full and shining halo about her face. She looked as fragile and ethereal as an angel in her soft white cotton gown. How could he ever have thought her anything but good and innocent?

"Cynthia told me to bring her some musquash roots from the woods. She said there were mice in her room. I told her she didn't need musquash for mice, 'cause it was too strong. She said for me to do what I was told; she said I couldn't play with little Woody anymore if I didn't do it. She said to keep my mouth shut. So I did it." She began to cry again. "I didn't know she was going to kill our Robert with it! I swear I didn't, Katie—you must believe me!"

"Shhh, Teresa," Kathryn soothed, taking the small woman in her arms. "Of course you didn't know . . . none of us knew how Cynthia was. You must not blame yourself. Is that why you kept the will, because you were afraid of Cynthia? You suspected what she had done?"

"Yes, I got it from his room. I didn't want her to find it. Then I was afraid, so I gave it to you."

"Was it you then who came to my room the night of the storm?"

"No, it was her, but I . . . I know how she got in," Teresa answered.

"How could she get in, Aunt Teresa? Both doors were locked," Matthew asked.

They watched as Teresa walked to the door to the sitting room. She pushed against one of the carved panels in the door just beside the doorknob. It moved aside, revealing a small square opening no more than six inches wide. Teresa pushed her hand through and turned the knob from the other side, causing the door to swing silently open.

"Easy!" she said triumphantly in her old manner.

"Aunt Teresa," Matthew said. "I don't recall that being there before."

"Joseph did it . . . before Robert came home." Then Teresa looked shyly down at her feet.

Sula came back into the room with a tray of tea, and, Kathryn suspected, to find out what was going on.

Teresa sniffled childishly. "I loved Robert so much," she said, looking guiltily at Matthew. "He wasn't like you. Him and me—we understood each other. He loved me even if I am stupid," she said in an accusing tone.

Matthew took her small hand in his. "You're not stupid, Teresa . . . and I love you, too. I'm sorry if I never let you know that. I know you miss Robert; I loved him too you know." His gray eyes glistened with tears.

Sula sniffed loudly at the scene, but Kathryn's look was for Matthew alone. His tenderness toward the pathetic little woman touched her as only he had the power to do. Just the look of him, his startling silver eyes so intense in his dark face, fairly took her breath away. She could not imagine ever loving anyone so fiercely as she did him.

"You do, Matthew?" Teresa asked. "You really love me? I never thought you liked me."

"Well, I do," he smiled at her candor. "Never doubt it, Aunt Teresa . . . I do."

Matthew embraced his aunt and kissed her cheek. "Everything's going to be all right now, I promise. I don't want you to worry about any of this any more. Why don't you let Sula take you to your room where you can lie down for a while?"

Sula took Teresa's arm and lead her from the room, her dislike for the woman apparently gone. She glanced back over her shoulder once and gave Kathryn a pointed look of approval.

Matthew sat by the bed, his dark head bowed as if he were searching for the right words. Kathryn knew he was going to tell her more about Cynthia.

"Well," he said. "Now at least I know *how* Cynthia killed Robert, although I confess I don't understand why. If she was in love with him why would she want to kill him? Am I tiring you Kate? All this commotion. Do you feel like talking, telling me exactly what happened?"

Kathryn clasped her hands tightly together, trying to still the trembling. "Matthew . . . I heard Cynthia say she killed Robert. But I think she intended to kill me instead. Robert drank the tea that was meant for me. I did not drink any tea that day."

"Thank God you didn't," he muttered.

"That's why she mourned for Robert so fervently. It was partially guilt and remorse."

He nodded. "I can only blame myself. I was the one who insisted that she stay here and that we bring up Woody. Robert never wanted that. But I . . . I always had to do what was proper, what was 'right.' God!" He looked away and she knew he was feeling a burden of guilt.

"Matthew, you must not blame yourself—I'm sure it's not that simple. How could you have known the difference between a simple-minded girl playing naughty little tricks and a madwoman? None of us knew."

"I should have known, dammit! All the little things she did, the tantrums, her cruelty to animals, the taunting little threats she used to make to Robert . . . and lately to Woody. But I felt sorry for her and partially responsible for her welfare. I even suspected all along it might be Cynthia who had left the red ribbons to frighten you, but when you were attacked that night I was positive it wasn't Cynthia. How could I have been so blind!"

"Matthew . . . you expect too much of yourself, and I think everyone else here does too. Could it be that you're still trying to fight your brother's battles?"

He looked at her steadily, his eyes shadowed with pain, then he nodded and looked down at the floor between clasped hands. "Probably," he said. Kathryn's heart ached for him. She wanted to reach out to him, to hold him, but this morning he seemed to be deliberately keeping her at arm's length. After last night she had not expected it.

Changing the subject she asked. "Then it was Cynthia who hit Woody that day and not Mrs. Spencer?"

"Yes," he answered. "I guessed that when I spoke to Mrs. Spencer about the incident, but she would not admit it even to me. Finally I warned Cynthia myself."

Kathryn remembered that day when Cynthia had fled down the stairs crying.

Kathryn told him about the note Joseph had delivered and of the bitter, crazed rantings of Cynthia as she stood above her in the darkness of the ice house.

Matthew frowned and Kathryn sensed there was more, but she was not prepared for the story he told.

On his way back from Salem, he had stopped briefly in Asheville, where he paid a visit to Dr. Logan. Something about Robert's death had been eating away at him; some vague uneasiness had plagued him since his return to Foxfire. He wanted the doctor to tell him everything he could remember about Robert's death.

Dr. Logan had said, "Matthew, I've seen so many mysteries with these young men who are so grievously wounded, or paralyzed, as your brother was. They sometimes have problems we've never encountered. Some of them just up and die for no apparent reason. Many of them have breathing difficulties, as your brother did, but . . . ," he seemed reluctant to continue.

"Yes? Go on," Matthew said anxiously.

"I don't mind telling you that Robert's death was a real puzzlement to me. His difficulty in breathing came on so suddenly—and the pain . . . I don't want to cause you any more grief, but the skin discoloration bothered me a bit too."

"What discoloration? No one mentioned anything about this to me," Matthew said, becoming alarmed.

"Why, his face turned dark . . . bluish. That happens with heart attack victims, but . . . I don't know. If I had not known better I'd have suspected poison of some kind. Seen that a lot back with the Indians. They used a special poison—quick it was.

Folks hereabouts call it cowbane, or musquash, but it's actually water hemlock . . . and it's deadly. But of course with Robert I knew it couldn't be anything like that."

Matthew told Kathryn that as he rode back through the darkness toward Foxfire, Dr. Logan's words kept going through his mind. He thought of Teresa and her constant gathering of herbs. But somehow, he said, he knew it couldn't be her. He kept remembering Cynthia's resentful glances at Kathryn. He prayed that he was wrong about his suspicions.

He arrived near dawn and raced upstairs to find that Kathryn's bed had not been slept in, and at that moment he was sure he was too late. Then Thursa had appeared in the doorway. "Matthew, why are you racing up the stairs in such an ungodly manner at this hour of the morning? What's wrong?"

Morning light was beginning to show behind the curtains when they spotted the piece of paper on the edge of the bed—the forged note to Kathryn.

As he continued his story of that night of horror, Kathryn could feel his frustration.

"I'm afraid there's more," he said. "Before we had time to look for you we found Cynthia's body not far from the ice house. She'd been killed."

Kathryn could only look at him with a horror and puzzlement at this newest revelation. "Killed?"

"It was Joseph, Kathryn. He and Cynthia were apparently lovers—but when he discovered she had used him to help seek her revenge on you he became infuriated. He dragged her away from the ice house . . . he intended to rescue you. They quarreled and he hit her and kept hitting her . . . he was the one who told us where to find you. He kept repeating over and over that he didn't know what Cynthia was doing."

Kathryn remembered that it was Joseph who had given her the note that told her Matthew was home.

"Apparently Cynthia told Joseph after Robert died that they could take the large sum of money she expected to receive from his will and run away together. She had not even planned to take Woody with her. Teresa knew about the will and knew also that Robert had left everything to you. She was afraid Cynthia would kill you too. I suppose Aunt Teresa reasoned that after I came home Cynthia would not dare harm you, and that's when she gave the will to you."

"But then Robert's will was read and Cynthia knew the truth. The small sum for Woody wasn't enough, and I didn't protect you . . . I was so blind!"

"No, Matthew . . ."

He continued. "After what you had told me of Cynthia's confession there at the ice house I can only assume that Joseph overheard her professing her love for Robert . . . and her words about me. He realized then that she had only used him and he flew into a rage, dragging her outside, where they fought. I don't think he intended to kill her. When I came he was still sitting there beside her, crying."

"This is all so unbelievable," Kathryn muttered, clutching her robe to her chest.

"Kate? Are you all right?" he asked quickly leaning toward her.

"Yes, yes, I'm fine—it's just so . . . so hard to believe," she gasped. "And Woody. What will happen to him now?" she asked.

"Woody will be fine. Really. I don't want you to worry about him. He's been told that you're sick and he thinks his mother's death was a terrible accident. When he's older we'll tell him everything. Of course it's going to be hard at first—but he's young and healthy and I'm convinced that he'll get over it much faster than we will. He's been asking every day to see you. In fact, when I leave he can come in and clamber all over you if you feel all right." For the first time a smile flickered across his handsome features.

"Yes, I would like that," she said. As he rose to leave she put out her hand to stop him. "Matthew, your mother has already told me that Woody is Robert's son. I feel like such a fool accusing you the way I did. Why didn't you tell me that night?"

He was silent for a moment. Kathryn could not read the flicker of emotion she saw hidden deep in his eyes.

"It's simple. I love the boy and I wanted to protect him from the scandalmongers as long as I could . . . and mother too, of course," he added.

"But I'm sure I wasn't the only one who saw the resemblance, which I know now to be a family resemblance rather than just yours. Didn't you care that everyone might think the same as I did?"

she asked.

"No, I didn't," he stated simply.

No matter how he denied it, Kathryn could see in his face that he was not as immune to the gossip as he would have her believe. She suspected he had always been hurt by the family's attempt to protect Robert at any cost. But she said nothing; she sensed there was more he had to say.

He chose his words with care. "I loved Robert . . . he was my only brother. But I guess I always knew that I was the one who would have to make the decisions that he simply would not. Perhaps I did not always make the right choices, who's to say? I know now that things were too easy for him, but then he never seemed to want as much from life as I did. He didn't really seem to care about the future of Foxfire or what the name Kincaid had come to mean in the community. When I argued that he was too complacent, he said he was content."

Kathryn understood perfectly what he was trying to say. His brother was a good man, the kind of man who was content to let the world go by, meekly accepting whatever fate gave to him. He wanted no responsibilities, no real commitments in life. Matthew was not the kind of man to ever let that happen to him, choosing instead to grasp fiercely for what he wanted—making his future what he wanted it to be.

Matthew continued, "So, I suppose I liked making things happen in life and taking what I wanted. I also knew long ago that if I'm to accept friendship, or more, from anyone, it must be on my terms—no half measures." He paused and looked at her steadily. "I'm not sure I've answered your question about why I didn't tell you, but I'm afraid that's as close as I can get."

"Yes, I understand . . . you need to be accepted for what you are, faults included. And if someone's to . . . to care about you, it must be with the knowledge of who you are," she said.

His eyes told her that what she said was true. Abruptly he asked "If Woody were truly my son . . . and Cynthia's . . . would it have mattered to you Kathryn?"

Before she could reply he walked from the room. She knew he did not want to hear her answer to that question. But he shouldn't have feared. She wanted to run after him and tell him that nothing he'd ever done could matter to her—as she had proven by loving him anyway, even as she considered him a complete scoundrel or the irresponsible father of little Woody, perhaps even a murderer. For even while her mind told her those things her heart had professed her love for him.

Two souls with but a single thought,
Two hearts that beat as one.
Friedrick Halm

Chapter Nineteen

All her thoughts were banished as Woody came crashing into the bedroom, anxious to see his Kat. He seemed all right—as normal as rain in springtime. The sight of his animated face made Kathryn believe that both of them would finally find happiness.

Woody kicked off his shoes and climbed into bed with her, hugging her tightly and making her laugh.

"I missed you, Kat! When will you be well so we can go fishing again?" he asked.

"Very soon, I hope, Woody. I'm feeling better each day.

Woody became quiet and looked up at her with his large brilliant blue eyes. "My mama died," he said.

"I know, darling," she said. "And I know how sad you must feel. But Sula and I love you, and your grandmother does too. We'll help you all we can."

"Matthew too," he said. "And Miz Kincaid and Teresa."

"Yes, that's right, Woody. Everyone here at Foxfire loves you. You are the joy of the household!" she said, hugging him close.

"I am?" he asked, grinning happily.

"You are," she declared.

There was a quiet knock at the door. Thursa came in and looked tenderly at Woody nestled in Kathryn's arms. She wore a black linen dress that looked unusually mournful on such a fine summer morning. Although it had not been mentioned to Kathryn, she knew instinctively that the funeral for Cynthia had been today.

Thursa stood beside the bed while Woody, anticipating grown-up talk, scampered from the bed to play with kitty.

"Mrs. Spencer is going away for a while, but she has no home, no relatives. I wanted to speak with you before she goes. I do not have it in my heart to hold her responsible for what her daughter did. My husband promised Mr. Spencer that his wife and daughter would always have a home here if anything happened to him. She is Woody's grandmother, but if you feel you cannot live in the same house with her I will of course tell her not to return."

Kathryn took a deep breath and her hands thoughtfully twisted the lace-edged coverlet that lay across her lap.

"Mrs. Spencer was never kind to me, but like you, I feel more sorrow than anything else for her. I couldn't turn her away even if I had the right to do so," Kathryn said.

"Are you sure?"

"Yes, I am." Kathryn looked into Thursa's bright eyes and they embraced, each shedding tears for the sadness of it all.

"Then I shall tell her to return to Foxfire whenever she's ready. Now Eugene is downstairs and wants to see you. Do you feel up to it?"

"Yes," Kathryn said. "Of course . . . if you will hand me that shawl?"

"Woody, sweetheart," Thursa said, ruffling the boy's dark, tousled hair, "let's go see Mom Sula and find out if she's baked any gingerbread men. Shall we?"

"Yes!" he said scrambling off the bed. "I'll be back soon, Kat. I'll bring you a ginger man!" he yelled as they went out the door.

When Eugene came in his face was drawn and worried. He rushed to her side and took her hand.

"Are you all right now, Kathryn? They tell me you will be fine, but I had to see for myself."

"Yes, Eugene, I'm feeling much better. You need not worry about me. Matthew and Thursa and Sula are taking excellent care of me," she smiled.

"I could not believe it when I heard," he said.

"I know, it's been very shocking for everyone. None of us suspected Cynthia was capable of anything like this."

Eugene released her hand and stood up, pacing restlessly before the window, his hands absently rubbing the window frame.

Kathryn looked puzzled. "Eugene?"

"Kathryn," he sighed, not turning from the window. "I blame myself for not warning you about her."

"What . . . what do you mean?"

"I knew she hated you," he said, walking back toward the bed. "I knew what she was capable of doing. I even warned her to leave you alone, but she only laughed and taunted me. She said I was too much a coward to risk opening my mouth," he said, head bowed in shame.

"Why would she think that."

"I never wanted you to know, never wanted anyone to know. I knew you'd hate me," he said.

Kathryn waited.

"Robert and I . . . we both teased and flirted with Cynthia when we were younger. It became another game, another competition between us. Robert loved it; he seemed to crave that competition over a woman."

Kathryn frowned as if she did not believe him.

"You didn't know him, Kathryn, not the way I did. And God knows even Matthew never knew some of the things. . . . Robert loved women . . ." He stammered, face flushed, and she realized this was something very difficult for him to say.

"It gave Robert some perverse thrill to share . . . things. Do you know what I'm trying to say?"

His words brought a sick feeling into the pit of her stomach and she did not want to hear where his conversation would take them. "Eugene, please . . ." she began.

"No, let me finish. We were young and irresponsible. And I . . . I would do almost anything Robert wanted to do. We both took advantage of the situation, the girl's youth and naiveté, her position here. He used her and then laughed about it. I felt guilty, ashamed, but Robert said she was a nobody. I hate telling you this, but I must if you're to understand why I did not come to you sooner, why I waited until it was too late."

"All right, Eugene," she said. "Go on."

"The fact is that Woody could have been my child. No one knew that except Cynthia and me. She always threatened to tell Robert whenever she wanted something from me. I know now he probably would not have cared anyway, but then . . . I was only concerned about our friendship. I thought Woody was mine until a few weeks ago. Then she told me that he belonged to Robert. She knew all along! She just used it as a threat all these years. Oh, she's not as crazy as everyone thought. She was clever in her own sick little way. I told her then that if she attempted to harm you in any way I'd kill her, and I meant it, Kathryn!" he said adamantly.

"But you couldn't have known . . . you didn't suspect that she killed Robert? And told no one?" she asked incredulously.

He looked away, unable to meet her accusing stare. "Yes, I did," he said.

"Eugene," she whispered.

"Kathryn, please," he babbled. "you must believe me. I never thought she meant to hurt you. Please say you will forgive me! I loved you, Kathryn!" he declared.

She ignored his declaration of love. "I don't know what to believe any more, Eugene. This whole thing is so complicated. I'm sorry for you. You seem to have lived your whole life avoiding responsibility, thinking only of yourself. I don't know yet if I can forgive you. Please, just get out of my sight," she said coldly.

"Kathryn . . ." he pleaded.

"You heard her, Eugene. I think it would be best if you leave now before I make a scene we might both regret." Matthew stood menacingly just inside the doorway, looking at Eugene as if he wanted to kill him.

Eugene left, his eyes still on Kathryn, silently pleading for her forgiveness.

"You heard?" Kathryn asked as Matthew came into the room.

"Yes," he sighed. "Forgive my eavesdropping, but I had seen him with Cynthia and I couldn't be sure how involved he was in all this."

"Oh, Matthew," she groaned. "Why has all this happened? This deceit . . . how could Robert or Eugene have ignored Woody if they thought they were his father. That's something I can never understand. Everything has become such a mess!"

Matthew sat beside the bed. He looked as if he wanted to touch her, comfort her, but he did not. His look was tender and pleading as he tried to reassure her. "It's over now, Kate. I know the worst is over. All we need is time. We all do. I suppose you must hate this place, this house. Foxfire has not been very welcoming to you I'm afraid."

His words surprised her, not because she had so often thought that herself but because it was no longer true. It *had* been at first . . . she was frightened of the house's strange, foreboding aura. But on the other hand, in many ways she had found it to be as beautiful and welcoming as anyone could wish. She had grown to love Foxfire and its surrounding splendor. Perhaps the evil she'd felt was only a premonition, not the result of anything to do with the house or its occupants.

"No, I don't hate Foxfire at all. In fact I've grown to love it and these mountains even more, if possible, than my own home."

"Good," he smiled, "Because this is your home, Kate, and I hope you know we want you to stay here, forever if you wish."

Not *I* want you to stay, but *we*, she thought painfully. "Thank you, Matthew," she said quietly, knowing in her heart she would never hear the words she had hoped for. She would stay then, for a while, until she could bear to leave him.

Kathryn did not see Matthew except briefly for several days, until the day Dr. Logan came and told them she could be up and about.

After she was dressed, Matthew came in and announced that he had come to escort her on her first venture outdoors—a walk to the overlook, her favorite spot.

He gently led her down the curved stairway and out into the coming sunset. Kathryn glanced at him from under lowered lashes, wanting to fill her memory with his face.

They stepped out onto the front porch and the warmth of the summer evening. Everything before her looked new and fresh. Being alive was more wonderful that she had ever dreamed. When she looked up the driveway she gasped at the sight before her.

"Matthew?"

There at the overlook was a beautiful stone structure—the sheltered bower he had said he'd build.

To her further surprise, Matthew pulled her to him. "It's for you, Kate." Then he bent and kissed her lips very gently, as if she were the most fragile thing in the world. Reluctantly pulling away from her he took a long breath.

"Kate . . . you know I'm not a patient man. I'm moody and sometimes selfish. I'm demanding . . ."

Kathryn's look of disbelief slowly turned to a smile.

"Don't look at me that way or I'll never be able to say this," he teased.

She found this reflective Matthew charming, and she knew how difficult it was for one as proud as he to make such admissions. She wanted to laugh aloud with delight. But she lifted her eyebrows, her face happy, and was silent while he chose his words.

"The night I found you . . . I thought I'd go crazy with worry. I don't think I could have lived if anything had happened to you. I suddenly knew what the most important thing was to me."

She reached up to touch his face gently.

"I'm often too blunt and I have a tendency to forget I'm a gentleman when I'm angry. Oh, hell, what I'm trying to say is . . . I love you, Kate, more than I love life. I won't be easy to live with. People will tell you you're crazy to marry me, to marry into this family. And after all that's happened, there will be talk. . . ."

"I don't care about that," she interrupted. "Matthew, do you know how long I've waited to hear you say those words to me? I love you—I think I loved you the moment I saw you standing in the doorway, scowling so fiercely at poor Eugene," she laughed.

"And *I* fell in love with *you,* against my better judgement I thought, that stormy day in the cabin," Matthew said. "You looked like a green-eyed sorceress, so angry and defiant," he laughed. "I was never able to get you out of my mind from that day on . . . and I tried . . . God I tried."

"How well I remember. You almost broke my heart! I don't care what anyone says. I know the real Matthew Kincaid and the real family at Foxfire, and I love them both."

They walked together out to stand inside the gazebo, looking back at the house. The lamps were being lit and they twinkled one by one through the windows. The lighted silhouette of the house glittered there in the darkening evening light, no longer forbidding, but a home awaiting them with its Foxfire glow.

Epilogue

It was a clear, warm June morning in 1875, with the scent of roses and freshly cut grass wafting across the lawn and into the open windows of Foxfire Manor.

Kathryn came out to the porch and smiled up into the eyes of her husband as he took her small gloved hand in his. She laughed aloud, the sound ringing merrily about the porch as he silently turned her around so he might inspect every part of her attire.

The high-necked, lace-covered bodice of her cream silk gown fit perfectly, accentuating her full breasts and tapering to a V at the slender waistline. The overskirt was draped gracefully back and caught up in a large bustled bow behind her, which moved seductively as she turned. In front the cream underskirt was sprinkled with tiny green flowers. Her long auburn hair was swept up behind her head, with one long curl falling stylishly over her shoulder.

"You take my breath away," he said, bending to kiss her waiting lips. "I think you've bewitched me," he murmured against her ear as she wrapped her arms around his waist and pulled herself closer to him.

"And you, my dashing husband, make me want to go back in the house and spend a quiet afternoon alone with you." She laughed against his neck as she spoke.

"You are shameless," he whispered, his husky laughter sending chills down her back.

"But . . ." his eyes twinkled as he set her firmly at arm's length. "It's a long drive into town and we don't want to miss the ceremony."

"No," she smiled, "especially since you're the guest speaker."

Through the open door to the house they could hear Sula as she bustled down the hallway.

"You boys is sure a handful! Now stop that gigglin' and get on outside. We don't want the major to be late for his ceremony! A respectable man, yessir, that's what your daddy is, a mighty respectable man in these parts."

Matthew grinned at Kathryn as they waited for the twins to catapult themselves through the door.

Stephen, named for Judge McClary, and Joshua, for Matthew's father, came bouncing out to join their parents. They were as curious and mischievous as Woody had been at their age. It was hard to believe ten years had passed since Kathryn came to Foxfire and discovered the little boy.

Thursa joined them, and beside her walked a tall, slender boy with thick curling black hair and eyes so blue that they evoked comment wherever he went.

Kathryn reached for him and put an arm about

his waist. Woody now stood several inches taller than she. Happy tears flooded her green eyes as she looked proudly up at him.

"You look so handsome, son," she said quietly.

He grinned and reached up behind her back to tug at a curl of her hair. "And you're very handsome too, Kat," he teased.

Thursa lovingly watched the scene before her, as Matthew put the boys in the large covered carriage that stood waiting. The years since the war had been good ones, better than she could ever have expected after Robert's death, but it had worked out, and now Foxfire rang with the joyous sound of children's laughter, just as she'd always hoped it would.

"You all best get goin'," Sula reminded.

"I wish you'd come with us, Sula," Matthew said, turning from the carriage.

"I ain't got no business at no such ceremony, even if they are puttin' up a big fancy war monument!" she huffed. "Besides, my old bones can't stand the long ride."

"More likely what your 'old bones' need is a rest from Stephen and Joshua," Kathryn laughed, leaning forward to kiss Sula's cheek.

"Now that ain't entirely untrue neither!" Sula hooted, placing her hands on her ample hips. "No sir, it ain't untrue!"

"Bye, bye, little sweethearts," she said as the boys waved from the carriage. "I'll have some gingerbread baked when you get back."

Kathryn shook her head at the woman's indulgence then turned and walked to the carriage, where Matthew stood waiting to help her and Thursa inside.

As they pulled away from the house and down the drive, Kathryn looked fondly at the stone gazebo at the view. It was now covered in trailing vines of delicate pink roses.

She remembered that day ten years ago when she and Matthew said their wedding vows there, and how even now the fragrance of lavender and late summer roses always brought that day back to her. How they had laughed when, just as the ceremony ended, a sudden summer storm swept up the mountain to envelop them and their guests in the mist-filled bower.

"Certainly a fitting end to our wedding," Matthew had laughed as they drove away to the old cabin for a quiet and isolated honeymoon. The stormy night that followed was hardly noticed as he initiated her into the final and most beautiful aspect of their love.

She turned her eyes toward Matthew sitting beside her in the carriage. He met her look with one of sweet remembrance and she knew he was also thinking of those early days.

Not that it had been all perfect bliss. A marriage between two independent people is bound to have its tumultuous moments, and theirs was no exception. But for all that, there were many more glorious moments, filled with ecstasy and love. Kathryn counted herself lucky each day to have found such a remarkable man as Matthew. And of course, Sula never let her forget that he was exactly the kind of man she needed to keep her in line.

She looked across at Woody, a mature, happy young man now and as much a part of the family as the twins. All three of the boys were blessed with three attentive "grandmothers." Thursa adored them as much as Sula and Matthew's mother, for after that day in Kathryn's bedroom when she confessed her guilt, Teresa had finally accepted the dark one, even becoming his champion in all causes once she realized how loving and tender the fierce man could be.

Kathryn looked through the dark forest surrounding the road and thought of the small cemetery there in its shadowed stillness. Lila Spencer had joined her daughter there within a year of the girl's death. They all were sure now that she must have been aware of Cynthia's secrets all along but that she was never able to accept what happened—never stopped feeling guilty for it. In the end it had killed her.

As they passed the Davenport farmhouse several miles down the mountain Thursa leaned forward to ask, "Are Eugene and Tilda coming to the ceremony today?"

"Yes, I think so, and the girls, too," Kathryn replied.

It was partly Tilda's influence and Kathryn's own forgiving nature that allowed her to welcome Eugene back to Foxfire and to influence Matthew to forgive and forget. That, of course, had taken a little more doing.

Just as Matthew had predicted, there were those who gossiped, more about Kathryn than about Matthew, and there was indeed some talk when he married his brother's widow. But the Kincaids had never placed a high regard on the opinions of others and the gossip soon passed.

Kathryn sighed contently, moving closer to her strong, handsome husband who always made her feel so safe and so wanted.

It was because of him that she finally accepted her happiness—no longer afraid that it might all end. Oh, there were still nights when she would awake suddenly, heart pounding, with the musty smell of the pit thick in her nostrils and the sound of mad laughter ringing in her ears. But Matthew was always there beside her, loving and strong. He would reach out for her in the night, pulling her close and assuring her in his husky, sleep-worn voice that he loved her and would keep her safe.

The face of evil on Foxfire manor was gone. Now it was simply a beautiful house—a home that Kathryn shared with the one man she would ever love—a home filled with the love and laughter of their children.